W9-BNG-051

The following is a work of fiction. Names, characters, places, events and incidents are either the product of the author's imagination or used in an entirely fictitious manner. Any resemblance to actual persons, living or dead, is entirely coincidental.

Cover and jacket design by The Cover Collection

ISBN 978-1-943818-88-4
eISBN 978-1-943818-92-1

Library of Congress Control Number: 2017963883

First hardcover edition February 2018 by Polis Books, LLC

1201 Hudson Street, #211S
Hoboken, NJ 07030
www.PolisBooks.com

POLIS BOOKS

THE DETONATOR

VINCENT ZANDRI

THE DETONATOR

"We are doomed! An implosion has taken place at the Earth's core. A war between denizens of the abyss. Our structures have been destroyed, our foundations shaken."

—Glauber Rocha, A Idade da Terra (The Age of the Earth)

"But the shameful thing has consumed the labor of our fathers since our youth, their flocks and their herds, their sons and their daughters."

—Jeremiah 3:24

THE DETONATOR

PROLOGUE:
OCTOBER 23, 1999
ALPHABET CITY
LOWER MANHATTAN
NEW YORK, NEW YORK

The warehouse is wired to blow.

A siren indicating the final five-minute countdown has already sounded for what promises to be the spectacular three-stage implosion of a fifteen-story downtown pre-war building constructed of reinforced concrete and steel. The first two floors have been gutted of its piers and structural beams to ensure multiple failure points. The building's interior has been cleared of useless debris—all bearing walls chopped out, all glass windows, bulbs, and panels shattered, the shards removed.

The piers on the remaining floors have been drilled with enough holes to make them look like Swiss cheese, the small, round, test tube–sized openings filled with more than seven hundred pounds of dynamite and linear-shaped, steel-slicing cyclotrimethylenetrinitramine, or what's also known simply as RDX.

The explosives have been wrapped with protective chain link fencing while heavy black geotextile material hangs off the scaffolding-covered exterior walls on the buildings immediately flanking the warehouse—a defensive maneuver designed to prevent and/or minimize shrapnel discharge damage. Even the weather has been checked repeatedly, the cloud cover having remained at the optimum twenty-five hundred feet. Anything less, and the shockwave from the blast stands a chance of ricocheting off the clouds and slamming into innocent people, vehicles, and surrounding structures.

Since "Safety First and Last" is Master Blasters motto, the precautions don't stop there. The surrounding blast area exclusion zone has been cleared, the window glass on nearby buildings taped over, the perimeter inspected and reinspected, the two-thousand-strong crowd of onlookers, gawkers, media pros, and just plain pyro and explosion junkies held at bay behind bright yellow barriers manned by a specially designated squad of NYPD in charge of maintaining order and security. More importantly, the explosive engineering blasting team has reinspected all electric charge strips and blasting caps, triple-checked the fuse and charge-to-explosive connections, double- and triple-checked powder factor calculations, and issued the final, yet always somewhat tentative, thumbs-up.

It's time to rock the house.

Sounding over the loudspeakers now, some serious rock 'n' roll. Throbbing bass, smashing drums, and buzzsaw guitar. The crowd gathered beyond the safety barriers are dancing, clapping, and singing along to the familiar classic rock refrain: BOOM BOOM, OUT GO THE LIGHTS!

This isn't a demolition job. It's a rock show. The Midnight Special played early in the day to a sell-out crowd of explosives junkies and groupies. A moment in time that will be etched on the brain of all those who witness it. Hear it. Feel its thunder. Smell its acrid explosive. Taste the fine dust that's about to rain down from heaven.

You, as the CEO of Master Blaster, hold the yellow electronic control box in your thick, callus-covered hands, its solid heavy-duty plastic construction somehow alive, its innards beating like an overworked heart, the black "charge" and the red "fire" triggers it houses possessing both the power of God (good) and the devil (evil). The power to initiate total destruction, and the power to stop it if need be.

The chatter of voices comes to you from over the headset while your body remains tense and rigid under a blasting uniform of Bell hard hat, Carhartt work pants, steel-toed work boots, denim work shirt, and tan Carhartt jacket. Your hands are protected with Uline non-slip grip construction gloves, while your eyes are shielded by yellow-rimmed DeWalt safety goggles. You've borne witness to enough controlled implosions in your adult lifetime to know that the word control is, at best, misleading.

There is no such thing as ultimate control when it comes to explosives. Best you can hope for is as much control as possible when it comes to taking down a massive block of concrete with explosives. Sure, you went to college (where you majored in beer, chewing tobacco, and weight lifting), but when it comes to handling explosives, you are strictly blue-collar. Your academic institution was the school-of-hard-knocks and unstable explosives. The school of blasted granite, the acrid odor of exploded dynamite, and choking dust clouds. Even with the dawn of the twenty-first century right around the corner, there's still no college degree for a master blaster. No special academic grade. No scholastic certification.

There is only on-the-job experience. You've been lucky thus far. You have all your limbs, all your fingers even. Thick biceps, barrel chest, shaved head, and dark goatee afford you the appearance of health, but also of a real badass. A man seemingly born for the job of crushing big buildings made of steel and concrete. And you've worked plenty hard at the job.

In the case of Master Blasters, Inc., your job experience isn't learned from a school book. It is entirely self-taught. The same holds true for your little boy, Henry. Or so you still hold out hope. The sickly little scruffy-haired, round-faced kid might be afflicted with progeria, one of those one-in-ten-million-births-affected genetic diseases that causes premature if not rapid aging. But you pray that a cure is on the way. Henry won't require college when it comes time to fill your boots, but he will require an education all the same. Which is why at four years old, the boy now stands by your side watching the show with anxious eyes (what little boy, sick or not, doesn't like to watch stuff blow up?). He will have grown up with the business, experiencing it firsthand, learning the ropes like he would a language or a religion. But always in the back of your mind, you know he has to live. He must survive if he is to become a Master Blaster.

Your partner, Brian Darling, co-owner and president of Master Blasters, Inc. couldn't agree more. He too insists on his one and only child accompanying him to the show. His child isn't a boy, but a nine-year-old girl. The sooner the short, stocky Darling can show his tall, skinny, happy-go-lucky, sandy-haired girl the ropes, the sooner the next generation of demolition experts will be prepared to take on even more challenging blasts, such as the coveted true implosion, a timed explosion that will cause a tower to collapse inward onto its own footprint.

"Knock knock," his jokester daughter barks.

"Who's there?" replies Brian.

"Dino."

"Dino who?"

"Dino Myte."

Master Blasters, Inc. knows how to unleash hell with their explosive demolition. But they are also one big happy family. Or so it appears, on the outside at least. The partners do have one thing in common, more than anything else: the fulfillment of the true implosion.

Only a handful of true implosions have been attempted in the history of timed demolition and nothing over twenty stories. You, along with the thirty-five-year-old Darling, had hoped that one day, Master Blasters would be the outfit that attempted the first thirty- or forty-story true implosion.

But Brian has been bombarded with some bad luck as of late. With a failed marriage sucking the life's blood out of him, along with what has become a daily fifth of vodka, it's been all you can do not to insist he stand down, take some time off, separate himself from all blast sites until the divorce is over.

"It's too dangerous," you've insisted. "Your head's not in the game and when your head's not in the game, Bri, you know what happens. Innocent people die."

But Brian has insisted to the point of tears, "Master Blasters is all I've got now. Don't take that away from me, Ike."

Brian is almost like a brother to you. The brother you never had. With reluctance and a heavy heart, you've acquiesced, given in to his need to work and stay busy. But not without serious reservations. After all, timed implosions are all about control. And once you've lost that control, you're finished. You might as well strap a suit of TNT to your chest like some whacked out terrorist and depress the detonator. Because what blasting a building to Kingdom Come comes down to is this: Once the detonator is triggered and the charged blasting caps begin to blow like a series of dominoes falling one on top of the other, you are no longer in control. The explosive charge is God now. Once it starts, there's no stopping it. All you can do is stand back and hope that hundreds of thousands of tons of blasted concrete and steel drop where it's supposed to, and not on top of the heads of so many innocent bystanders.

The siren sounds again.

One minute.

Your hands tremble. Even after all these years, your cold hard hands sweat and shake inside their gloves as you await the final go-ahead. With the countdown now reduced to the final sixty seconds, you take hold of your binoculars for one final review of the structure. Bringing them to your eyes, you start at the top and scan the building's exterior, moving downward slowly so you are sure to spot anything that should not be there.

Something two-legged. Human. Alive.

You've been lucky thus far. In the thirteen years since you and Brian started in the demolition business, not so much as a stray cat has been caught up in one of the spectacular implosions. Your bonding company loves you for that, and in turn, they've issued you the highest rating possible. Something that hasn't gone unnoticed among the New York developers. Something that has only bolstered your reputation among your peers. Something that's allowed you to seek out top dollar. Something that's even landed you an episode on the Discovery Channel's hit reality show, The Detonators.

But none of that matters right now as the clock whittles down to thirty seconds. The point of no return is fast approaching. The time when the electric charges are initiated and the timed blasts commence.

"Dad," your boy speaks up suddenly, yanking on your sleeve. "Where's Uncle Brian?"

You pull the binoculars from your eyes, look down upon the boy. A little boy you love with every muscle fiber in your heart, but also a boy who breaks your heart.

"He's where he's supposed to be, Henry. I just heard him joking with Alison."

"I don't think so, Dad. I don't see Uncle Brian anywhere."

You glance over your shoulder, eye the spot where your partner is expected to be standing some thirty feet away along the safety perimeter. But all you spot is his little girl. She's wearing a fluorescent-Tonka-Truck-yellow Master Blasters hard hat and protective eyewear while standing as stiff as a steel beam, her eyes locked on the warehouse.

Under normal circumstances, she might be rattling off her made-up knock-knock jokes to the many workers who surround her. But right now, she appears to be closed-mouthed and anxious. Rather, more anxious than usual only mere moments prior to a shooting of this magnitude, this importance, inside the most important city in the world.

Reaching for your collar-mounted radio, you bark, "Brian, come in…Brian, you hearing me, brother? Over."

But the hip-mounted speaker only produces static.

"Twenty seconds," your chief foreman shouts. "Clear the way!"

"Brian," you repeat. "Brian, come in, man. Speak up."

But there's no answer.

Heart beating. Pulse pounding. Reaching for the binoculars once more, you scan the building's third floor, peer into the glassless windows. That's when you spot him. He's seated on the floor, his back pressed up against one of the I-beams rigged to explode.

"Stand down!" you shout into your headset. Reaching for the bullhorn, you press it against your mouth. "Stand down! Abort! Stand down!"

"Dammit," you curse under your breath. "I should have known something like this would happen. It's all my fault."

Turning to your boy, you press your hand on his shoulder.

"Stay right here, Henry. You understand me? Stay right here. Don't you move an inch."

Henry nods, but his eyes do a strange kind of roll inside their abnormally small sockets. The child is only four, but already he's showing signs of getting older. Not by the year, but seemingly by the day. You and your wife, Ellen, have taken the necessary steps, had him poked, prodded, and MRI'd by the best doctors money can buy. But all they can come up with is that his disease is degenerative in nature, and by the time he's twenty, he will be the equivalent of a ninety-year-old man. That is, if he's still alive at all. Because all the doctors have concurred: statistically speaking, Henry has almost zero chance of seeing his twentieth birthday.

Statistically speaking...

But your son is not a statistic. He is your blood. Your flesh. He is you and he is Ellen.

You jump down from the small podium, begin sprinting toward the warehouse. You feel the collective gasp coming from the onlookers as much as you hear it. Blood races through your veins. Pulse soars. Mouth goes dry. The building you are about to enter is wrapped in enough lethal explosive to evaporate your flesh and bone should it spontaneously detonate. But you can't think about that right now. Right this very second you can think only about rescuing Brian. Rescuing Brian from himself. From his despair.

Barreling through the wide open entrance, you race up the stairwell to the second floor. You spot him seated on the floor of the empty space.

"Brian, for God's sakes. What the hell is happening here!?"

Your old friend and partner turns, looks up at you with his

round mustached face, smiles. He's gripping a pint-sized bottle of vodka in his right hand. In his left, he's holding a sheath of papers.

You go to him, drop down onto one knee, grab hold of his arm.

"Well, hello there, partner," he says, slurring his words. "Shouldn't you be working right now?"

"We're about to shoot this place, Bri," you say, yanking on his arm. "Did you think I wasn't going to spot you before I hit the triggers? You should know me better than that by now. Jesus, how long we been shooting together? We gotta get the hell out of here. Then we can talk about it."

"Talk about it? What's to talk about? She's already filed for divorce, Singer. Don't you get it? She doesn't love me anymore. She's in love with another. That's the way it's always going to be."

His words strike you with more explosive power than the TNT stuck to the beams.

"Then let her go, Bri," you say, yanking on the arm once more. "You've got so much to live for. You've got Alison. Your sweet little girl. Let's just get out of here before we both go up with the place."

"But that's the point, isn't it? To go out in a blaze of glory. I can't think of any other way to go, can you, my partner and my lifelong friend?"

Brian brings the bottle to his mouth, proceeds to take a long, deep drink. So deep, some of the crystal clear booze runs over the sides of his mouth, down his cheeks, down his neck.

"You don't want to die, Bri. You're just upset. You're the best blaster on earth. You've got a gift. This will pass, trust me."

Brian smiles, his eyes glassy, tears rolling down his cheeks.

"I trust you, Singer," he says. "Or, trusted you anyway. Once upon a long time ago. But the question is: Should you trust me now?"

He reaches into his jacket pocket, pulls something out. It's a second electronic control box. It appears to be wired to the main detonation line that runs throughout the entire structure.

Your insides slide south. Your steel-toed, engineer-booted feet don't feel like they're touching the concrete floor.

Brian looks up at you, smiles. "I know it was you, pal. I know it was you who bedded down my wife, made her fall in love with you. I…know…it…was…you. And the hell of it is, I should have seen it coming a long, long time ago."

The warehouse is still standing, but you feel it shifting. As if the bedrock beneath it is sliding dramatically. A severe seismic event. Your world…your personal world…turning upside down.

"Brian…don't."

"Goodbye, partner," he says, his fingers coming down on both the black and red triggers. "Figured in the end, there's no one I'd rather see hell with than you." He grins coldly. Then, "Oh, and fire in the hole."

The first blasting cap detonates, setting off a second and a third, the short sharp blasts powerful enough to rattle the structure and knock you off your feet.

You jump up, heart in your throat, the deafening blasts invading your ear and rattling your brain, echoing like a big brass bell inside a tower.

"Brian!" you shout, but he can't hear the words exiting your mouth.

You can't hear your own words. You can't hear Brian's words when you squat, grab hold of his jacket collar, attempt to pull him up off the floor. You only see his mouth open and close as he slaps your hand away, then shatters the bottle, creating a jagged knifelike edge he won't hesitate to thrust into your flesh should you touch him once more.

You do the only thing you can do with mere seconds to live. You turn for the stairwell entrance, and you run. You run as the explosives detonate, as the blast-furnace-like fire erupts, as the entirety of the oxygen is sucked up like the starlight inside a black hole.

You run like hell. Run for your life.

FIRST STAGE

THE DETONATOR

CHAPTER 1

AUGUST
BASS RIVER
CAPE COD, MA
PRESENT DAY

The tower is wired to blow.

Or, more accurately, the five-foot-high vertical sand tower is about to blow sky high, even if it did take Henry and me most of the morning to construct it.

"Take your position along the perimeter, Henry," I insist while squatting and strategically positioning my hands along both sides of the tower's base. "Sound the one-minute siren. Time to implode this sucker, make way for something new."

In an unusual display of energy and enthusiasm, Henry jumps up and down, megaphones his hands around his mouth, and sings like a trumpet, causing some of the other folks on the beach to lock eyes on us. He might be unusually short and small, if not frail, his bones brittle, his face wrinkled, his hair thin, gray, and rapidly receding, but you can still see some of me in him. My brown eyes, my solid square jaw, and my barrel-chested build acquired not entirely inside a weight room at some Gold's Gym (although bench pressing three-fifteen on a flat bench can be the next best thing to sex), but on hundreds of demolition jobsites I worked with my hands prior to finally realizing my dream: the privilege of working with explosives. Okay, maybe Henry doesn't have much in the way of a stocky build, or a square jaw accented with a salt-and-pepper goatee, or the healthy tan skin that I inherited from my late mother's Asian Indian side. But sometimes you see what you want to see in your boy. And I see a magnificent, beautiful young man.

"What's our motto, Henry? The Master Blaster prayer."

"Safety first and last, Dad."

"Amen, son. Gospel if I ever heard it."

"Thirty seconds, Dad."

"Hey, don't forget the tuneage."

"Oh yeah," Henry says. "I almost forgot." Bending down, he picks up the plastic sand shovel, positions it across his little belly, starts strumming it, air guitar-style.

"Boom, boom," he sings aloud in a high-pitched rattle-filled, elderly voice. "Out go the lights!"

"Clear the area, Ellen," I say, "this is going to be the world's first true implosion of a one-hundred-story high-rise. The one that's gonna put Master Blasters back on the map."

"Oh, for God's sakes, Singer," Ellen says from her beach chair beneath the blue umbrella, "can't you please act your age? Or at least leave the job at home?"

"I'm like twenty dog years older than Dad," Henry points out. "And I'm having a blast…Get it? A master blast."

Suddenly, an itch in my left ear. One of those impossible-to-get-to itches since it's actually located inside the canal and not on the ear itself. Careful not to get any sand into the opening, I gently finger the tiny hearing aid that I've been wearing for sixteen years now. Since the…well, let's call it accident…that occurred in Manhattan's Alphabet City when the warehouse I was contracted to implode was detonated by a second, illegally operated device.

"Earth to Singer," Ellen says, brushing back her thick, shoulder-length black hair with her fingers. An action that even now, after twenty-three years of marriage, never fails to take my breath away. "Did you turn up that hearing aid?"

"Roger that, Ellen, baby," I say, removing my finger from my ear. "I can now read your lips, loud and clear."

Not too tall, but not too short, Ellen fits my five-feet-ten-inch frame perfectly. Daily morning jogs and even some strength training in our home gym has allowed her to maintain the identical sexy figure she bore when I first met her during our junior year at Bates College back in '85, where I studied engineering and she plowed through a major in music theory. The short of it was that I would demolish buildings while she pursued a creative career in the musical arts. More precisely, piano performance.

But what we didn't anticipate at the time was that our one and only child, Henry, would be afflicted with progeria and his slow but sure debilitation would become as heartbreaking as it would be time consuming. While Ellen had hoped for a thriving career as a concert pianist, she ended up spending the bulk of her days and nights seeing to Henry's needs, even if he is about to turn twenty in a couple of days. She has, however, managed to maintain a part-time career as a professional pianist and piano teacher. I also suspect she spends much of the day just plain having a good time with Henry, since he is arguably one of the funniest, most gentle souls on earth.

"I just wanted to remind you that your building-blow-up days are behind you," Ellen goes on, staring up at the sun while her dark round sunglasses shield her deep brown eyes. "You lost your license, remember? You almost got killed, remember that too? You almost left me a widow and Henry a half orphan. It's important to move forward in life. Besides, you have a nice new thriving line of work."

"The new job is boring," I say. Then, "Were you aware they're going to implode the old Wellington Hotel in a few days in downtown Albany? That could have been my baby, El. Word up is they called in a Chinese company to shoot it. A Chinese company, for God's sakes."

"Might I remind you, you're part Indian," my wife says. "Blasting seems to run in your Asian blood."

"Okay whatever, but they're gonna have fireworks, food vendors, a block party, media from all over the state. They even set up a grandstand for the mayor. Oh, and I'm one hundred percent born and bred Americano."

She finger-combs her hair so that the bulk of it rests sexily on her shoulder.

"Let it go, Iqbal Lamba—"

"Ike, if you don't mind. And drop the Lamba. You remind me of my mother."

"Okay, Ike, breathe in, breathe out, and let it all go. You're here, you're alive, and that's what's important."

"Easy for you to say. You have your concert piano career. You have your fans, your shows, your future. You have Lincoln Center."

"I'm a piano teacher who gives a concert at the local Jewish Community Center gymnasium now and again." She laughs. "But thank you for making it all sound so glamorous."

Behind me, Henry still has his hands cupped around his mouth.

"Ten seconds!" he bellows.

The waves crash onto the beach, while the sunbathing vacationers who flank us pretend to ignore our very existence.

"Working for the Albany Police Department bomb disposal is boring?" Ellen says. "It's dangerous and glamorous."

She says this with an almost defiant tone in her voice. But here's the truth about bomb disposal: Disarming an explosive device requires heavy bomb-resistant body armor, robots, and plenty of safety procedures. Demolishing buildings by timed implosion, on the other hand, doesn't require much more than safety goggles. It also once came within a hair's breadth of killing me. I survived, but with a right shoulder to left hip purple scar that runs the length of my back. A stark reminder of the hot steel that sliced through me as the old warehouse in Alphabet City went boom when it wasn't supposed to.

"Nothing happens in Albany," I go on. "I haven't disarmed anything in two years, and even then, the last bomb I put down wasn't put down by me personally. It was a teenager's M-80 that was neutralized by the robot. I got to work the controls like it was a video game. The entire APD made fun of me. Called me M-80 Man for two full weeks."

"That happens to me too, Dad," Henry says. "People are mean. Sometimes you gotta let that shit go."

"Henry, mouth," Ellen scolds.

"Oops," he says.

"They also used to call me The Robot," I add. "Like the robot in the Lost in Space reruns."

"Why, Dad?"

"Because my blasting suit makes me look like…well…a robot."

"But the important thing," Ellen interjects, "is you came home that evening happy, healthy, and wise. No more wiring up unstable buildings with even more unstable explosives. No more traveling half the year. No more nights awake in bed worrying if the building was going to implode or drop the wrong way onto a whole bunch of bystanders including yourself and our son."

She makes a wide, ear to ear smile that smells like victory. I can't blame her, of course. What wife doesn't want to be free of worry when it comes to their husband's day job? But what I wouldn't give for the chance to resurrect Master Blasters. To finally get a shot at that coveted true implosion. One never seen before (or felt, or heard, or smelled…). Something to put me in the record books and maybe even secure me a second episode on The Detonators.

Ike Singer, the Master Blaster dreamer…

"Five seconds!" Henry shouts, his thinning gray hair as disheveled at nineteen as it was at ten when it was much thicker, his oversized Tommy Bahama bathing trunks hanging off narrow, fragile hips, smaller than normal brown eyes bright but plagued by cataracts, thin lips surrounded by fleshy cheeks marked with age spots. My God, sometimes when I look at him, I still see the small, round-bellied toddler playing in the sand on this exact patch of Cape Cod beach. Time flies for me, but like sand inside an hour glass, it's running out for Henry.

"Go to it, Ike," Ellen says from her chair. "Don't keep your public waiting."

Here's what I do: I drop to my knees, assume the position by once more placing both hands on opposite sides of the sand tower at its base.

"Wait," Henry says. "Final equipment check, Dad."

"Safety first and last, son."

"Hard hat," he says.

I pull back my hands, straighten up, make like I'm putting on a hard hat. Henry mimics my actions precisely.

"Safety goggles."

I pretend to put a pair of goggles on.

"Ear protection."

I slip on some invisible behind-the-head earmuff-style protectors. Again, Henry does the same. In fact, this is the most important safety step for him since, like me, his hearing is fading.

"Electronic control box detonator."

Holding out my hands like they are gripping a box no bigger or smaller than a video game remote, I place one finger on the black trigger and one on the red. The triggers in my mind, that is.

"Fire in the hole," Henry goes on. "Three, two, one..."

Thrusting myself forward while bending at the knees, I slice my hands through the bottom of the sand tower so cleanly, the structure seems to hang on in suspended animation for an extended couple of seconds. Long enough for me to know that all eyes belonging to the beach-going bystanders located within a radius of twenty feet are locked in on the action. It's no longer possible to ignore us.

Something happens, then. The five-foot-high tower begins to wobble, from one side to the other, until just like that it collapses into its own center and crashes down onto its own footprint. A perfect true sand tower implosion.

The crowd applauds. One man even whistles. As incredible as it is to believe, I feel the rush of excitement flow through me, like electricity through the veins. The rush I never get sick of. The rush I only crave more of now that it's been taken away from me by a crotchety New York State judge. The rush that has eluded me for going on sixteen years. The rush I've secretly vowed to get back one day in the form of my reissued license.

I stand, raise up my right hand, high-five Henry.

He attempts to jump up and down, but in his prematurely aged condition, it's all he can do to stand in one place for more than a few minutes at a time.

"We did it, Dad," he bellows. "A true implosion."

"Call the press," I say. "We've made history."

The crowd begins to disperse, smiles on their faces. I catch a look at Ellen. She's grinning, but shaking her head like she's trying to convince herself that boys will be boys at any age.

"Can we be done now?" she says.

I cock my head, take one last look at the pile of sand that just seconds ago was a five-foot-high tower.

"Show's over," I say. "But wasn't that spectacular?"

"Call the New York Times, Singer," Ellen says. "There's gotta be a reporter who will drop everything to grab up the scoop."

A young woman approaches us then from the direction of the ocean.

"Funny you should say that, Mrs. Singer," the young woman says. "I'm here to speak with your husband about what it's like to blow stuff up for a living."

CHAPTER 2

She's a tall young woman, with fine sandy blonde hair, but clipped a couple inches above her shoulders. She's not wearing a bathing suit, but instead tan shorts and a button-down shirt with no sleeves, the tails of which are hanging free. A canvas bag hangs over her shoulder and she's holding her leather gladiator sandals in her left hand. Her skin is fair, which tells me she hasn't been in the sun for very long and probably shouldn't remain in it without some serious sunblock. Her gray-blue eyes are bright and youthful, and looking into them, I can't shake the sudden wave of déjà vu that tells me this isn't the first time we've met.

She holds out her hand.

"Allow me to explain," she says. "I'm actually a freelancer doing some research on the most dangerous jobs in the world. One of which is the brave demolition crews who take down those mammoth towers with dynamite and a prayer."

Pulse picks up, because I'd love nothing more than to talk about my career. Or, former career anyway. Glancing down at Ellen, who's still seated in her lounge, I spot her smirk. I imagine her eyes rolling in their sockets under those dark sunglasses.

"You've come to the right place, young lady," she says. "My husband loves to talk about himself. Don't you, Ike?"

"Dad is da bomb," Henry mutters under his breath. "If you don't believe me, just ask him."

"Easy, you," I say. "Nothing wrong with a little healthy self-confidence."

The young woman laughs. I take her small, gentle hand in mine, give it a squeeze, then release it. The sensation washes over me for a second time. I'm not entirely sure what it is, but I can't help but feel like I've been introduced to her on some prior occasion. But where and when?

Ellen picks herself up, brushes some sand off her thighs, and holds out her hand.

"I'm the wife," she says with a grimace. "Ellen Singer."

The stranger giggles.

"The wife with a terrific sense of humor." She takes Ellen's hand in hers. "You're probably wondering how I found you here on this beach."

Ellen cocks her head over her left shoulder.

"Crossed my mind," she says.

"Me too," I say.

"Me three," Henry says.

Brushing back her hair, the stranger nods in Henry's direction.

"Well, if you have to know," she says, "Henry's Facebook account helped me out."

Ellen and I immediately turn to our son.

"Henry," we say in unison. Then, with me taking over. "What did we say about handing out personal info on social media, son?"

Henry pouts, peers down at his tiny, sand-covered feet. For an individual who, in terms of his condition, is thirty to forty years older than his parents, he is still very much a goofy kid.

"Oopsies," he says.

Eyes back on the mystery woman. "So you drove all the way out here to interview me?"

She shakes her head.

"My boyfriend has a time-share at the hotel right next door," she explains. "So I'm killing two birds. Hope you don't mind."

"What is it you wanna know?"

Raising her wrist, she glances at her watch. "Is it okay if we go somewhere more comfortable to talk?"

I point with my thumb over my shoulder. "There's an outdoor bar up there. On the patio above the beach."

"Perfect," she says. "I understand your present job is pretty dangerous too. Bomb disposal specialist. Maybe we can talk about that also."

I turn to Ellen. "You okay with Mr. Facebook for a few minutes?"

"Aren't I always?" she says under her breath.

"Mr. Facebook," Henry says, once more waving his arms. "Take a look at Mr. Facebook....Take a good look 'cause he won't be here forever."

"Not funny, Henry," Ellen says.

"Lead the way," I say, holding my hand out for the stranger.

She starts walking in the opposite direction of the crashing waves. But something dawns on me before she gets too far.

"Hey," I call out. "What did you say your name is again?"

She stops in the sand, turns.

"Alison," she says, "Alison Darling."

CHAPTER 3

The name hits me over the head like a piece of shattered concrete. The same must hold true for Ellen. Funny the effect time has on little girls. It makes them grow up. Grow up into attractive young women. I'd be tempted to give Alison a great big long-time-no-see hug, just like Ellen is presently doing, if it weren't for the bad vibes that now wash over me like a tidal wave. Waves of guilt. Of sadness and remorse.

I'm not a perfect husband by any means, and there was a time when I was even more imperfect. Imperfect to the point of being downright ugly. There's a dozen excuses I could give and another dozen euphemisms and sugar-coated descriptions of my mistake, but it would only serve to insult one's intelligence. So, I'll just say it straight no chaser.

Back in 1999, I conducted a brief affair with my partner's wife—Alison's mother. It's nothing to be proud of. Nothing I fondly recall. Nothing I want to recall at all for that matter. Like I said, I'm not looking for excuses here, but if it's possible to sight one, it would be that Ellen and I had grown apart to the point of collapse over the matter of Henry and his irreversible physical condition. In a word, Ellen was looking for me to face the reality of the situation and all I wanted to do was bury my head in the sand. I sought escape. That escape ended up with me in the arms of another woman.

How long did the affair last?

One single solitary night.

But brevity didn't prevent my partner's wife, Patty, from falling in love. Or so she insisted at the time, the dirty-blonde-haired, hazel-eyed woman even going so far as to persistently call me at my home and on my cell, long after I'd made it perfectly clear through my dogged silence that it was over. So to say my mood just went south at the sudden and unexpected presence of Patty and Brian's daughter on the beach in Cape Cod, of all places, is putting it major league light. I guess, in the end, you can try and escape your past, but no way in hell does it ever escape you.

I buy us a couple of cold beers at the outdoor bar while Alison grabs us a small table that overlooks the beach, including the backs of both my wife and my son in the near distance while the sound of the waves gently crashing on beach provides a somber soundtrack.

Sitting myself down, I place Alison's beer in front of her, and mine in front of me. We both crack the tabs, take respective sips of the ice cold beer.

"No knock-knock jokes?" I say, the words coming out forced and hoarse, as if they were peeling themselves from the back of my throat.

"Excellent memory," she says, staring contemplatively into the opening on the top of the can. "My dad loved those corny jokes."

"You still think about him?" I say, picturing the short, stocky, black-haired and thick-mustached Brian.

"Every day," she says. "Sometimes more than that." Then, looking up at me, her face bright and smiley. But somehow not happy. "And what about you, Mr. Singer? Do you remember my dad?"

My mind fills with images. Brian and I tossing a Frisbee on the big green outside our lower campus dorm at Bates back in the mid-1980s. Brian, wearing a black tuxedo at my wedding, standing beside me as my best man, and me standing at his side, just a few years prior as he wiped moisture from his brow with the back of one hand while checking his pockets with the other for a wedding ring he was sure he'd lost.

Brian and me signing our first contract for the explosive demolition of an abandoned refrigerated warehouse on Albany's north end--a job no one would touch because of the possibility of contaminating the area with old and still very toxic Freon. Brian staying up all night to create a detonation sequence that could be construed as a work of pure explosive art. Brian high-fiving me when the building imploded onto its own adjacent parking lot as planned, the press interviewing us for what seemed like hours afterward, and even some of the younger bystanders asking for our autographs. Brian and I sweating out our first big demo jobs in Scotland, West Africa's Benin, Paris, and New York City, celebrating our first huge bonus at a steak house with our wives dressed in sultry black evening gowns. Brian and I shouting out in joy at the birth of our kids, and watching our plans… our collective hopes and dreams…come to fruition.

But then I also see the defeated Brian sitting on the concrete floor in the wired-to-blow warehouse in Alphabet City, one hand gripping divorce papers, the other a second electronic control box.

"I know it was you, pal. I know it was you who bedded down my wife, made her fall in love with you. I…know…it…was… you."

Now it's me staring into my beer can like it's a crystal ball that can't see the future, but instead, is doomed to replay the mistakes of the past.

I attempt to paint a happy smile on my face. "So, Alison, you're a journalist now?"

She shakes her head, pulls something out of her bag that looks like a pen, only larger. But when she thumbs a switch on the metal cylindrical device and brings the other end to her mouth, I realize it's not a pen at all.

"E-cig," I say. "That do it for you like real cigarettes?"

"Nothing replaces the tobacco blast of a real cigarette. But I don't want cancer."

"Better watch yourself. Those things have been known to explode. Could do one hell of a job on your pretty face."

Grinning, she says, "I was raised in the explosives business, remember? I'll be sure to take every precaution possible."

"I'm sure you will," I say. Then, "And what is it you want to know?"

"I'm researching a story for non-professional reasons," she says, exhaling a breath of blue steam. "It's a very personal story involving you, me, my mom, my dad, and the past. But..."

"But what?"

She drinks some beer. Not because she's thirsty, but because what she's about to tell me is going to hurt. Or so my gut tells me.

"Well, Mr. Singer—"

"You're not a kid anymore, Alison. It's Ike."

"Okay, Ike Singer. There is something you should know, I suppose."

I glance out at the beach, spot Ellen seated in her lounge. From all appearances she hasn't moved an inch since I left her alone with our son, who is currently digging a great big hole in the sand. The old-man-kid enjoying his beachside vacation, like it's his last. I would gladly die before I ever hurt my wife and son again.

"It's about my mother," she says.

Just like I saw the many faces of Brian, I now see Patty. Her big eyes, her shoulder-length hair. I feel her touch. Even after all this time.

"I'm listening."

Alison steals another, longer sip of her beer, exhales.

"She's dying," she says.

I love my wife. Love her more than myself. Need her more than the air I breathe. So why does news of Patty's mortality feel like a swift kick to the gut?

Now it's my turn to drink. I finish the can, get up from my chair, grab us two more, set them down on the table.

"I haven't finished my first yet," Alison comments.

"Drink up."

But she just stares at the condensate running down the sides of the two cans placed in front of her.

"What's Patty dying from?" I ask.

"Cancer. It's in her liver and her lungs."

"Radiation?"

"She's finished with it. It helped for a while. Shrunk the tumors. But they came back. Doctors say it will reach her brain before Christmas."

I do the math. Five months.

My mouth is dry, pulse pounding not in my chest but in my temples. Why does Christ give us a life only to snatch it back up before we're barely halfway through?

"Is that why you're here, then? To tell me your mom is dying?"

She pauses to smoke more of the e-cig, then stares down contemplatively at the two drinks set before her. She pockets the e-cig, raises her hands back up, locks her gaze on mine.

"I know about you two. About what happened that one night in 1999."

Another powerful kick to the stomach, my lungs suddenly emptied of their air.

She goes on, "I know now why my father died inside that imploded warehouse all those years ago. Why he did it. Why he wanted to take you with him."

A third kick.

Don't deny it, Singer, I tell myself. That will only make it worse. Best just to hear her out. Best just to accept the fact that you have this coming.

Cracking the tab on the second beer, I drink half of it down in one gulp. Getting good and soused feels like the perfect medicine right about now. But then, that would be like feeling sorry for myself over something I have no right to feel sorry for myself over.

"She still loves you, Ike," she says. "She never stopped. She fell in love with you, but then felt abandoned by you. What hurt her more than anything was your not calling her or returning her calls. Not even once. I thought you might like to know that, now that she's dying."

"I appreciate it," I say. But it's a lie and she knows it.

She steals a glance down at the beach.

"You know, Ike," she says. "You and the missus and your boy, you really do make a picture-perfect family. Even if he is sick. Really special. Norman Rockwell couldn't have painted it any better."

Exhaling. Feeling sad, agitated, and anxious.

"Thanks," I say. "But I have to ask. What's your point, Alison?"

"Course, it's too bad the boy won't live long," she says in place of an answer. "You know, way back when, I knew there was something not quite right with him, but I just couldn't put my finger on it. I thought he looked like a cartoon character or something out of the Muppets. Like Elmo." She laughs. "But then, I was what, nine years old?"

"He suffers from Hutchinson–Gilford progeria syndrome, thank you very much. You're right, he has very little time left and I'd appreciate you not talking about him or referring to him as a Muppet."

"We have that in common you and me."

The mix of emotions running through my veins now channels into outright anger. Anger at myself for screwing up. Anger at Patty for getting sick. Anger at Alison for showing up suddenly in my life unannounced while I'm on vacation with my son, arguably for the very last time.

"What do we have in common?" I ask.

"Loved ones with very little time left."

It's not the words themselves, but the way she says them that forces a steely cold tremor up and down my entire system of nerve bundles. This is not the sweet little kid I once knew. The kid with the bad knock-knock jokes.

"Anyway," she goes on. "You are very lucky. If you could have seen what my family life was like after my father died. After my mother lost you. I don't think a day went by when she didn't drink herself to sleep." Shaking her head. "Did you know that for many years, I was moved around from foster home to foster home during those periods when my mother couldn't take care of me? Do you have any clue how very little the city of Albany cares about its neglected and abused children?"

Neglected…Abused…

A slow burn replacing the cold Freon in my veins.

"No. I wasn't aware," I say. "But I'm quite certain you won't be appearing in any 'I love Albany' public relations TV spots anytime soon."

"Well, why would you be aware since you broke off all communication with us? After all, my dad tried to kill you. I can't blame you." She drinks more beer. "It lasted for a period of maybe five or six years. From time to time my mother would break down and be hospitalized, and from time to time those horrible social services Nazis would send me away, whether I liked it or not. My God, some of those homes were hell on earth. Trust me, Ike, the system is cold, calculated, and corrupt." Peering into my eyes, smiling once more. Like she's capable of an instantaneous emotional sea change. "I really like calling you Ike. I…Like… Ike."

"That so."

"Listen, Ike, you know what it's like to be forced to walk the woods at night with a crazy foster father? You know what it's like to feel his naked body pressing down on yours? To feel his hand covering your mouth so his wife can't hear the screams coming through the trees?" She laughs, drinks, sets the can back down. "I wonder sometimes, Ike…I wonder sometimes if your sweet, precious, gorgeous wife, Ellen, knows the whole truth and nothing but the truth about what happened sixteen years ago. Would it upset her if she knew the truth? If she knew who you really are?"

"That's enough," I say. "What the hell do you want from me?"

"Hey, everything okay here?" Ellen says.

I raise my head up quick. My wife is fast approaching along the concrete walkway. After a fleeting moment, she stands before the table, a black cover-all shrouding her torso, leaving just smooth tan legs exposed. The legs of a twenty-five-year-old. Her hair is neatly parted above her left eye, her sunglasses giving her the look and feel of someone famous and glamorous.

I stand, nearly knock over my can of beer.

"Sure," I say, the hoarseness having invaded my throat and voice once again. "Why wouldn't it be?"

"Maybe Alison is asking some tough questions. Putting you on the spot."

I swallow something cold and bitter.

"I have indeed been hard on Ike," Alison says, sliding out her chair, standing. "But your husband has responded like a real trouper. Haven't you, Ike?"

I nod, the slow burn having completed its mission of filling every vein and capillary in my body.

"Alison was just leaving."

"I was?" She giggles. "Oh yes, I guess I was." She takes hold of her beer, drinks down the rest, crushes the aluminum can in her hand, just like her father used to do inside our dorm room while we watched episode after episode of old Twilight Zone reruns. "That's what Ike and my dad would do even to the meanest, oldest, toughest building there was. What did you two call it? A true implosion?"

"We never actually got to perform a true implosion," I say, more under my breath than out loud. "Your father—"

"Yes, we know what happened to my dad."

She sets the crushed can on the table, grabs her bag, places the strap over her shoulder.

"Well," she says. "I'd better be going."

She walks around the table, goes to Ellen. Holding out her arms, she gives my wife a big, tight hug. Caught by surprise, Ellen purses her lips. I know that behind those sunglasses her eyes have gone wide. She makes a half-hearted attempt at hugging back.

"Nice seeing you again, Alison. Don't be a stranger."

The two separate.

"Oh, I won't be," she says. "I won't be a stranger at all, believe me."

Shooting me a wink of her right eye, she walks past me, her shoulder brushing against mine.

Ellen comes to me.

"You okay, Ike?" she says. "You look a little pale."

Glancing out toward the beach, I spot Henry standing in the newly excavated hole. It's deep enough to hide his thin legs almost entirely.

I say, "I guess remembering the past…remembering what it was like to work day in and day out with explosives and shooting buildings and bridges that could fall on your head if you didn't do things right…remembering what happened on that final day…took more out of me than I thought."

More lies to hide my shame, my guilt, my remorse. So many wrongs don't stand a chance in hell of making a right out of what happened all those years ago between Patty Darling and me.

"Maybe you shouldn't answer any more of her questions."

I shake my head. "It's okay. She's Brian's daughter after all."

Ellen nods, contemplatively. "Amazing how much she looks like Patty back when we were all in school together. Same eyes and hair." Then, forcing a smile. "Head back down to the beach? It's our last day of fun in the sun before reality settles in."

"Not yet. I think I'll have another beer, then meet up with you guys in a few minutes."

"Don't get drunk, Ike Singer," she says, bringing her hand to my face, gently caressing it. "I was hoping to sneak in a shower break with you later when Henry falls to sleep."

In my mind, thoughts of Patty dying. Bad thoughts. Disturbing thoughts.

"Sounds good," I say. Under normal circumstances, I would be counting the minutes and seconds until later tonight when I will finally have Ellen all to myself. But now I am frightened over what might become of Alison's sudden appearance.

Leaning in, Ellen kisses me on the mouth. Then turning, she heads back toward the short flight of steps that leads down to the beach.

I go back to the bar, order a third beer. And a whiskey chaser to go with it.

CHAPTER 4

When night falls, we head out for lobster at a restaurant retrofitted from an old three-masted whaling schooner. We're seated at a booth that's got its own brass porthole which opens onto a narrow inlet. The briny-smelling breeze blows in through the round hole. We can hear the seagulls and the occasional hum of an outboard motor while the night fishermen flock to the bay with their spinning rods for sea bass and stripers.

The lobsters are a bit cold by the time they get to us, the mashed potatoes lumpy, and the salads limp. But Henry just loves this place because it makes him feel like a ship captain. It's at once heartwarming and heartbreaking to see Henry happy. Sometimes it's easier when he isn't feeling good. Or he's in pain. Because then we have the option of giving him something to make the pain go away. We are in control. We are able to help him. But seeing him happy reminds me…reminds us…that soon the time will come when he won't be so happy. The happiness is temporary. Staged. Fleeting.

After dinner, we play miniature golf, eat soft ice cream cones, ride the go-carts. I'm not saying much of anything, not because I'm not enjoying a night accented with a cool breeze that blows off the ocean, but because I can't get Alison Darling's face out of my head. Can't shake the image of her mother from my brain. Patty, lying on her back inside a dark hotel room, only the red and blue light from the neon-lit sign mounted to a metal pole in the parking lot, oozing though the breaks in the curtains, flashing on the popcorn ceiling…

On several occasions, Ellen asks me if I'm feeling okay. Would I like to go back to the hotel early? Lie down?

"You have a long drive in the morning," she reminds me. "Maybe you need to get some rest."

But I plant a smile on my face. As genuine a smile I can muster.

"I'm fine," I lie. "Just a little too much sun today."

My mind is racing with words. Words that suddenly, and very unexpectedly, come at me in the voice of Patty Darling. They invade my brain like a thousand fire ants.

But after more than two decades of marriage, you know your wife, isn't that right, lover boy? And your wife knows you. Trust me on that. She knows you're thinking about Alison, and the conversation you had today. But then, what Ellen doesn't know is the truth. Maybe that's the way you have got to keep it, Ike. That is, if you want to keep your family together.

By the time we get back to the hotel, Henry is already fast asleep.

Carrying him into the room over my shoulder, as if he were just four years old, I set him gently on the bed, pull off his too-big jeans, slip him under the covers, kiss him goodnight. Not like he's a nineteen-year-old young man living inside an old man's body, but instead, a little boy who refuses to grow up.

My body in need of a nightcap, I retrieve a seven-dollar beer from the mini bar and pop the top with an opener while Ellen packs her and Henry's bags, sets them by the door for easy access to the Suburban in the morning. Mission accomplished, she tells me she's taking a shower tonight so the chore won't have to be bothered with in the morning.

"How about you?" she says, shooting me a wink while taking hold of my hand, squeezing it tightly.

Message received, loud and perfectly clear.

"Good idea," I whisper, setting my beer down on the dresser.

We run the water until the bathroom is steamy. We then slowly undress one another, all the time our mouths and tongues connecting, our hands exploring one another's bodies like we only just met at some no-name Hyannis bar and are about to make love for the first time. I run my hands through her hair, and she runs her fingernails down the length of my spine as we kiss one another softly, but hard too.

Stepping into the shower, we continue to kiss, but let the water soak our bodies and the steam coat our faces. Ellen uncaps a small bottle of body wash and proceeds to massage her soft flesh, starting with her breasts, which are pale against her tan skin. I quickly take over, soaping her body for her, my hands and fingers massaging her breasts, drifting down past her tight tummy, to her naval, and finally her sex. Leaning forward, her left hand pressed against the forward wall, she reaches around for me and allows me to enter her from behind. We make love slowly, but passionately too, careful not to wake Henry, but all the time wanting and needing one another.

In my head, I try to see only Ellen. But Patty's face flashes through my brain. In my imagination, I see a very sad Patty. Her hair disheveled, her face bloodless and pale, eyes filled with tears. Whatever excitement I had for Ellen goes irretrievably limp. I close my eyes tightly, keep them closed, try to erase Patty's memory from my brain. I don't want to ruin this perfect and all too rare moment.

But it's too late. I can't seem to function.

"What's wrong, babe?" Ellen whispers. "Is it me?"

I open my eyes. "I'm sorry, honey. I'm not sure what's gotten into me."

"You're nerved up," she says. "Henry. His sickness. A grown-up Alison visiting you out of the blue today, churning up all those old memories of Master Blasters and Brian. Maybe it's all too much."

I kiss her on the mouth. "Give me a few minutes. I'll be back in fighting shape."

But the water is already going from hot to lukewarm. Within a minute or two it will be downright cold.

"Tell you what, Singer. I'll take a rain check on this one. But as soon as we get home, I'm gonna ravage you."

"I like it when you talk dirty," I say. But I'm making light of sad situation.

"Oh, and I'm gonna get you a Cialis prescription."

"Very funny."

I shut off the water. We step out of the shower. Ellen hands me a white towel. She dries herself, then steals another towel, which she turbans around her wet hair. She goes to open the door, but I place my hand on the opener.

"I love you, El. More than anything in the world."

"I know," she whispers. "I've always known."

She kisses me gently on the mouth.

With that, I open the door and step out into the cold, air-conditioned darkness of the hotel room.

Later that night, I dream.

I'm standing on the top floor of a high-rise that's set to blow. The walls have been stripped of their glass and the place scraped down to the naked concrete. The half dozen vertical bearing I-beams are injected with explosive and wrapped, while the blasting caps are set in position.

In my hands I hold a remote electronic control box, my fingers on the triggers. Now appearing at the opposite end of the floor are two figures. As they step out of the shadows I see they are Ellen and Henry.

"What are you doing here?" I say. "It's too dangerous."

"We didn't want you to be alone," Ellen says, from across the floor.

Three more figures appear, not from out of the shadows, but like they've been standing there the entire time, and only now have I noticed them. It's Patty, Alison, and Brian.

It hurts my head to look at them, because Patty is naked, with only a cheap motel bed sheet covering her sex and torso, her dirty blonde hair mussed up, her eyes bloodshot, like she's been crying all night. Drinking and crying.

Alison is nine years old again, but her T-shirt has been torn down the front, the button on her blue jeans popped off, the zipper opened, revealing a hint of pink panties. Her left eye is swelled shut and black and blue. Without her having to say it, I know she's been victimized by her foster father.

Brian's body is mangled, his arms blown off, his legs pretzeled, a large gaping hole in his chest. His lower jaw is blown away and a portion of his skull is missing, exposing his brain. He's been blasted to bits, but somehow, he's alive.

Ellen steps forward, holding Henry's hand.

"I know what you did to these people, Singer," she says. "I know what you did to us."

My eyes well up with tears and I press the triggers on the controller. I don't know why I'm doing it, but I can't seem to help myself. The sirens sound while the tune to "Boom Boom, Out Go the Lights!" blares from the loudspeakers below.

"Knock knock," says Alison.

"Who's there?" I say.

"Goto."

"Goto who?"

"Goto hell."

The first of the blasting caps detonates…

I wake. Rise up. My body soaked in a cold sweat.

Reaching out with my left hand, I feel for Ellen. Her chest is inflating and deflating slowly up and down and in rhythm to her slow breaths. I look over my right shoulder, see that Henry is also fast asleep, his little body curled up in the fetal position.

I lie back down, roll onto my side away from Ellen, my eyes focused on my sick son. From outside the open window come the lonely sounds of waves crashing onto the beach.

"Christ almighty, what have I done?" I whisper to myself, as my eyelids fall.

CHAPTER 5

In the morning, the sun shines bright on Cape Cod.

She sits tight behind the wheel of her four-door BMW while the nice family finishes packing the black Suburban to the breaking point with numerous pieces of luggage, shopping bags bearing stylish logos belonging to shops in downtown Hyannis and quaint seaside Chatham, and even the beach toys that Henry used perhaps for his final time. There's also a couple of extra bags filled, no doubt, with meds for the boy. An old boy of nineteen going on ninety.

Such a sweet kid. Such a sweet old man. Such a shit sandwich he's been dealt by the good Lord above.

Life's a bitch, Henry old boy. Then you die way before your time.

It will be a shame to break up his family. The only thing he's got left on this earth.

Lifting the center console, she rummages through her old CD collection, finds the cracked and stained plastic cover that once upon a time belonged to her dad. Pat Travers, R&B guitarist and all around general troublemaker. A musician with an explosive anger, or so rumor has it. She pops the CD into the dash player and fingers the fast forward until she comes to the one song Master Blasters, Inc. would blare over a mic'd up boom box just prior to starting the countdown to one of their implosions.

Boom Boom, Out Go the Lights…!!!

She recalls sixteen years ago and the electricity that would pervade the air when the gathering crowd danced to the over-amplified guitar, throbbing bass, and pounding drums, their collective voices sending a chill through her nine-year-old flesh and bones as they collectively sang along with Mr. Travers, "BOOM BOOM, OUT GO THE LIGHTS!"

The song she'd listened to ten thousand times before begins. The fast but steady beat mimics her pounding pulse. She eyes the happy family as they exit their bottom-floor motel room for what will be their last time this summer. When they pause for one final selfie, angling themselves awkwardly so that they can get the beach into the background, she finds herself smiling. How wonderful it might have been to experience the same thing when she was growing up. A photo by the beach with her mom and dad. A selfie of the three of them, having just enjoyed a wonderful vacation together.

Instead, all she knew was the shame of her father's suicide and attempted murder…the shame of her mother's alcoholism, breakdowns, and hospitalizations…the shame and agony of one foster father after the other staring at her with hungry eyes from across a strange dinner table, in a strange house, occupied by a strange family who had no real love for her. A foster father who would impregnate her with his evil offspring. She remembers it all. But most of all, she remembers the woods.

She watches while Ike helps the elderly but yet oh so young Henry climb up into the back. Watches Ike wrap the seatbelt around him. Watches the father gently brush back what's left of the boy's severely retreating hair, revealing an age-spotted scalp. Watches him close the Suburban door and do something she never would have expected: the raising of his hand to make the sign of the cross. In the name of the father, the son, and the unholy ghost of a woman you used up like a piece of meat.

"You're going to lose Henry soon and you know it," she whispers under the thrashing music. "Now you know what it feels like to be me. To live in fear of what you will lose."

When Ike goes around the back of the Suburban, opens the

driver's side door, hops in, she fires up the BMW. She waits while Ike backs out of his spot, then pulls out of the lot onto the river road that will lead him to the Cape Cod highway and, eventually, the Mass Pike.

Careful not to let him get too much of a head start, she shifts the transmission into drive and proceeds on down the road.

"Boom, boom, Ike Singer," she sings, "out go the fucking lights!"

CHAPTER 6

Traffic is light on a Friday morning.

It takes me only twenty minutes to get off the Cape and over the steep, arching Sagamore Bridge which spans the Cape Cod Canal. From there, it's a straight shot up Route 495. Then finally, the long westward drive on the busy Mass Pike. Traffic becomes heavier as we pass through small industrial towns like Worcester and Springfield, Henry fast asleep in the back, Ellen glued to her iPhone.

"That's interesting," she says after a time. "I don't think Alison Darling is a real journalist."

Just hearing the name of my partner's daughter coming from her mouth causes a start in my heart.

Patty's voice sounds off inside my head again. She's speaking to me exactly how she used to speak to me once upon a time. Same word choices, same spicy, if not humorous, take-no-prisoners tone.

Knock knock…Wait, don't answer, lover boy, I'll do it for you. Who's there? Goto…Goto who?…Goto hell…Now tell me something, Ike, have you ever heard a more stupid joke? I relinquish any and all responsibility for my one and only daughter's sense of humor and her psychosis…

"How do you know that?" I say while silently trying to brush off my stupid thoughts. "That Alison isn't a real journalist, I mean."

"I can't find a single article or byline with her name on it," Ellen says, fingering the screen on her smartphone. Today she's wearing a short, white, summer-weight dress that sports a V neck, revealing more than a hint of cleavage and a black lace Victoria's Secret bra. Her smooth legs and manicured feet protected by leather sandals make the package complete. It also robs me of my breath. Shifting my right hand, I set it on her leg.

But she swipes it away like it's an insect.

"Henry will see," she whispers, not without a smile. "Pay attention to the road, Mr. Singer."

She continues to glare at her phone while I battle the traffic.

"Here's something," she says, just as we pass a sign that advertises a rest stop ten miles ahead. Feeling the pressure in my bladder from the large Dunkin' Donuts coffee I polished off prior to scaling the Sagamore Bridge, I'm setting a course straight for the exit.

"Something what?"

"There's an Alison Darling…and how many Alison Darlings can there be in the world…who isn't a writer at all, but a scientist."

"A scientist," I repeat, glancing into the rearview, spotting a metallic silver BMW coming up just a little too close for comfort on the Suburban's behind.

"Well, she's an assistant professor at the College of Nanoscale Science and Engineering in Albany, more specifically. There's a small bio with her picture on it."

She reaches over with the phone, like it's at all possible for me to take the time out to study it what with the jerk on my tail. But that doesn't mean I don't see the smiling face of the woman who sat across the table from me yesterday, threatening me, maybe not directly but threatening me all the same.

"That's her," I say, quickly shifting into the right lane without using my directional. Take that, silver Beemer. "What's her area of expertise? What's she teach?"

"Nano-thermites or what's also known as super-thermites. Which, according to this anyway, is the study of…get this… metastable intermolecular composites such as metal and metal oxide for high and customizable reactions." She looks up. "I can hardly even pronounce this stuff much less picture it."

The fine hairs on the back of my neck prick up.

"Explosions," I say. "Explosions, pyrotechnics. She's studying major league explosions created by very small explosives. Super-duper small. I suppose that's why she wanted to talk with me." Shaking my head. "When I was young, the closest you could come to a college degree in explosive demolition was going to war. Nowadays you can get a masters or even a doctorate in Explosive Engineering."

"Small explosives," Ellen presses. "Like how small?"

"Like as small as a pinhead in some cases. I've done some reading up on them…their development…since I started subbing for the APD."

Ellen shakes her head. "I don't get it. How can something as small as a pinhead make a huge explosion?"

"You mess with the order of molecules on a nano-scale and then add a little propellant to them along with a shot of pure oxygen, and an ignition switch for a cherry on top, and you've got a bomb that will fit into the pocket of my Levi's that's also powerful enough to take down an airliner. Those ISIS bastards downed that Russian airliner over Egypt with a nano-scale bomb stuffed into a soda can."

"Oh, great. Terrorists are gonna love this nano-scale stuff. Make them even more murderous."

"Luckily this science is very, very expensive right now. But the military implications are huge. They're so small and the materials are essentially odorless and undetectable by traditional methods like dog sniffers and automated colorimetrics like DataChem and SEEKERe machines. We've been training on them for a year now. Training how to counter them."

"A bomb so small you can fit it into your pocket and that can go undetected. That makes me feel better."

"Unfortunately it's reality, and what's worse is this stuff will be getting cheaper as time goes on. Used to be all a terrorist had to do was mosey on down to the local Home Depot, purchase a length of pipe, some low-burn explosive like black powder, a trigger device like an alarm clock, and you were done. You could build it for twenty bucks. But it was cumbersome and didn't pack a lot of firepower. Relatively speaking, that is. With super nano-thermite tech, however, an IED will cost you a lot more, but you can take out a city block with a mini pipe bomb that will fit into the core of an average Bic pen."

Ellen stares out onto the highway. "The world is truly screwed, you know that?"

"People seem intent on killing one another. Mutilating them. Always been that way."

"You sound almost excited when you talk about it. Admit it. It turns you on."

I cock my head. "Well, just imagine the good use super-thermite bombs could be put to. I could take down an entire concrete tower with just a small amount of controlled charge. Be a lot quicker, safer, and cheaper than shoving pounds and pounds of detonation cord and TNT into the walls and bearing beams. Course, I'd have to figure out a way to get my license back first."

"Let's hope you don't," she whispers, her eyes peering out the window.

We're quiet for a moment while I peek once more into the rearview. The silver BMW is back on my tail. But this time I'm getting a clear shot at the driver. My heart flies up into my throat when I see that the person behind the wheel is Alison Darling.

The green sign for the rest area says one mile.

"Mind if we make a pit stop, El? I'm about to burst."

"What I'm trying to figure out in my head," she says in place of an answer, "is why Alison would present herself as a reporter or journalist?"

A quick glance into the rearview. She's still on my tail, a sly smile on her face, her eyes shielded by aviator sunglasses.

"I'm not sure she ever used the title journalist or anything else," I say. "Research. I think she said she was doing research."

I'm not defending Alison. I'm more interested in keeping my wife's suspicions at bay. Better that she just forget about Alison altogether. Better that she not have the slightest suspicion about my mistake. My crime against her love and trust.

Ellen nods. "Scientists do research, right?"

"Exactly."

The rest stop is now coming up fast on my right. My pulse is pounding, far faster than it should. I'm doing my best to remain calm. Like nothing is happening right behind us.

"Aren't you stopping here?" she interjects.

"That's the plan."

I'm doing almost eighty. The turn-off is only about three hundred feet on my right. The right lane splits off onto an exit ramp.

"Ike," Ellen says, voice raised a decibel, "you're going to miss it."

I stay in my lane.

"Ike Singer." Her voice is louder, more anxious.

The exit is only twenty feet away. It looks like I'm about to drive right past it. Until I suddenly and abruptly twist the wheel to the right, jerking the Suburban over the grassy meridian and onto the exit ramp.

"What the hell are you doing, Singer?!"

Henry jerks awake. "Are we dead?"

The Suburban bounces while I toe tap the brakes.

"Sorry, guys," I say. "Guess I spaced out."

"Space Mountain," Henry says. "That's what you are, Dad. Ike Singer from Space Mountain."

"More like shithead behind the wheel," Ellen grouses.

"Mom said the S word." Henry laughs.

"Tattletale," Ellen says. "I'm gonna make you take extra Geritol tonight, young man."

"Very funny, Mom. Haha."

I find an empty parking space, pull in, cut the engine. My pulse is still pounding, but at least I lost Alison.

“Let’s go, all,” I insist. “Still a lot of road left to cover.”

Opening the door, I slip on out of the Suburban, content to breathe in some fresh oxygen. But instead, my heart goes south. Because pulling into an empty space behind us is a silver BMW.

CHAPTER 7

"Let's make this quick," I say, opening up the back passenger's side door, undoing Henry's seatbelt.

"I'm not a cripple, Dad. I can unbuckle my own seatbelt."

"What's the rush, Ike?" Ellen says. "You gotta give us a chance to stretch our legs."

"Just want to get back on the road ASAP." Taking hold of Henry's hand, pulling him along.

"Easy, Dad. Remember, I'm not as spry as I used to be."

I slow down, allow him to walk at his own pace. Sometimes Henry insists on doing everything himself. Then, a mere moment later, he'll realize his limitations. It's a difficult, if not contradictory, existence for him. Sometimes I get frustrated over it. But those are the times I need to catch myself. Rein myself in. Show a little patience and compassion.

"What's gotten into you?" Ellen whispers. "You're suddenly Singer the very strange."

I breathe in, breathe out. Heart be still.

"I'm sorry, guys," I say. "Just contemplating heading back to work. You know how it can be."

"Boring," she says. "Remember, you said it yourself. Finding hidden bombs is boring. But somehow safer since it's the robot that gets blown up. Not you. Which, of course, I greatly prefer. I'll take boring over blown to bits any old day."

Her sarcasm doesn't go unnoticed. But I know it's her way of masking anxiety. And who can blame her? I wrap my arm around her shoulders, plant a kiss on her cheek.

"I love you," I say.

"Get a room, kids!" Henry bellows.

We come to the doors of the facility. I grab hold of the opener, open the door for Ellen and Henry.

"Nathan's Hot Dogs," he says. "I'll have two with mustard."

"I'll take one," Ellen says. "I'm famished."

"Okay," I say, looking over my shoulder. For the moment I've lost Alison. Who knows, maybe she decided to move on to the next rest area after all. "I'll meet you at the Nathan's stand after I hit the bathroom. Henry, you coming?"

"Right behind you, Dad."

Together, my son and I disappear into the men's room.

When we're finished, we head back into the general area of the rest stop. Turning toward the Nathan's Hot Dog stand, I spot Ellen. And the woman standing beside her.

Alison Darling.

Her smile is matched by Ellen's. It's a benign smile, filled with the surprise and wonder that can only come from running into someone you haven't seen in years and years, not once in twenty-four hours, but twice.

"Look who the cat dragged in," Ellen says with a wink of her eye. Without her having to say it, I know she's a little weirded out by Alison's presence. If only she knew what I knew about Alison. About her father. About her mother. She would not only be weirded out. She'd be screaming at me. Hitting me. Leaving me. Leaving me for good. I might do the same if the tables were turned.

"Well, hello there, Ike," Alison says, hugging me tightly, planting a peck on my cheek. "Nice duds," she adds, referring to the last remaining black and red Master Blasters T-shirt I'm wearing. "Strictly old-school, dude."

I stand stone stiff. No words. No signs of affection. Only rage, which of course, I'm forced to swallow.

"Better make it look good," she proceeds to whisper in my

ear. "We wouldn't want the wifey to know what happened, now would we."

It takes all the strength in my body, but I try my hardest to paint a smile on my face, but what I truly want to do is scratch her eyes out.

"And hello there, Henry, my old friend," Alison says, releasing me. Then, pressing her fingers up against her lips. "Errrr, well, you know what I mean."

"Hi to you too, young friend," he says, happily. Innocently. "Are you having Nathan's hot dogs too?"

"I was certainly thinking about it."

"Dad, can Alison join us?"

A pain throbs in my stomach. I shoot a look at Ellen. She finger-combs her dark hair, crosses arms over her chest. Nervously.

"Henry," she says, "Alison is very busy. I'm sure she wants to get home."

"Nonsense," she says, "I'd love to join you guys for lunch. That is, if you'll let me buy."

The throbbing in my stomach turns into yet another slow burn that starts from the tips of my toes and runs all the way up to my brain. Maybe there's steam rising up off my scalp and I don't even know it.

I nod.

"Sure thing," I say, through grinding teeth. "Alison, lead the way."

Together, we get in line for Nathan's Hot Dogs. Like one big happy family.

CHAPTER 8

We small talk our way through lunch. The benefits of Cape Cod over Maine. The shorter drive, the nicer weather (in general), the warmer ocean temps. But of course, Maine kicks ass when it comes to lobster. Hands down, you can't beat State-O-Maine (as Henry calls it) for the freshest lobster in the world. Not that he's ever been there. Or so he's quick to admit.

As hard as I try, I can't take my eyes off of Alison, even for a full ten seconds. It's as if she might belt out the truth about our shared past at any moment. She's dressed more like an in-lander today than a beach-goer. Jeans, cowboy boots, loose black button-down shirt over a black bra. A plain silver necklace matches the silver bracelets on her left wrist. She keeps a pen in her pocket that I initially confused for her e-cig device. I'm guessing she wants to be prepared if she's suddenly overcome with the urge to write something down.

Eventually, Ellen gets down to asking the one question that has baffled her since we left the Cape.

"Alison," she says, while taking a tiny bite of her ketchup-, relish-, and mustard-covered hot dog, "I could have sworn you said you were a journalist when you met us on the beach yesterday."

"I did?" she says, her own hot dog held in both hands, a small thin line of yellow mustard gracing hers. She takes a big bite out of it. "I think I might have said I was doing research."

Ellen swallows, contemplates a second bite, but decides against it.

"I stand corrected," she says. "My ears are getting as bad as my husband's." Then, "I must confess, I did a little checking up on Google to pass the time during the drive and I see you're quite the scientist. A professor, even."

"Wow," Henry says, mustard stuck to his lips, while he polishes off most of his second hot dog. "You're a real professor? How come I didn't know that, Mom?"

"You were sleeping, kiddo."

"I am indeed a teacher, Henry," Alison says. "An Explosives Engineering professor." Then, holding up her free hand. "Correction. An associate professor. I'm only just getting started."

"So why say you're a reporter?" Henry presses.

I shift my focus to Alison. Is she shaken up by the question? By all appearances, not in the least. She calmly smiles, gives her head a slight shake so her soft hair falls behind her ear.

"What I meant was, I'm researching a report on dangerous jobs that require daily contact with violent explosives. Sometimes I don't communicate as clearly I should. That's the problem with us lab rats. Long hours spent in solitude researching and experimenting. Plus, there's a method to my madness. People like to talk about themselves especially when they think they're going to be in the paper or on television. If you knew I was a scientist right off the bat, you might not have been so willing to engage,if you get my drift."

"Ahhh, classic bait and switch," Ellen says. "You work on nano-bombs? Am I getting that right?"

Alison chuckles. "Not exactly. But I do study nano-thermites. The super bombs of the future. Also, super bullets, if you can believe that." She shifts her focus to me. "Something you might be interested in, Ike. Both as a bomb disposal man and a demolitions man."

I nod.

"Bullets," I say, playing along. "Wouldn't the heat generated from a thermite round melt the gun barrel?"

"Well, the bullet itself is more or less conventional." Her eyes wide, like she's finally inside her element, she pushes aside the Nathan's garbage and spreads out a white napkin on the table. "You can't even see the super-thermite tip with the naked eye. But a bomb is a bomb once it goes boom. Isn't that right, Henry? You and I witnessed more than a few explosions and implosions back when we were little kids. Our dads had the greatest job in the world." Her expression suddenly sours. "Until, well, you know..."

A start in my heart. As if that was the segue she needed to start spilling the truth to my family. Instead, her spirits seem to suddenly lift.

"I need a pen," she says.

"What about the one in your pocket, Alison?" I say.

"Oh, it's out of ink." She looks over one shoulder, then the other until she spots what she needs. Getting up from the table, she goes to the counter, comes back with a pencil. She proceeds to sketch a firearm cartridge that appears fairly garden variety to me, aside from the tip which she darkens, as if to illustrate a very tiny, almost pinhead-sized warhead.

"And the gun you fire it out of?" I press.

She exhales, bites down on her bottom lip. "We use the most durable, heavyweight model handgun we could find currently manufactured in the global ballistics marketplace. Something that should, conceivably anyway, handle a very, very high-caliber round."

"There's still the issue of propulsion heat," I offer.

She peers up at me quick, like I'm pressing too hard.

"We're dealing with it," she says. "For now, it's imperative that only one round at a time be fired from the gun. Anything more than one round...or should I say, anything fired rapidly...and the thermite charge will overheat and explode in the shooter's face while evaporating his or her shooting hand." She grins as if something's funny. "In fact, that kind of explosion would probably cut the shooter in half at the waist or at the very least, blow his or her head clean off."

She folds up the napkin, stuffs it into her chest pocket selfishly, like it's a government secret.

Henry swallows the last of his hot dog, looks up at us with a pensive expression. He issues me the nod and wink which I automatically interpret as, I need to use the men's room, now!

Poor Henry. Because of his advanced progeria, he no longer produces some of the digestive proteins and amino acids we normally take for granted as adults, decades away from old age. The result is a fragile digestive tract.

"Let's go, partner," I say. "Race you there."

He gets up slowly. Soon, he will need a walker. The realization brings tears to my eyes. But I hold them back. Ellen and I have become experts at holding back the tears.

"Might need your help on this one, Dad," he says.

"How much is it worth to you?" I say, taking his arm, gently helping him to his feet.

"How much do I owe you so far?"

"I haven't added it up. But it's got to be somewhere around a million and a half. Give or take."

"Tell you what," he says, "I'll leave the entire estate to you and Mom."

"Not if we go first," I say.

Alison laughs. But nothing's funny.

Talking the way we do to one another…making fun of the situation we've been dealt. It might seem crass or even insensitive to some. Certainly we're not the PC family. For Henry, his mother, and me, it's like our defense mechanism. A way we let the cosmos know, without question, that even though my son is getting his ass kicked physically, he really can't be beat. Not by a long shot.

"Off we go," I say. "Alison, good seeing you again. Don't be a stranger."

She shoots me a wink. "Glad you said that. I was hoping to come around from time to time, maybe spend some time with Henry."

My boy turns. "I'd love that, Professor Alison. I don't get to hang out much with people my own age. If you know what I mean."

"I do, Henry," she says. "I'm not all that much older than you." Then, turning to Ellen. "Why don't you give me your cell number and I'll put it in my phone."

"Absolutely," Ellen says.

"Ellen!" I bark.

The two women shoot me a look.

"Sorry," I say, quickly toning it down. "I was just going to say, we can get in touch with Alison easily enough. You don't have to do that."

"Nonsense," Ellen says, eyes wide, like, What the hell is wrong with you, Singer? "What are we going to do? Send out a homing pigeon, Ike?"

Alison shoots me another wink, her lips pressed together. Her face says, Gotcha!

Henry and I turn toward the bathroom as my blood begins to boil.

I hope never to see Alison again. See her alive, that is.

CHAPTER 9

She exits the facility while the nice little family deals with Henry's overly sensitive stomach. The old boy's timing could not have been more perfect. What she must do, she must do quickly. But she must also do it alone, far from the prying eyes of the Singers.

Outside in the parking lot, she passes by the many vacationers and travelers. The cute nuclear families on the way to the beach are pale-faced but excited to the point of giddiness. The families on their way home from vacation, however, are tanned and in some cases burnt. The energy is sucked from their souls while all that awaits them is the daily routine and more credit card debt. It's the latter group of people who are in no special rush.

She often wonders what it might have been like to have a family of her own. What it might have felt like if she'd been brave enough to bring to term the offspring of the man who raped her. She wonders if the child would have been sweet and gentle, or more like a monster, like his father.

She recalls the horror of first discovering her pregnancy. The pregnancy test kit she snuck into the bathroom, peeing onto the blue plastic thermometer-like test indicator stick. She was just fourteen years old. She still shudders at the helplessness, knowing she could never approach her foster mother with the news or else face the woman's wrath. "You tempted my husband," the short, overweight, salt-and-pepper-haired woman would accuse while lashing out with fists. "You forced yourself on him."

She couldn't go to her mother. The woman was already close to death from drink and drugs and depression. Her only alternative had been to visit the family court on her own, to request a meeting with the judge who presided over her case. A judge who not only worked for the appellate court, but who also made the time to serve on family court as his civic duty. When she stood before him in his court and she expressed, in vivid detail, her mistreatment, the judge promised a thorough review, only to inform her two weeks later that there was nothing the court could do to alter her living situation. After several interviews with social services, her foster parents were deemed good people and she should feel lucky to be taken in by them. She should learn to follow their rules.

"Is rape and abuse a rule?" she screamed before being forcefully removed from the courtroom, fully aware of the beating that awaited her when she returned home later that evening.

Still she had the baby to think of, and still she would not give up. She visited a priest and explained the dire situation to him. But all he could manage was to shake his head and insist she go home, pray for God's mercy and forgiveness. A child was a wonderful thing, regardless of how it came into this world.

Finally, in a desperate attempt to put an end to the matter once and for all, she scraped together enough babysitting money to hop the bus to Planned Parenthood down on Lark Street in the center of the city. There she personally spoke to the woman in charge. A woman who seemed to speak down at her, as if disbelieving her fiction about a rape, about being chased around the woods in the night by an evil foster father. A woman who seemed to believe that her pregnancy was more the result of carelessness and of relying on the system as a means of contraception. Still, the woman planted a smile on her face and agreed to help her. Help her for no cost. In the end, they terminated the pregnancy and then politely showed her the door.

No one gives her a second glance as Alison approaches Ike's

big black Suburban. Walking around to the back end of the gas guzzler, she pulls the pen from out of her pocket, takes a knee directly behind the passenger's side rear tire. Bringing the tip of the pen to the interior of the brake drum which is bolted to the metallic tire rim, she presses the top of the pen with her thumb pad.

Under normal circumstances, an ink-tipped ballpoint would pop out of the bottom, business end of the writing instrument. But in this case, the pen is not a pen at all, but a retrofitted dispenser which she developed in secret inside the Albany University Nano-Tech laboratory. With a steady, unwavering hand, she thumbs the button, careful not to press too hard while dispensing a translucent sol-gel composite energetic material directly onto the taut rubber.

"One cc," she whispers to herself while releasing her thumb from the device. "That's more than enough."

Standing, she replaces the pen to her shirt pocket and calmly crosses the lot to her own car. Unlocking the driver's side door with the electronic key device, she slips back inside, turns the engine over. The sunbaked seat is so hot it feels as if she will burn up. Opening the window, she also blasts the AC. She's reminded that the pen in her pocket contains enough heat-sensitive material which, if spontaneously ignited, would not only evaporate herself and the car, but would take out almost all the cars in the lot, plus much of the rest stop structure.

She's been taking a real chance by carrying the pen around in her shirt pocket. But truth be told, she enjoys the challenge of carrying it. The danger. The control she has over it. The feeling of knowing that at any second, the world around her...her world... could simply cease to exist in a single brilliant, super-heated flash of white light. Like she heard her father say to his partner and best friend, Ike Singer, not long before the detonations that disintegrated his flesh and bone, "Sometimes you control the blast as best you can. Most times, as best you can is good enough. But then there are the times, as best you can doesn't come close."

The summer heat, if respected, can be a blessing. Under normal conditions, she would require a flame or even a laser pulse to ignite the material placed on the interior of the Suburban's back passenger's side wheel. But in this case, the heat generated from both the external temperature and the friction from the tire spinning at high speed against the road will be enough to create the super-thermite reaction she's looking for.

She might tail the Suburban like she did earlier, but this time she knows the prudent thing to do is to hold back a ways. Allow nature to take its course. Once that happens, she'll be there to pick up the pieces.

It will be Alison Darling to the rescue.

Now, coming out of the rest stop, the Singer family. That's her cue to pull out of the parking spot, drive around the back of the facility, await the moment when Ike pulls back out onto the highway, oblivious of the fiery danger that awaits him and his loved ones. A danger he will no doubt handle as best he can.

CHAPTER 10

Approaching my big, black, all-wheel drive Chevy Suburban, family in tow, I try not to be entirely obvious when looking for Alison's car. When I see the spot she occupied is empty, I breathe a sigh of relief. Maybe it's possible she's gone for good and I'll never have to be reminded of what happened between me and her mother again, or what happened between me and her father.

But then I once again see Patty in my head and I know that my past isn't going anywhere soon. Of course, Alison is going to show her face again. Alison has got Ellen's phone number for God sakes. For all I know she's liable to show up at my front door this week. She's angry, wants revenge for what happened. I feel something cold run itself up and down my backbone. Maybe I should think about doing something about her. Maybe I should do something before it's too late and before she exposes me for who I really am.

"Earth to Ike," Ellen says, standing outside the front passenger's side door.

"Yeah, earth to the old man," Henry says.

Suddenly snapped out of my trance, I pull the key ring from my pocket, thumb the lock release. The chirp sounds, the locks release.

"I'm not old," I say, opening the back door for Henry.

"That's what I keep telling myself," he says. "But then I look in the mirror and it ain't pretty."

"You're our handsome young son," I say, offering him a hand

to help him up into the back seat. "Never forget that."

The expression on his face is pain-filled as he settles himself in. I know that soon, I'll have to trade in the Suburban for something he can more easily climb in and out of. I go to help him with the seatbelt, but he slaps my hand away.

"I can do it, Pops," he says, proudly.

Holding my hands up in surrender.

"I know when I'm beat," I say, closing the door.

Ellen is standing beside me, stone stiff, her hand gripping the opener, her face looking forward, staring at the pavement. When she looks up at me, I see that her eyes are glassy, tear-filled. She gives her head a quick shake.

"He doesn't have long to go," she whispers.

My chest feels as if it were a balloon that's unexpectedly been pin-pricked.

"We've got to prepare ourselves, babe. We have to be ready. But not yet."

I might say something more, but that's all I can get out.

Ellen opens the door, inhales a deep breath, paints a smile on her face. A smile that's about as happy as a cancer. But a smile that she bravely wears anyway.

I head around to the front of the vehicle, slip myself in behind the wheel, and start her up.

"Everybody good?" I say, backing out of the spot.

"Dad," Henry says, his eyes wide. "I wanna thank you and Mom for the vacation. Best. One. Ever." I see his shiny smile in the mirror. It's surrounded by pale skin and age spots. "Can't wait till next year and we can do it all over again."

Over my shoulder, I catch a glimpse of Ellen, and the tear running down her cheek.

"Me too, Henry," I say, voice cracking, choking. "Me too, kid."

I pull out of the lot back into heavy traffic, my eyes searching the rearview for a silver BMW, but spotting nothing of the sort. Hands gripping the wheel, I shift into the left lane to pass a gasoline tanker that's going too slow. My eyes naturally focus in on the high combustion warning painted onto the backside of the big tanker. A somewhat alarming illustration of red/orange flame.

"You know, she's really very nice," Ellen says, after a time.

"Who's nice?" I say, as I attempt to pass the tanker. But it's speeding up as I speed up, like the operator is deliberately preventing me from passing. I press down on the gas, the big Suburban engine churning out the rpm's.

"Alison, silly," she says. "Who did you think I was talking about?"

"Associate Professor Alison," Henry says. "Give credit where credit is due."

"Associate Professor Alison," I repeat, picturing her father seated on the bare concrete floor of an Alphabet City concrete warehouse that was wired to blow. "Her dad would be proud."

The tanker is still speeding, and I'm still trying to pass it. But now there's a pickup truck on my tail. The driver is flashing his lights on and off, as if he doesn't already have my full attention. I see his bearded face in the rearview, his tight mouth moving in anger. Shouting something out. Something four-lettered.

I grip the wheel more tightly. Give the Suburban more gas, manage to pull up even with the tanker truck.

"What the hell's going on?" Ellen says, concern tainting her voice. "Why won't he let you pass?"

I lean in toward her, lower my head while looking up toward the driver. That's when I hit the horn. The middle-aged, baseball-hatted man peers down at me through the driver's side window glass. He's wearing sunglasses on a face that bears no expression at all, so it's hard to judge what he's thinking.

"Eyes on the road, Ike," Ellen says, elbowing me in the chest.

"Yes ma'am."

I straighten back up.

"You're making me nervous," she says.

"Yeah, Dad, let's lose this asshole."

“Henry!” Ellen barks, shooting a look over her shoulder.

“Hey, I’m old. I can swear.”

The pickup truck is so close now, I feel like I’m wearing him. The driver is flashing his lights again while the tanker is still taking up my entire right side.

“Good Christ, El. I’m pinned in here.”

That’s when something explodes beneath us.

CHAPTER 11

The Suburban bucks severely to the right.

It's cutting off the tanker.

For a split second, I feel like we're going to slam into it and the whole thing is going to blow. The operator's got no choice but to hit the brakes, swerve sharply into the left lane, narrowly missing the pickup truck. The operator punches his horn as he attempts to regain control of the big truck, veering past a half dozen cars, nearly slamming into them with a tank filled with hundreds or even thousands of gallons of combustible fuel.

Ellen shrieks while out the corner of my eye, I catch Henry as he flops over onto his left side, his small, lithe body having slipped out of the shoulder strap. Why the air bags haven't released, I don't know.

"Blowout!" I bark, holding as tightly to the wheel as I possibly can without dislocating my fingers. Inching over to the soft shoulder, I pull off the highway.

"Hold on, everyone!"

I pump the brakes. The vehicle bucks and bounces, the gravel spraying up against the metal undercarriage as we skid to a sudden stop.

I kill the engine, thrust myself back against the seat. "Shit!"

Ellen frantically releases her seatbelt, flips around onto her knees, goes to Henry's aid.

"Are you okay, sweetheart? You okay?"

I turn, peer over my shoulder. I see him slowly sitting back up, dark round eyes opened wide. But in typical Henry fashion, he's got a small grin planted on his face.

"Jeez," he says. "That was bitchin'. Like Fast and Furious number ten or something."

"Vin Diesel's got nothing over me," I say, my heart pumping in my throat. Then, "Everyone stay put while I do a damage check."

The cars and trucks whiz past, no one bothering to slow down or pull over to offer up assistance. Maybe a cop will be coming by soon. A Massachusetts State Trooper.

Opening the door carefully, I slide out, close the door behind me. Heading around to the back of the Suburban, I immediately spot what's left of the rear passenger's side tire. Nothing but a steel rim, frosted with remnants of a steel-belted tire. Even the brake drum appears to be busted up. A severe blowout if I've ever seen one. In my head, I see the sparks that must have shot out of the wheel as I skidded across the concrete highway.

I go around to the front passenger's side seat, knuckle tap the window.

Ellen puts the window down. "How bad is it?"

"You don't happen to have a Triple A membership, do you?"

"That bad? What about the spare?"

"The wheel drum is bent to hell. The brake's gone. Spare is entirely obsolete. We need a tow."

"So much for getting home on time."

I reach into my jeans pocket, pull out my cell phone. "I'll call for a tow. Sit tight."

"Good idea."

I can't help but smile, despite the…let's call it…less than convenient situation. I pull out my cell phone. At the same time, I make out the sound of a car pulling up behind me. Turning, I spot the very car I'd rather not see.

A silver BMW, its driver wearing a broad smile on her face.

CHAPTER 12

"Oh my Lord," she says, eyes wide. "Are you all right, Ike?"

Ellen must sense the car having pulled up behind us, because she gets out.

"Alison," she says, "thank God you weren't far behind."

My late partner's daughter approaches Ellen, gives her a tight hug, like she's just survived a plane crash.

"Are you all right?" Alison begs, her face tight and filled with concern. "Is Henry okay? He must be so frightened."

The cars and trucks continue to speed past us. You can feel them punching through the air as they shoot on by at seventy, eighty, sometimes ninety miles per hour. You can hear their engines roar as they come and go in direct proportion to their speed. What do they call that? The Doppler Effect?

It takes several tries, but it takes only a few minutes for me to connect with a local outfit that will come to our location and tow the Suburban to their garage. The mechanic informs me that he won't do shop work on the Lord's day of rest and therefore can't get to the job until the morning, necessitating an overnight stay.

"Plus there's the Red Sox game," he adds.

I explain the situation to Ellen as we stand outside Henry's open back seat window. The expression of disappointment on both their faces tells me how badly they want to get home. Home and settled.

"Mind if I interject something?" Alison says after a beat. "If it's okay with you, Ike, I can give Ellen and Henry a ride home while you do the manly thing and stay with the truck. How's that sound?"

The manly thing...Alison is most definitely picking a fight.

"Thanks for interjecting, Alison," I say.

The fine hairs on the back of my neck rise up once again. My mouth goes dry. I know precisely what Alison is doing. Asserting control. Dominance. Taking over. Where it's all leading to, I have no idea. But whatever it is, it can't be good.

Just then, the sound of another car pulling off onto the gravel shoulder, approaching us. I turn quick, spot the blue squad car of a Massachusetts State Trooper.

Turing my attention back to Alison, I look into her eyes. She returns my gaze, her eyes hidden behind sunglasses. But I imagine they don't blink, that they're ice cold in the early afternoon summer heat. The gaze says, If you know what's good for you, keep your damned mouth shut.

The door opens on the cruiser. A trooper climbs out. He's tall, uniformed, stoic in manner and movement. He's wearing high, brown, lace-up boots and his sidearm is holstered on his left hip. I don't know why this should give me comfort, but it does.

When he comes to us, he asks the obvious question. "Who's the owner?"

"That would be me."

Ellen is standing to my left side. She's leaning up against the Suburban, as if attempting to stay as close to Henry as humanly possible without getting inside and sitting beside him. To my right is Alison. She's standing a few steps behind the trooper, who occupies the center. Like I said, she's wearing her aviator sunglasses, so her eyes are impossible to see. But I feel them. Feel them burning holes in me.

Here's what I want to say: "Officer, this woman is following me and my family. She's stalking us. She's threatened to tell my wife the truth about my past. Threatened to reveal things that would not only upset her, but that would cause her not to trust me anymore. Cause her to leave me. Most certainly I am guilty for my transgressions, but this young woman has evil intentions.

She feels cheated, violated, and wronged. Now she wants vengeance."

But here's what I say instead: "My back tire blew out."

"You have the right amount of air in it?" he asks, as if air pressure matters at this point.

"I checked before we left home for the Cape last week," I say. But it's a lie spoken to make me appear more responsible than I really am.

"New York plates," he observes, sticking both thumbs inside his utility belt. "Where's home in New York?"

"Albany."

"Still a couple hours away," he says. Then, "It's Sunday. You found a shop that will take you in?"

I give him a nod.

"Not gonna get those calipers and rotors fixed today." He's shaking his head like something's wrong besides the obvious.

"I already know that. Red Sox game."

The shaking of his head ceases. "You sure a simple blowout caused all this damage?"

"The tire blew up. We ended up on the side of the road. That's all I know."

Trooper, nodding, biting down on his bottom lip.

"Listen," he says, "I can recommend a decent hotel in town for you and your family."

"Thanks."

"It will just be him," Ellen interjects.

"Excuse me, ma'am?"

"We're going back with our young friend here," she explains.

Trooper turns to her. "So you're not family?"

"That's my BMW back there," Alison says. "I too live in Albany. I've offered a ride."

Trooper's eyes back on me. "You know this woman?"

"Yes," I say, peering into her eyes, through the dark sunglasses. "I know her."

In my head, I hear Patty's voice so clearly it's as if she were standing right beside me.

"Play this one straight, Ike. Don't say anything to this officer of the law that might make him suspect Alison is stalking your shiny happy family. Don't do it, or there will be hell to pay later… Trust me on this one, lover."

"You're okay with her transporting your family back home?"

I bite down on my bottom lip.

"Sure," I say. Fucking choice do I have?

Trooper's eyebrows perk up then as he gets a better look inside the car. A closer look at Henry who, no doubt, is staring back at him, a big smile plastered on his face, as if to say, "Yup, I'm young, but I look really, really old. You wanna make something out of it?"

He turns back to me. "Your boy has special needs? Maybe it's better your family sticks together."

"Nonsense," Alison says, stepping forward. "We're all very close. Our families used to work together. Isn't that right, Ike?"

"Yeah," I say, deadpan. Not happy. "She's right."

Trooper nodding again. "Okay then, it's settled. I'm going to wait in the car for the tow truck. State law requires a trooper on site for the duration of the breakdown."

He steals one last look at Henry, nods, touches the brim of his hat like he's a cowboy, then excuses himself and walks back to his cruiser.

"Singer, honey, you mind transferring our bags into Alison's car, assuming there's room?" Ellen says.

"I have plenty of room," she says. "I only take an overnight bag when I visit my boyfriend. The trunk is empty."

Alison raises up her hand, her keys set in her palm.

"Time for you to go to work, Ike," she says. "As if you don't already have enough on your plate. But then, a Master Blaster thrives under pressure. Don't you…Ike?"

I snatch the keys from her hand, a lit stick of dynamite settling itself in my stomach.

CHAPTER 13

It's all going according to plan. The tire blowout, the severe damage not only to the tire rim but the entire wheel base, the splitting up of the shiny happy family. How nice it will be to get some good old-fashioned quality time alone with Ellen and Henry. Time to get to know one another better. They haven't laid eyes on her since she was a little girl. A little girl who used to follow her dad to every one of the Master Blasters implosions. How she wished to follow in his footsteps one day. How she wished to make Master Blasters world famous.

Even as a youngster of eight or nine years old, she knew Henry didn't have a future in the business. Henry didn't have a future at all. She remembers so vividly watching the four-year-old boy who, in her eyes, resembled a character from out of The Lord of the Rings. A miniature old man with a receding hair line, wrinkled skin, pointy nose, beady eyes, and lips so thin you swore you could just peel them off his mouth like chewing gum from the foil.

Master Blasters was going to be hers and hers alone. Rather, she would get one half of it, while Ike Singer got the other. But then, that was okay too. She liked Ike. That is, she liked him until she found out the truth about him and her mother. Until her father found out the hard truth and what had seemed like a happy, healthy family unit blew up in their faces.

Ike Singer owed her mother for the way he fucked her and dropped her like a bad habit. He owed her father for cheating on him in so many ways and causing his self-destruction. Ike owed her for killing off her family. Killing off her future. Subjecting her to unspeakable abuse, unspeakable neglect inside a cold, city system.

Now it's time to pay for his sins. But the reimbursement will start small, like the first, basement stage of a detonation sequence.

It will start with Ike's very foundation. His wife and child.

CHAPTER 14

Pulling Henry's and Ellen's suitcases from the Suburban, I lug them the fifteen or so feet to the BMW's trunk, set them on the gravel-covered soft shoulder. I thumb the electronic key device, spring the latch on the trunk. It opens.

Like Alison said, it's empty, other than a half-filled gallon of blue windshield wiper cleaner and gear for changing a flat tire. Lifting the suitcases, I set them inside, lay them one atop the other. I'm about to close the trunk when I spot something in the far corner.

A slip of white paper.

I'm not sure why I would be concerned with a piece of paper, but my explosive disposal specialist's gut speaks to me, tells me to at least take a look.

I pull the slip of paper from the depths of the trunk and immediately discover that it's a sales receipt. A quick glance at it reveals the items of purchase. A plastic bucket. Five sheets of packing Styrofoam. A roll of duct tape. I stare at the date on the receipt. June 13. Three years ago.

There's nothing in the receipt or the date in which it was produced that tells me to hang onto it. Obviously, Alison was packaging something. Maybe something to send somewhere far away. But again, I listen to my gut. I shove it into my jeans pocket, close the trunk.

Back at the Suburban, I attempt to plant a smile on face.

"All set," I say.

Just then, the flatbed tow truck turns off the highway, pulls up in front of the Suburban, comes to a stop. The driver jumps out and approaches the vehicle. I go to him.

"I'm Ike Singer," I say. "The one who called."

"Back wheel?" the short, black-haired, t-shirted young man says.

"That's right."

He approaches the disabled vehicle's rear passenger wheel, drops down to one knee, takes a good look. Reaching out with his hand, he gently touches the rim and some of the blasted-apart carnage inside the rim. When he shakes his head like a medical technician who can't get a pulse from a hopeless case, I know I'm in for a world of hurt. Financial hurt.

He looks up at me. "A blowout caused all that shit? Calipers are shredded, brake drum punctured and busted up, brake bracket is probably still sitting on the highway somewhere. Looks like you ran over an IED." He laughs, stands up straight. "Sorry, did two tours in Iraq. Lots of things to fuck up your wheels out there, not to mention your head." Then, "Oops, my apologies, ladies."

"No need to apologize," Ellen says. "Just glad you can help us out."

"And thank you for your service to our country," a gleeful Alison interjects.

He backsteps to the flatbed, reaches inside the driver's side door, comes back out with a clipboard. Hands it to me.

"Need you to sign here and here," he says, index finger pressing down on the form attached to the clipboard. "It's all about the insurance these days."

I pat my chest, as if I have any chest pockets on my old Master Blasters T-shirt and a pen stuffed inside one of them. That's when I see that Alison has that same pen I noticed during lunch stored inside her left chest pocket.

"You mind?" I say, holding out my hand.

She glances down at the pen, quickly. As if I've startled her.

"Oh, sorry," she says, taking a step back, like she's afraid I'm about to snatch the pen right out of her pocket. "There's no ink in it. Remember? I told you that already."

"Guess I kind of forgot. So why carry it?"

"I know, I know." She grins. "I'm such a geeky scientist. But the pen is an expensive Mont Blanc. When I get home I'm going to buy another ink cartridge for it."

"That's something your dad would have done," I say.

She grins. "You did know my dad so very well. You were his best friend. He loved you like a brother." Suddenly her smile fades. The smirk that follows speaks loud and clear.

The mechanic finds another pen in his truck, hands it to me. I sign off on the documents. He tears out the pink carbon copy, hands it to me. I stuff it into my jeans pocket.

"Okay," he says, slapping the clipboard against his hip, "I'm gonna put her up on the truck. I guess you'll be coming with me, Mr. Singer?"

I nod. Turning to Ellen, I kiss her on the mouth.

"Be careful, El."

"Of course, I will be," she says. She opens the door for Henry, reaches in with her arms to help him out. But the ever stubborn boy brushes her off.

"I can do it, Mom," he insists.

I see his eyes focused on Alison, and I know he's trying to impress her. Or, at the very least, not look like a helpless case. Can't say I blame him.

I walk Henry and Ellen to the BMW, watch them get in. I close the doors for them, then place my hand to my mouth, blow them both a kiss apiece. They each blow kisses back my way.

Turning to Alison, as she sets her hand on the driver's side door opener. "Mass Pike can be dangerous this time of year. I'd hate to hear of anything bad happening to my family."

She laughs, bites down on her bottom lip.

"I'll take extra special care, Ike. Don't you worry about your family. Oh, and don't call them every five minutes. I wouldn't want to be coerced into revealing our little secret to the wifey."

I can't see her eyes, but I know she's throwing me a wink. Pulse soars, blood speeds through the veins. For a quick moment, I see myself shoving her into oncoming traffic. Even a compact car doing seventy mph would crush her flesh and bones on impact. It would be an accident. Plain and simple. A tragic accident.

Alison opens the car door.

"Let's get some AC going," she says, closing the door behind her.

I stand and watch as she fires up the BMW, pulls up to the highway and then, seeing an opening, spins her wheels and pulls out. That's when I hear the tow truck engine revving and the black Suburban being pulled by a heavy duty cable onto the now angled flatbed. I turn to the state trooper, who is still parked behind me, his blue flashers flashing, engine idling. I toss him a wave goodbye.

He nods like, Roger that.

As I make the short walk to the tow truck, open the passenger's side door, hop up inside, I can't help but feel like my world, however humble, is collapsing all around me.

CHAPTER 15

The Suburban is unloaded off the flatbed and mounted on the mechanical lift inside the garage. The mechanic is so impressed with the damage done to the rear wheel, he invites the other mechanic on duty to give it a look.

"Thought you didn't work on Sundays," I say, nodding in the direction of the second mechanic.

"We don't," the mechanic says. "Sundays are for catching up with the overload, which just got more overloaded, thanks to you, friend."

Gasoline and oil vapor might pervade the air, but he lights a cigarette anyway, and gathers around the damaged wheel base with the other grease monkey like they're watching the last few minutes of a tied up Red Sox-Yankees game. But after a few beats, the second mechanic—a heavyset, tan-skinned man with long black hair pulled into a tight ponytail—raises up his hand, touches the exterior of the damaged brake drum with his fingertips.

"Feel this right here, Tian," he says, to the mechanic who rescued me. "You recognize that?" He pronounces Tian like Chin. As in Christian.

Tian reaches out with his hand, touches the same spot Ponytail just touched. He nods, as if the two men are conversing not with words but their thoughts. Their combined automotive experience.

"I'll be a dumb son of bitch, Billy," he says. "I should have gone with my gut on this one." He turns to me. "Hey, mister, what'd you say your name was?"

I tell him yet again.

"Well, Mr. Singer. Looks to me like your tire wasn't the problem here."

I feel a coldness envelope me. It's like I know what the mechanic is going to tell me before he says it. And I do. I'm a man whose life revolves around explosives. I should have a sixth sense about these things.

I place my fingers against the shattered drum, exactly where his fingers and the fingers of Ponytail Billy placed his. My entire body goes stiff, like a jolt of electricity has just passed through it.

"Explosive," I say. "Somebody booby-trapped the wheel with explosive. At least, that's what you're thinking, isn't it?"

"It's not what we're thinking," Billy says in a low, baritone voice.

"It's what we know," Tian confirms.

Leaning down, I press my fingers against the severely damaged tire rim, bring them to my nose. Sniff. Then I do the same with the brake drum. Touch the spot that looks like it was seared with a great heat. There's no particular odor on either of them other than old oil and gas.

"But if this were an explosive," I say, "it would leave behind a residue. And the residue would possess a distinct odor. Acrid and toxic."

Unless it was liquid thermite. Unless it was a super liquid nano-thermite that came directly from Alison. Maybe she booby-trapped the Suburban. Maybe she caused the wheel blowout. A blowout that might have killed my whole family. She works with the shit. It's not a farfetched idea to believe she had something directly to do with it.

Tian looks at me with squinty eyes. "You know something about explosives, Mr. Singer?"

I tell him what I used to do for a living and what I do now.

"You should know what you're talking about then," he points out.

"Apparently not enough to realize my wheel was blown up," I

say. "I thought I was better than that."

"Who wants to believe that someone or something sabotaged their ride?"

"Good point," I say. "Not that that makes me feel any better."

"What I can tell you for sure is that a blowout didn't cause this kind of damage. Somebody fucked with you and did it with something that could explode without leaving much trace of itself. Or much of a smell anyway. That's my humble opinion. Like I said, I saw a lot of busted rims just like this one on Humvees in Iraq."

I've seen steel twisted, bent, sheared, and even melted steel that resembled candle wax back when I was shooting buildings. But I've never seen a wheel so wrecked due to a simple tire blowout.

Alison. It was you…

Tian just looks at me with a stone face, like I'm from another planet.

"You got any enemies to speak of, Mr. Singer?" He steals a drag of his cigarette. "You, being a cop and all."

I shake my head. But the gesture is just for show.

"Not that I know of," I say. "And I'm not a cop. I'm a subcontractor for the cops. Basically I sit around and wait for nothing to happen."

"Maybe that's why you didn't recognize the obvious," Ponytail Billy says.

But Alison's young, grin-filled face fills my head and I know I'm lying to myself and the grease monkey when I claim to have no enemies. But would she really go out of her way to put my entire family in danger by planting what amounts to a bomb under my Suburban? Would she take a chance on incriminating herself in a court of law should I find out she is directly responsible? Or is she so confident that one, the bomb would only blow out the wheel? And two, that I would never alert the police to the matter since the only thing I fear more than her, is her letting my wife in on the secrets of my past?

My eyes locked on the misshapen rim and the damaged drum.

"What the hell kind of explosive does that kind of damage but leaves no residue?" Tian whispers, more to himself than anyone else.

"Experimental blaster," I say. But that's as far as I take it. As far I want to take it.

"Something small, but powerful," Ponytail Billy adds. Then, turning to me. "I'd watch my back I were you. Somebody out there doesn't like you very much." He turns, heads back to the racked car he was working on.

"Listen, Mr. Singer," Tian says, exhaling a cloud of blue cigarette smoke, "you want I should call in the local cops? Or maybe you can handle it on your own once you get back to Albany. Seeing as you're a sort-of-cop."

His face is painted with genuine concern.

Maybe I should grab hold of somebody's car. Maybe Tian's. Get back on the road as fast as I can. Go after Alison. But then I tell myself to hold on. If I confront Alison in front of my family, there's no telling what she'll do. What she'll reveal to Ellen. My only choice is to find a way to neutralize her before she says anything at all. And that could mean shutting her up forever. My God, what the hell is it I'm saying here? Am I contemplating physically assaulting Alison?

"Hello, Mr. Singer. You hear me?" Tian presses.

I turn to the chief mechanic.

"Sorry," I say, bringing my finger to my right ear lobe. "Sometimes my hearing's not so great. Price of one too many detonations."

In my head, I see my family riding with Alison back to Albany. I try and work up some moisture in my mouth.

"I just want to get it fixed and be on my way." Pulling my smartphone from my pocket. "You going to start on her today? Even though it's Sunday?"

"I had to call for a new tire rim, new tire, new brake drum, and a half dozen other assorted components. I can put the whole thing together in about an hour, believe it or not. But the parts won't be here until the morning even if they are in stock. It's late and it's Sunday. But I'll have you back on the road by noon tomorrow." Glancing at the smashed rim set on the floor. "For now I'll set the damaged rim in the back for you to deal with however you wish. Sound fair?"

"Fair enough."

"Let me know you need a ride anywhere like a hotel."

"Can you suggest one?"

"Motel 6 right down the road. Be honest, you can walk to it. Hook a right once you leave the garage and you'll spot it within five minutes." Dropping his cigarette, stamping it out with the tip of his boot. I can't help but imagine a spark flying free from one of those lit cigarettes one day, and lighting the entire joint up. "Need anything out of the Suburban? I can drop her back down."

I shake my head. Not worth him going to the trouble just for a toothbrush. Besides, I'm not sure how much sleep I can look forward to tonight, knowing now what I know.

"I'm good."

"Well then see you tomorrow, Mr. Singer."

Exiting the garage, I go right, and walk alone in the opposite direction of my hometown.

CHAPTER 16

Dialing the number for the APD, South Pearl Street Precinct, I await the connection. When it comes I ask for Detective Nick Miller in Homicide.

"Thought you were on vacation," says the dispatcher. A pleasant young man named Jack recently diagnosed with a heart condition and therefore assigned to dispatch.

"I am," I say. "Or, was anyway. Had a tire blowout on the way home, so now I get an extra night in a small town outside Worcester."

"Lucky you, Ike." Then, "Hang on, Miller's light just went off. Here he is."

"Singer," Miller says, as the connection is made. "How was the beach?"

"I'm tanned to perfection."

"So why the call? You're not required to check in with anybody here. We get a bomb threat while you're vacationing, the staties can take care of it. That kind of constant-up-my-ass-communications responsibility is above your pay grade."

What Miller is referring to is that, technically speaking, I'm not a cop, but instead a subcontracted employee since the city of Albany doesn't possess the resources or the manpower to mount an official bomb squad (bomb threats are usually handled by the State Police and/or Department of Homeland Security). So what they do to plug up the vacuum is hire me, full-time/part-time. In turn, I'm granted access to a used Ford F150 extended van outfitted with mostly outdated equipment, an eleven-year-old explosive-sniffing dog named Nemo, and support staff consisting of a single rookie cop named Ted. If and when I go out on a call, I usually work not with homicide but instead, arson. Course, if a bomb were to go off in Albany and it resulted in fatalities, I'd work with homicide as well. But thus far, it's been all quiet on the northeastern front.

"Ran into a bit of problem. You got a minute, Nick?"

"For you, of course."

As the sign for the Motel 6 up ahead begins to take shape, I fill him in on the events of the past twenty-four hours. About Alison showing up. About her veiled threats of revealing everything that transpired back in '99 to Ellen.

"Have you thought about telling your wife everything?" Miller says. I see him seated behind his desk in his first-floor office outside the general booking room, the venetian blinds closed on the windows. He'll be wearing tan, neatly pressed trousers, and a maybe a light blue button-down, the sleeves rolled up to his elbows. His full head of gray/white hair will be cut military short and his smooth, boy-like face, clean shaven. He'll have his feet resting up on his desk beside his holstered sidearm, which he will have removed from his belt before taking a load off. Having jogged his standard five miles this morning, the old dogs need a rest.

"Would you tell your wife about an affair you conducted when your only child was four years old and that led directly to the suicide of who was then your best friend and business partner? A suicide by building implosion that nearly took you along with it while robbing you of your livelihood? It's too late for a full confession, Nick."

I see him shaking his head.

"My wife died on the operating table," he says, exhaling. "There's so much I wish I'd told her before she passed on."

Nothing but breathing coming over the line. In my mind, I can't help but picture Henry...picture him laid to rest. It's a vision that makes me shudder. I feel a knot in my stomach and I quickly try to erase the vision from my consciousness.

"You want me to look into her for you?" he says after a time. "It's really a job for arson or traffic, but I'm not particularly overwhelmed at the moment."

"I can look into her on my own. What I was hoping is you might make a check on my wife and kid tonight."

"You think this Alison character might, ummm, overstay her welcome? Make things uncomfortable for Ellen and Henry?"

"It had crossed my mind."

"Sure thing. I'll call you later if there's a problem."

"Thanks."

"Don't mention it. Least I can do for the APD's favorite subcontractor."

"Now you're making me blush."

"Good to know I still have the touch," he says. "But do yourself a favor and think about telling Ellen the truth. Or at least, a version of the truth. You keep lying to her, you're also lying to yourself. That ain't good. She'll be angry at first and hurt as all hell. Shit, she might even make you sleep on the couch for a week or so. But it would stop Alison in her tracks if she is, in fact, planning on doing something hurtful. You destroy her leverage, you destroy her will."

What I want to do right now is destroy Alison. But I'm not about to tell Nick that.

"I'll definitely take that into consideration. Talk to you later."

"Roger that, Ike."

He hangs up.

I pocket the phone and head into my home away from home for the night. The beautiful Motel 6.

CHAPTER 17

After checking into a second-floor corner room, I head out for a few supplies, which include a six-pack of beer, a mixed submarine sandwich (they call them "grinders" out here in Massachusetts), plus a toothbrush and toothpaste. After I set everything onto the bed back in my room, I decide to text Ellen, make sure everything is okay. Alison warned about calling too much. Her threat wasn't direct, but I perceived it as one, and its message was clear enough. But maybe I could sneak in a text.

Home yet? I type into the smartphone.

I wait for a reply and drink a full beer while staring out the window onto a long row of three-story wood clapboard houses. Blue-collar neighborhood. Red Sox and Pats fans. Mostly from Irish stock. Heavy drinkers. When the chime indicating a response comes through, I open the text.

We are home and all good, reads the texted response.

For the moment I feel a wave of relief. Until a second text comes through.

This is Alison. Thought I asked you not to call or text Ike, you silly man.

My body goes rigid. Acting on instinct, I press the telephone-shaped green indicator that will immediately place a call to Ellen's cell phone. I count three rings before what sounds like someone answering the phone. But as soon as I speak, the phone is hung up.

I dial again, but this time, I get Ellen's prerecorded message.

"This is Ellen Singer. Sorry I can't take your call, but at the beep leave your life story. Have a great day."

I dial it again. And again. Same thing. Just the message. I would have tried the landline next. That is, if we still had a landline. But we got rid of that after buying a new cable television-slash-cell-phone package from Verizon.

I pop the tab on another beer, drink that down. Then open a third and wait. My heart beats in my throat and my brow breaks out in beads of cool sweat. Could Alison have physically harmed my family? Is that what this is all about? Is it time to call Miller back, have him send a couple squad cars to the house? What if I do that and it only makes Alison angrier so that she kills my wife and my son?

Maybe I should think about what Miller suggested. Maybe it's time I stopped lying to myself and Ellen and just fess up the truth. Maybe Alison will still come after me, but at least my conscience will be clear.

Patty's face in my head.

"How come you never told Ellen?" I say aloud, as if she can hear me.

Because I loved you too much. I didn't want to hurt you, even if you were hurting me.

"Any other reasons?"

Ellen was my friend. Had been since college. You remember. You were there, Ike. What good would it have done to hurt her just after she gives birth to a little boy who would be lucky to make it out of his teens?

Cell phone chimes, breaking me out of my spell.

I snatch it up, peer at the digital face. A multimedia text from Ellen. I open it. The video shows the interior of my house. Someone is walking with the cell phone in hand through the kitchen, into the front hall and vestibule, up the stairs, all the way down the narrow corridor into the master bedroom. For a quick second or two, the phone flips around showing Alison's smiling face while she brings an extended index finger up to her lips as if to say, Shhhhh.

Then, flipping the phone back around, she focuses in on two objects laid out on the king-sized bed. Two human objects. They are Ellen and Henry, snuggled up together, asleep. At least they appear to be asleep.

But how do I know for sure?

I text, Put Ellen on. Do it now.

A text comes back a few seconds later.

Beauty sleep time. No more texts…Catch my drift, Ike?

"You bitch!" I shout.

But there's no one around to hear me.

CHAPTER 18

I try calling again, but it's no use. All I get is the message machine. Knowing I have no choice, I call Miller back. Jack, the dispatcher, claims he isn't in. But I have his cell phone number in my speed-dial, so I try that. When he answers, I can tell right away he's in his car since I make out the sound of traffic behind his somewhat distant voice.

"What's wrong?" he says. "You're all out of breath."

I tell him what had happened when I called Ellen's cell phone. About the hang-ups and the video.

"Calm down," he says. "It's probably nothing more than what it appears to be. Alison decided to answer Ellen's phone while she was asleep. Maybe she's having trouble using it since it might be a model that's foreign to her."

"I don't like the feel of it, Nick."

"You been drinking, Singer?"

The question catches me by surprise.

"I had a couple of beers. Just a couple."

"Okay, tell you what. I'm on my way home. I told you before I'd make a check on things and that's exactly what I'll do now."

"Thanks. But do me a favor. Don't make it obvious."

"How can I not make it obvious?"

"You're a cop. Can't you sneak around the house, make a check through the windows with no one being the wiser?"

"Jeez, that's illegal. And last time I checked, I carry a real honest-to-goodness cop badge and a real honest-to-goodness Smith & Wesson 9mm."

"I'm telling you it's okay. I'm giving you permission."

"Okay, okay, but I'll have to wait until nightfall to do what you want."

"Fine by me. Let me know something as soon as you know something."

"I will. And, Ike..."

"What is it?"

"Don't worry."

"That's like asking me not to breathe."

CHAPTER 19

Options. Either sit here while the dusk approaches and drink the rest of the six-pack. Or do something with my time. Which is why I decide to head down to the lobby to utilize their quote "Business Center" unquote, which in reality is nothing more than an old Dell desktop computer set out on a thrift shop kitchen table in the far corner of the lobby.

Clicking on the Google search engine, I type in Dr. Alison Darling, wait for the results. There isn't a whole lot to speak of. A LinkedIn profile seems the best bet, so I click on that. There's a picture of the young professional, hair neatly parted on the side, her expression confident, her lips neither smiling nor frowning. If I don't already know her for who she is, I would find her attractive and smart. I might even hire her. That is, if I was looking for someone with expertise in both commercial and military applications of super nano-thermites.

I peruse the description, find that she worked for a several big demolition outfits across the country after college before returning to school for a master's. None of this seems particularly shocking, but it's the last line of the description that gives me pause. It says she's currently working not only for the University at Albany in the nano-tech research facility, but that she also subcontracts for several private sector explosive demolition outfits. Including BigBlast, Inc.

...BigBlast, Inc....

"Where do I know that name?" I whisper to myself.

Opening up another Google Search screen, I type in Big-

Blast, Inc. The website comes up for the New York City–based but apparently Chinese-owned company. The home page for the website features a slideshow that might as well double as an advertisement for some HBO action/adventure series featuring big bombs, big explosions, and lots of crazy death-defying stunts.

The first photo shows an old hotel being imploded in Las Vegas under colored lights while the caption below it reads "Las Vegas illusionist Criss Angel pulls off an elaborate escape from a downtown strip hotel mere seconds before its demolition."

I find myself shaking my head.

"Why didn't I think of that?" I whisper inside the empty Motel 6 lobby. "No wonder the Chinese are kicking our fiscal asses."

The next picture reveals an old hotel being shot on a Palm Beach oceanfront. The one after that, an old metal-span bridge that connects Vermont and New York's Lake Placid being blown to bits. Then, a final photo displays charges being set inside the Wellington Hotel in my hometown of Albany for an implosion that's to take place the day after tomorrow.

I can't help but feel envious of this last photo. Knowing in my bones that the project would be mine if I were still licensed to perform explosive demolition, I can't help but feel my stomach sink at the sight of BigBlast, Inc. barging in on my territory. And now, to be made aware of Alison's probable involvement in the project while she stalks my family is doubly troubling.

Shutting down the BigBlast website, I go back to Alison's LinkedIn page. Having scoured the entire listing, I click back to the Google results. I see a listing for her dad's obituary way back when in 1999. I click on the link for the Times Union newspaper and peruse the short article that accompanies the round, rugged face of my old college roommate and then Master Blasters partner.

"A loving father and devoted husband was lost in a tragic accident last Friday," the article begins. But that's where I stop reading.

It wasn't an accident, now was it? I whisper to myself.

Sitting back in the chair, I picture the words "devoted husband" like they've been spray-painted on the plain white wall before me. In my head, I can't help but play out the events of that one night in 1999 that changed my life forever. My meeting Patty Darling at a nondescript bar in downtown Albany. I remember how she reached out to me for advice on how to handle a husband who all but ignored her now. As Brian's best friend, was there anything she should know about? Was he conducting an affair behind her back? If he was seeing someone, who was she? Was she young? Was she beautiful? Was the other woman more interesting than her?

I looked into her eyes while she sipped her drink and brushed back her dirty blonde hair. Hair that, other than the color, was not all that different from her daughter's today. She was so beautiful, I thought. So sweet. I'd always found her to be beautiful and sweet. I'd even nicknamed her Patty Cakes. I couldn't imagine how in the world Brian could shove her aside emotionally. But then, what the hell did I know? I was suffering through my own turmoil. My own absence of domestic tranquility. And who knows what really goes on inside another man's castle? Who was I to judge?

My own life had taken a nosedive since the birth of my son.

Since his diagnosis, frustration filled my veins and sadness plagued me. What hope other than a slow, cruel death awaited my little Henry? Better that he'd not been born at all.

I took my despair out on Ellen, lashing out at her or worse, pretending she didn't exist. The bottle became a near constant off-hours companion. All too often I slept in the construction trailer parked at one of the no-explosives-required mechanical demolition job-sites I had going on in the city. The sad truth is that I isolated myself not only to avoid my family, but to avoid myself. The hatred I had for myself over the way I was acting. There were no mirrors to be found inside a job-site trailer. No pictures, no mementos, no reminders of the affliction that now overwhelmed my son, overwhelmed my wife. Overwhelmed me.

So that night, when I listened to Patty, and I watched her dry her tears with the backs of her hands, I saw something in her that I needed so very badly. I saw a beautiful woman who was in trouble. Who was vulnerable. And I reached across the table, took hold of her hand, and held it tightly.

I'm not sure how it happened exactly, or how it was agreed upon. But one thing led to another, and soon we were out the door of the bar and in my car. We pulled into the first discreet motel we could find. Naturally, I parked around back. I paid for a room with cash and then we made a kind of love that wasn't really love at all, but more like a primal release. An explosion or implosion of pent-up frustration and sadness.

We did it in that rented room for much of the night. Until our bodies were coated in sweat and our flesh ached and there was nothing more for me or Patty to give. When it was over, our respective demons returned to haunt us. We had no choice but to retreat back inside our protective shells and we slept, or tried to sleep, one beside the other in the cramped, old bed.

We slept, but not together.

When I opened my eyes in the cold morning darkness, and the hangover had set in, I stared up at the popcorn ceiling…a ceiling stained with the memories of countless couples who had used this small room for the very same purpose…and I cursed myself for what I had done.

I slid out of bed, got dressed as quickly and quietly as I could, left fifty dollars on the table for Patty's cab fare. Sure the money might have been confused as a payment. As a gratuity. But I didn't care. I just wanted out of there.

Unlatching the chain on the door, I succumbed to the urge to steal one more glance at her. She was lying on her stomach, her soft hair settled on her neck and back, her elbows out, her hands hidden under her face. In the stark red light from the exterior neon sign that leaked in through the narrow, vertical openings in the drapes, I saw her eyes open and then close. I knew then she was faking sleep.

How could either of us possibly sleep?

All I wanted was to leave that place. Leave town. Leave my own skin and bones and my broken heart behind.

That day I drove beyond downtown to the abandoned Port of Albany. I pulled up to the edge of the dock, so that all I could see out the windshield was the river, running gray and flat in the cool, damp morning. A layer of gray fog hovered above the water like a mustard gas that threatened to poison everything within its reach. Opening the glove box, I pulled out the semiautomatic I stored there. I pulled back on the slide and cocked a round in the chamber. I stuffed the barrel in my mouth. The gunmetal tasted sour against my tongue. It scratched the soft skin on the roof of my mouth. I began to cry, weep, the tears running down my face onto the pistol barrel, onto my lips, the gunmetal taste now seasoned with my own salt.

I knew I couldn't possibly escape. That no matter where I went, the memory of my infidelity and the constant pain of my dying boy would torture me. What I wanted was peace and a forever long sleep, free of dreams, free of nightmares, free of broken hearts. I yearned for that one final, split-second explosion of triggered primer and detonated gunpowder, the bullet burrowing its way through soft tissue and bone. The result would be painless and immediate. In a flash of brilliant white explosive light, I would simply cease to exist.

But in my head I saw only Ellen and Henry and I knew they needed me. I was so sorry for having wronged them that I couldn't possibly pull the trigger. Not now. Not when I had already been so selfish.

Pulling the barrel back out of my mouth, I got out of the truck and stood on the far edge of the pier. So close to the water, the tips on the steel-toed engineer boots hung over the edge. The seagulls flew in and out of the fog, and a fat green fish jumped out of the water, snatching an insect out of the air. It landed with a quick and decisive splash. For a brief moment, I found myself smiling. I don't know why exactly I was smiling. But I was smiling all right, and it was the first sign of life in an otherwise dying man.

I tossed the gun into the river. It made the same sound as the fish had. But this time, the water drowned it with all the indifference of a buried casket.

Later that night I went home and made love to Ellen for the first time in a year. It was something I had to do. Something I needed to prove to myself and to Ellen. I slept in my own bed not as a stranger, but as a married man who held onto his wife's hand the entire night.

Now, if you don't believe a word of what I'm saying…if you don't for a moment believe that Ellen would welcome me back into her arms as fast and apparently thoughtlessly as she did, you're wrong.

Dead wrong.

Because not only did she take me back, she never asked me where I'd been the previous night. Not once. Maybe she assumed I'd slept on the job-site again, or maybe she just didn't want to know where I'd slept. That was a good thing, because so often in ignorance, we find peace, even if only for a little while. Because although the desperation now resided with that semiautomatic at the bottom of the Hudson River, the fear did not. One day soon, the fear would come back to haunt us, and the peace would be gone forever.

What I'm trying to say is, I knew that if Ellen ever made me confess my actions, she'd walk out on me. Probably for good. Maybe she harbored the same exact fear. Because, in the end, she just accepted me back into her bed like nothing bad had ever passed between us. Her strength was remarkable. It was matched, measure for measure, only by my weakness.

Patty called me, of course. Called me many times. Countless times. And I ignored the calls. Every single goddamned one of them. What the hell else is there to tell you, other than she and Brian split up two months later. Something that caused me further heartache and guilt. But not enough to cause a personal setback or to once again send me on the downward spiral toward total and irreparable collapse.

One month after that, we were set to implode the warehouse in Alphabet City. It was one of our first real big breaks in New York City. It seemed like the entirety of lower Manhattan came out to witness the spectacle. So did the major media. We sold Master Blasters T-shirts and vendors sold red and black Master Blasters ice cream with chunks of debris (cookie dough) in it. It was a carnival atmosphere, until Brian took his own life in the implosion, and I barely survived with my own.

A nine-year-old Alison Darling was there to witness the whole thing. So was my dying boy.

I decide to give the Google results one final scan before calling it a night. The second obituary is located about halfway down the page. It's for Patricia Darling, 44, who, not unlike her late husband, was lost in a tragic accident at her home in Albany.

"What's Patty dying from?" I ask.

"Cancer," she says. "It's in her liver and her lungs."

Heart jumps into my throat. Inhaling a breath, I pull out my cell phone. My hand trembles as I punch the number in for Miller. His answering service comes on. I don't bother with leaving a message before hanging up. I need to speak with him about Alison's lie in real-fucking-time.

A quick glance outside the glass door reveals darkness. If the homicide detective is good to his word, it makes sense he's not picking up his phone. He's checking out my house in the wooded outskirts of Albany, like he promised.

Stand. Dizziness kicks in, like there's not enough oxygen reaching my brain. I stare into the picture window and see not my own reflection, but instead, Alison's.

"You lied to me, you bitch," I say aloud, like she were truly standing inside the room. "You lied about your mother."

Sitting back down, I type the name Patricia Darling into Google Search. A Times Union piece appears. "Tragic Boiler Explosion Takes Woman's Life." The date on the story is June 14, 2012. A short article stating, "The badly burned remains of Patricia Darling, the wife of the late Brian Darling of the now defunct Master Blasters, Inc. demolition company, were discovered in her bedroom late last night by emergency medical and fire personnel after the old water boiler in their West Albany home exploded and caught fire. Although Alison Darling, the twenty-four-year-old daughter of the deceased, was questioned by authorities at the APD, no foul play was suspected." The remainder of the article goes on to explain the dangers of old boilers. How without proper maintenance, they can become ticking time bombs.

I wasn't working for the cops back in 2012. I was still working on construction sites as a demolition contractor. Taking buildings apart mechanically without explosives, using only basic tools and equipment like ninety-pound jackhammers and an old JCB backhoe. Until one day, I said to myself, "Enough is more than enough, Singer." No more working crap jobs for crap money. Maybe the courts had taken away my license to shoot buildings, but that didn't mean I had to give up explosives for good.

So here's what I did.

I gave up mechanical demolitions altogether and enrolled in a year-long trade seminar at a local community college for bomb disposal. It wasn't all the education I would require for putting down IEDs and other explosive devices. But it was enough to land me the subcontractor job with the APD. And that was fine by me. After all, the gig would be temporary until I could finally get my blasting license back.

I haven't been at the job for very long, but I've learned a lot about explosives in my time as a bomb disposal man. And my gut is telling me that something doesn't smell right about Patty's boiler explosion death.

Digging into my pocket, I pull out the receipt I found in Alison's trunk. The date printed on it is June 13, 2012. Once again I read the items on the list. Styrofoam, an empty bucket, a sheetrock knife, clear plastic, and a roll of duct tape.

Thoughts speed through my brain: Alison wasn't using this stuff as packing material at all. I should have seen through the fog earlier. As a professional detonator, I should have recognized the ingredients.

Clicking back onto Google, I type in all the items on the same line, separating them only by commas. When I press the Enter key with my index finger, I not only get the result of my search, I also get a picture to go with it.

What do you get when you combine Styrofoam and gasoline inside an empty bucket? A bucket you then cover for a few days with clear plastic held in place with duct tape? Ask any old Vietnam vet bellied up to the bar inside some old corner gin mill.

Napalm. That's what you get.

SECOND STAGE

CHAPTER 20

Ellen has no idea what awaits her.

Henry has no idea what awaits him.

It's almost too easy.

But it's only seven in the evening, Alison reminds herself while driving back to her lab. Eventually, the wifey will want to do a little practicing on the piano. She's been away for a week, after all. A professional piano player and teacher will need to practice. It's what she does. It's who she is. As a skilled pro, she might not make much in the way of mistakes anymore. But all it will take is playing the wrong song and it's, Boom Boom! Out Go the Lights! The lights and, in this case, a finger or two, or perhaps even a hand.

At least, that's the way she wired the piano while the two floated around never-never land during their afternoon naps. All it took was a little non-electrical motion-sensitive shock tube detonator she's stored inside the metal casing of her e-cig device, and a one-quarter-cc drop of the transparent super liquid-thermite from her pen.

But this time, the explosion won't be triggered by touch or heat alone. This time the explosion will be triggered by a specific number of touches. If Ellen fingers the black C-minor key on the black baby grand one hundred times, she won't get the chance to "Play it again, Sam." Most of her hands will be spattered all over the living room wall behind her.

Why bother to trigger the super nano-thermite explosives this way?

"Well, I'm not against giving a person a fighting chance," she says aloud while turning into the parking lot of the Albany University nano-tech lab. "This isn't about shooting fish in a barrel. It's all about the challenge. All about the fun."

Besides, she's got her money on Ike returning home not tomorrow, but tonight. That's what a concerned family man would do. He wouldn't use tonight as a get-out-of-domestic-jail-free pass. But once he figures out the Suburban tire didn't blow from normal wear and tear, he'll do everything in his power to get home quickly.

Get home tonight.

She enters her keycard at the door, stares directly into the electronic retinal security scanner. The front steel and glass door opens. Inside the smooth marble finished lobby, a uniformed security guard sits at the big round reception desk playing a game of electronic cards on his laptop.

He looks up at her. "Don't tell me you're working late again, Ms. Darling?"

He's a late-middle-aged man whose wife died a long time ago. Now his new wife is his work and his cards. His lonely nighttime existence.

"Always working, Stanley," she says, while pulling a pair of leather gloves from her pocket, slipping them on. "I'm standing on the bottom rung of the ladder. I gotta work my way up."

"You know something, Ms. Darling?" Stanley poses.

She stops, turns to him. "What is it?"

"Why isn't a pretty girl like you married?"

She smiles, recalls her foster father chasing her through the woods in the night, recalls her pregnancy. Recalls the fear of being alive inside a cold-as-ice city and an explosively hostile world.

"My guess is I haven't met the right man, Stanley," she says. "Why? Don't tell me you're proposing."

He laughs, turns back to his laptop and his never-ending game of electronic solitaire. Reaching into her jacket, she slowly slides out her e-cig device.

"Well, forty years ago, I might have done exactly that," he says, shifting some cards around on the screen.

"Too bad," she says, sliding a fresh stainless steel cartridge into the e-cig device. "I might have said yes." She approaches him. "Oh, I almost forgot, Stanley. I brought you a present." She hands him the device. "I know you can't smoke inside the building, and what a pain it is to keep heading outside every five minutes, especially when you're the only one on duty. So I thought I'd give you the gift of indoor-friendly tobacco."

Stanley's face lights up as he takes the e-cig in hand.

"Well, I'll be damned," he says. "How's it work?"

She shows him.

"Brand new cartridge is already loaded," she adds. "Flavor contains just a hint of strawberry."

"My favorite," he says, switching the device on so that a blue light illuminates at the device's head. He brings the tube to his lips, inhales.

She goes to the elevator, presses the going-down button.

"Doc," Stanley says, exhaling blue vapor along with his words, "you've made my night."

"Glad to be of service," she says at the precise moment the e-cig explodes in Stanley's face, obliterating his entire lower and upper jaw.

Boom Boom…Out Go the Lights…

The elevator arrives. She goes to it, steps casually inside.

The door closes. She slides her ID card through a reader that will allow access to a subbasement level that isn't identified on the elevator's enunciator panel. When the door slides opens, she walks out into a brightly lit corridor, walking its narrow length until she comes to an area enclosed by another steel and glass door.

She once more slides the ID through the digital reader and stares obediently into the retinal scanner. The solid, bullet/explosive-resistant door opens. A few doors down is another solid metal door. This one says, EXPLOSIVES. Authorized Personnel Only.

Taking hold of her semiautomatic, she aims for the security camera, presses the trigger. Then, sliding her keycard into the door, she opens it and steps inside. Surrounded by all manner of explosive components, from det cord to computerized detonation systems, she retrieves her smartphone and thumbs a number on the speed dial.

"How much longer?" says the Chinese-accented voice. "I am growing impatient while you carry on with this charade of personal vengeance."

"My personal business is exactly that and it will be accomplished before the dawn and the Wellington Hotel implosion. You can pick me up at our designated rendezvous. I trust I won't require a passport or visa?"

"You have to ask, Dr. Darling?"

"That's what I thought," she says. Then, "You know, I really am going to miss the country of my birth."

"You will be wealthy beyond your wildest dreams. You will be treated like a hero in the People's Republic. Just keep that in mind."

But that's not what's on her mind right now. What's on her mind is revenge, and making sure Ike Singer and his entire family know the precise meaning of payback before their bodies are blown to smithereens.

CHAPTER 21

Standing up from the table, I pull out my phone, dial Tian from the garage.

He answers.

I ask, "How much will it cost me to get my vehicle back tonight?"

"Jeez, I'm already drinking beers," he says.

Oozing over the phone, the sound of beer bottles clinking, jukebox music playing, men and women laughing, yelling, carousing.

"I need that new wheel tonight."

Exhaling. Sighing. "I suppose I can get it if I call a guy who knows a guy who knows a guy. But Jesus, Mr. Singer, it'll cost you." He pauses, maybe to steal a swig of beer. "Why don't you rent a car you wanna get home that bad?"

"By the time I do that, you can have my ride ready, and I'd rather not have to come back here tomorrow. I have a sick kid who needs my attention. You said it will only take you an hour to put it all together."

An abrupt beep sounding off inside the phone indicating a new text. Pulling the phone from my ear, I see it's from Ellen. Heart in my throat, I click on the MMS text. It's a photograph of dark blue suit–jacketed Miller, sneaking around the exterior of my farmhouse. Ellen didn't snap the photo. Alison did.

"You make the repair tonight, now, ASAP, I'll make it worth your while. Understand?"

"Understood. Meet me in front of the garage in twenty minutes."

Hanging up, I head back up to the room, drink one more beer. Once again I try Miller's number. Once again I get his message service.

"Miller, it's Singer. Call me when you get this. I'm coming back tonight."

Cut the connection.

Slipping into my jacket, I close the door behind me, leave the Motel 6 without checking out.

CHAPTER 22

As promised, Tian is already in the garage with the overhead door open, the bright white light from the ceiling-mounted fixtures spilling down on the oil-stained concrete floor.

"You must really wanna get home, Mr. Singer," he says, detaching the old, damaged brake drum from its axle, setting it down. "I could have saved you a grand or more if you just waited until morning."

"It's not about the money," I say, bending, picking up the drum, examining the spot where a tiny amount of explosive material appears to have detonated, leaving a black scorch mark, the metal having melted and warped inward, like it were constructed not of strong steel alloy, but flame-heated candle wax.

Phone rings.

"You'll store this for me in the back along with the damaged rim when you're done?" I say, retrieving the phone.

"It's your dime. I'll gift wrap it in latex you want."

Eyeing the cell's digital display.

Miller.

"Jesus, where you been?" I say, stepping outside, phone pressed against my ear.

"And hello to you too, Singer," Miller says. He's back in his car. I can tell by the sound of his voice, the background noise that accompanies it.

"Two things," I say. "First. I got a picture of you in a text just a little while ago. You were walking around the exterior of my house in the dark. It was sent from Ellen's phone. When I called it back, nobody answered. I think Alison Darling is using it."

"That's one," he says. "And for two?"

"Alison's mother, Patty, isn't dying of cancer. She's dead already. The boiler blew in her house three years ago. It mashed up her brains pretty bad and it was also accompanied by a fire. You can look it up in the old Times Union newspaper archives. By time the fire was done with her, there wasn't much Patty Darling left to pull evidence off of."

Miller, pausing for a beat. Digesting the information.

"Why would Alison lie about that to you? Doesn't make sense."

"She's playing with me. It's part of her game. Her stalking game."

"What do you want me to do?"

"Arrest her ass."

He laughs. "Jeez, I don't mean to make light of the situation, Ike. I know you're freaked out by her reappearance into your life and what it could mean for you and Ellen if she decides to spill some very overdone beans. But I can't arrest her for what amounts to joking around."

"She wasn't joking."

"You described her as a jokester when she was a kid. Always making up her own knock-knock jokes."

"That was then. She's an adult now and she's not so funny. There's more."

"What is it?"

I tell him about the receipt. About the items it contained and the date. I also tell him about what Alison told me about Patty being careless after Brian died. About her heavy drinking. Her drug use. Her manic depression.

"Okay, that's interesting I'll admit. But I'm sure APD arson was all over the scene if there was a burn death related to the blown boiler. Tell you what, I'll check the files and see what I can see."

"Napalm, or versions of it, burns very hot. It can destroy any evidence that would lead an expert to believe the boiler didn't just blow on its own, that the fire accompanying it wasn't the result of a busted gas line. Done right, it can erase its own trace evidence."

"Okay, pal, slow down," he says. "Funny, but if I wanted to rig a boiler to blow and burn the house down along with it, I'd make it look like Patty got drunk and did it herself."

"That's not the way Alison would do it. She'd want to control the situation. Create a work of art."

"How do you know?"

"Trust me. I used to blow shit up for a living with her father. I'm going with my gut on this one."

"Like I said, I'll look into it. So what's next, pal?"

"I'm coming home tonight."

"What's the rush?"

My temples flare. I like Miller, but he's not grasping what I'm trying to tell him. That I consider Alison a direct existential threat not only to the state of my marriage, but to my family. Their physical safety.

"I don't like what's happening with Alison. I don't trust her."

"Listen, Ike, all kidding aside, if you feel there's a real problem, I'll make sure a squad car makes a pass every hour on the hour tonight. Hopefully it will be a quiet night and the chief can spare the car and support staff without pissing off the mayor and the city council. You have a long, hidden driveway, but they'll do their best. When will you be back?"

"Couple hours give or take."

"Okay, give me a ring when you get in," he says. Then, "Oh, and Ike."

"Yeah?"

"Knock knock."

Is he fucking kidding?

"Who's there?"

"Cargo."

"Cargo who?"

"Cargo beep beep."

He laughs.
I hang up.

CHAPTER 23

Before Tian can release the vehicle, I'm forced to hit up two separate ATMs to hand over one grand in cash, just to cover the grease monkey for his troubles. The pretty green doesn't cover the cost of the repair either, including the new tire, the new rim, the brake drum, the calipers, the pads, and the labor associated with putting it all together. That's another twenty-two hundred, which I slap onto my Amex.

"Pretty steep," I say.

"Price of doing business after hours," Tian says. "Plus, take into account I've missed five innings of the Red Sox-Spankmes game."

He grins a crooked gray-toothed smile. Like he's baiting me, the New Yorker.

"Luckily I don't give a fuck about baseball, Tian, or is it Christian?"

"Just Tian," he says. Then, slapping me on the arm. "Just jokin' with ya."

I pay him, snatch my keys from his hand, cross the lot to the now repaired Suburban.

That was an hour ago.

Now, as I approach the New York state border I try dialing Ellen's cell for what has to be the twelfth time since I started the nighttime drive. But all I get is the message service.

The road passes under my wheels. Maybe it's my imagination getting the best of me, but I can't help but see my family dead. Slaughtered by a young woman who wants revenge for something that happened when she was a girl. Something that occurred in the span of one single night, and that led to a whole lot of bad nights and days for her, her mother, and her father. A night that I've come to regret with all my heart. But a night that has yet to escape me.

Maybe I should have at least kept in touch with Patty after the night in the motel room. Maybe I should have called her when her husband died, acknowledged her when they buried him. Certainly I saw her at the funeral. But I was too beat up myself for us to say much of anything to one another. I was in a wheelchair, my back bandaged and braced, my hearing all but gone while my eardrums began their long healing process.

But I wanted to keep my distance from her. A distance matched by my shame for what I'd done with her two months prior, knowing that all I wanted was escape from Henry's condition. Instead of running from her, I should have found a way to approach her at the funeral, apologize for catching her at a time when she was most vulnerable, as her marriage with Brian was unraveling.

The past can't be undone. Once the implosion sequence starts, the stages commenced, there's no going back.

But that's not right either. Because what if I had been able to speak with her? What the hell would she have said to me as she witnessed Brian's dark brown casket being lowered into the earth on a cold, wet day?

Oh, it's okay, Ike. No harm done.

Go ahead, Ike, say it. Say the truth. Patty, casually speaking inside my head while I drive. Her imagined voice comes to me so clearly, it's almost like she's seated right beside me. Like sixteen years haven't gone by since I last laid eyes on her. *You took advantage of me. You wanted escape and you wanted your own particular brand of revenge not only against Ellen for bearing a child like Henry, but also against God for allowing the boy to be born with a disease that would cripple him and render him a slow death over a period of two decades.*

But then, it wasn't God's fault any more than it was Ellen's. Any more than it was yours. Bad luck happens and that's all it was. Ruining my life and the life of my daughter was no way to make it right in the eyes of the world and heaven above. I was in love with you, Ike. Had been from a distance for a long time. You knew I loved you from as far back as college. You saw it in my eyes when I'd come up to the dorm room to visit your best friend, Brian. Or when we'd all go out for beers. Or when we'd hit up a basketball game. I always found a reason to sit next to you, to press up against you, to set my hand close to yours.

"I remember," I whisper inside my head. "It was awkward because Ellen was with me. But then, I guess I kind of liked it too. Isn't that right, Patty Cakes?"

Patty Cakes…Oh my God, do you know how long it's been since you called me that? Truth is, I think it used to make Ellen and Brian a little jealous when you'd say it. Tell me, Ike, do you remember that one Saturday in the fall of our senior year when the four of us got together for a long, lazy lunch? We drank all the beer in the fridge and then drew straws to see who would make the very necessary beer and cigarette run. You drew the shortest straw and sure enough, as if it were scripted that way, I volunteered to ride shotgun with you. I didn't think it was fair you had to go all by your lonesome, after all.

This was around the time that Ellen and you had decided to spend your lives together. At the same time, she was getting suspicious of my crush. As for Brian, he was oblivious, his world revolving around beer and football. But we weren't parked in the liquor store parking lot inside your old blue Chevy three-on-the-tree pickup for more than a few seconds before I pressed my body up against yours.

You were attracted to me and you knew it. Your Patty Cakes. No, that's not right. Let's call a spade a spade. You were very attracted to me. But I was still Brian's girl and you were Ellen's guy and right was right.

You kissed me then. But the kiss was meant as a friendly kiss. When you shook your head no, you didn't have to say another word. I backed off like a good girl should.

But when we finally got back to the campus apartment with the beer and cigarettes, Ellen could see the truth painted on your face as plain as the sun shining down on the golden-leaved trees on that brilliant New England fall afternoon. She could see it on my face too, I'm sure. Something happened between us. What exactly happened, she had no idea and surely did not want to jump to any conclusions. She never said a word about it for the rest of the afternoon and evening. But that night when you were tucked in bed together, she spoke her mind. Didn't she?

"If you ever fuck her," she whispered in your ear, "I will leave you. Do you understand me?"

"How do you know what she said? You weren't there."

You see, I know these things now because I'm dead. It's one of the perks of being a ghostly figment of your imagination. I can gain unfettered access to your thoughts. Your memories. Good and bad.

Ellen's words frightened you that night because deep down in your heart of hearts, you loved Ellen more than anything on God's earth. Did it matter that you'd popped the question and she'd already said yes? That you'd already bought the ring with the paltry savings you managed to scrape up? That her well-to-do father was willing to fund your business with Brian? Yes, but what really mattered was this: to lose her over me or anyone else, was to lose everything.

So yes, it's true. You knew how much I still loved you when we got together at that bar back in 1999, and you took advantage of that love at a time when you needed an escape the most. Now look at the mess you've created for yourself, and your family. Vengeance doesn't know time. It only knows violence. It only knows explosiveness.

Driving. Not aware of the road speeding under me. Tears filling my eyes.

I wipe them from my cheeks with the back of my hand.

"I don't know what I'd do without you Ellen...Henry...You make me complete." I say this aloud and it makes me feel odd. Bad. Like the thought on its own isn't enough to convince myself. But I want to say it aloud because I want Patty to hear it. If she can hear it in heaven or where ever it is her soul has ended up.

Really? says Patty's voice once more in my brain.

For a fraction of a moment, I imagine her buckled into the empty shotgun seat. I shoot a glance over my right shoulder, see her sitting there. Patty, wearing a pink T-shirt and a pair of black panties, like she wore on the night we last saw one another. Only, she doesn't look like she did back then. Now there's a bead of blood running down her forehead, dripping off her eyelids, onto her cheek. Half her body is badly burned. Blackened. The skin charred and disintegrated. So badly, the bones on her rib cage are visible.

You really expect me to believe you're sorry for what happened to me after you used me and hung me out to dry?

"You're not real," I whisper quietly. "I just have a vivid imagination sometimes. Especially when I drive. Alone."

Well, imagine this, lover boy. Imagine a man tenderly making love to me all night. Telling me at least three times how much he has always loved me, but was afraid to say it. Knowing how much it would hurt my husband. How much it could hurt me, my child. How much he loved me, even in college. Even when we parked outside that liquor store, how much you wanted to pull down my panties and fuck me there and then. But you couldn't. You wouldn't hurt Ellen like that. But it was all bullshit, wasn't it?

"Takes two to tango, Patty Cakes," I whisper. But this doesn't seem to make me feel any better. "You asked me for a drink on that night in '99. Not the other way around."

I'm still imagining her sitting beside me, riding with me along the long stretch of Massachusetts Turnpike. A second stream of blood is running over her other eye, the split in her forehead from the boiler explosion more visible in the overhead highway LED lanterns.

You refused to wear a condom that night, Ike. That turned out to be a bad decision. But what was worse was refusing to answer my calls. Refusing to call me back. Even when you knew Brian and I split up for good. You know I left him for you. I guess I thought that if I made the move, you would come to me, and we would finally be together. And then, when he blew himself up and I was left behind to bury the body parts, you made sure as hell you occupied one end of the cemetery and I the other. Let me guess, you were shitting yourself in that wheelchair, praying to God above I didn't blow your cover to Ellen.

"I loved...love...my wife. I'm sorry for what happened. I'm not proud of it. But it happened. Now I have to move on from it."

Like Brian moved on? Like I moved on? Like Alison moved on? Like our unborn child moved on?

"What the hell do you mean?" I'm shouting. Shouting aloud like Patty is truly seated beside me.

What I mean is, this: How do you know we didn't make a baby inside that motel, Ike? A baby boy, perhaps. A boy who might have turned out to be happy and healthy, with a long life ahead. Unlike poor Henry, whose days are numbered.

"Now you're just fucking with me. Fucking with my head. You never got pregnant. That's impossible."

You know what is impossible, Ike?

"This conversation."

Okay, maybe this conversation is all made up. A figment of one man's never-ending guilty conscience. But what isn't made up is this: A big boom is in your near future.

I shake my head, make a fist, punch the empty passenger's side seatback.

"Turn your brain off, Ike," I say. "Turn it off now."

Up head, a big green road sign. Welcome to New York State, it reads. A second smaller sign appears immediately after. It reads, Albany, 22 miles. Slowly, I twist my neck, catch a quick glance of the shotgun seat. Of course, it's empty. But that doesn't mean she's not still there embedded inside my brain like the memory of an imploded building down in Alphabet City.

"Fuck you, Patty Cakes," I say. "And fuck me too."

CHAPTER 24

At half past nine o'clock I make the turn onto the country road that takes me to my farmhouse. It's located on a patch of five acres surrounded by an old apple orchard, the far eastern perimeter of which consists of a two-hundred-foot-high cliff wall that's a part of the one-thousand-acre Thatcher State Park. In other words, I live out in the sticks, even if those sticks happen to be located within Albany County.

I pull into the gravel driveway, drive the quarter-mile length lined with tall pines on both sides. Avenue of the Pines Ellen calls it. Until the trees open up onto a large front and back lawn, a white clapboard two-level farmhouse taking up the center space.

I park outside a red barn that we use mostly for housing our vehicles and some lawn cutting equipment. Hopping out of the Suburban, I go to the back door off the kitchen and head inside.

"Ellen!" I shout. "Henry!"

My spirits lift and a shockwave of relief washes over me when I hear the piano playing.

I head into the music room, just beyond the kitchen and off a center corridor that leads to the front door and a staircase accessing the second floor. At the far end of the room, beyond the stone fireplace, is a baby grand piano that Ellen has owned since she was a teenager growing up in West Albany.

Watching her, oblivious to my presence at the opposite end of the big, open room, I wish I had never strayed from her for even one night. Her long dark hair beautifully draped against her narrow shoulders, the smooth skin on her neck and chest visible beneath her summer-weight dress, a simple chain supporting a small silver angel set against it, I want nothing more than to crawl inside her body and snuggle up against her heart. But I know that if she ever found out the truth about Patty and me, the likely outcome would be too ugly to contemplate, too painful to visualize. That in mind, I have to do my best to shield her from it.

Shield us.

Ellen, Henry, and me.

Suddenly, as if now sensing my presence, she looks up at me, her brown eyes filled with surprise and wonder.

She lifts her hands from the keyboard.

"What are you doing home?" she says. Then, realizing what she just said, she laughs. "Well, that didn't sound too entirely gracious, now did it?"

I press my lips together. Smile.

"Let me start again," she says. "To what do I owe the distinct pleasure of having my friend, husband, and lover home a day earlier than expected?"

"Turns out all I had to do was pay just a little extra for Sunday evening service."

"How much extra?" she says, cynicism in her tone.

Raising my right hand, I extend index finger and thumb, create a narrow space between the finger pads.

"Just a teensy bit."

"I'll bet," she says. "Thank God my boyfriend didn't come over tonight." Again she laughs, because of course it's a big joke... her having a boyfriend on the sly. "Or, hey, wait just one minute. Maybe it's your girlfriend who didn't show up?"

A dull pain settles in my stomach. I know she's kidding around. But her words are hitting a little too close to home.

She moves in close to me, her lips nearly touching mine. "You wouldn't ever cheat on me, would you, Singer?"

She waits for an answer.

I feel myself tensing up.

"Of course not," I say. "Why would you even ask a question

like that?"

She raises up her hand, makes like a pair of scissors with two extended fingers.

"Good, because you know what I'd do if you did." She brings the fingers together. "Snip, snip. And then I'd take you for all your worth."

The dull pain now becomes a sharp one.

"You don't have to worry," I say. "I'm not worth all that much now that Master Blasters is history." But I'm putting on an act and I pray it doesn't show on my face. "Henry's okay?" I say, quickly changing the subject.

"Yes. He's in the den watching television."

I listen for the sound of SpongeBob SquarePants reruns. Or maybe a Batman cartoon. I hear the television, but I can't make out what's playing.

Taking a step inside, I slowly approach the piano. I'm not entirely sure why, but I feel as if I'm walking into a minefield. That at any second, a blasting cap will be triggered and my leg will be blown off at the knee.

"I called and called, El," I say. "You never answered."

Her eyes go wide.

"Oh my God," she says, walking around me to the small catch-all table set by the front door. Snatching up her iPhone, she stares down at the screen. "Well, that explains that," she adds. "It's turned off."

"I received a picture of you and Henry, asleep."

She nods, while pressing the start button on the smartphone.

"Alison's phone was out of charge so she asked if she could use mine. She was nice enough to give us a ride home, so I thought, why not?"

Alison. My overactive mind paints a picture of the dirty-blonde young woman sneaking around my house while my exhausted family slept.

"You know, Singer," Ellen goes on, "Alison really is a nice person. Hard to believe she's Brian and Patty's daughter. Now I feel really badly about not keeping in touch with them after all these years. But after what happened. That explosion down in New York. The way you were caught up in it. What he tried to do to you. I guess it was better to let it all go. Plus…"

"Plus what?"

"This is silly, I guess. But Patty has always had a thing for you. We both know that."

"I've always loved you."

"But you never made a nickname for me like you did Patty Cakes."

"There's that," I say, reminded of the whacked-out conversation I had with Patty in my head all the way from Worcester to the New York state border. "And then there's something else you should know."

She just looks at me, perplexed.

"Patty's dead," I say.

Her eyes grow wide. She exhales, but doesn't inhale.

"How is that possible?" she says, genuine sadness tainting her voice. "I thought she had cancer and was in the process of dying, if that makes any sense. I don't understand."

Shaking my head. "I thought she did too. But I did a little checking up and she's already dead."

"Alison," she says. "Why would she lie about a cancer? What would motivate her to make up something so horrible? It seems so totally out of character."

"I don't know, El." Touching the Miracle Ear hearing aid in my right ear. "Could be I didn't hear her right."

She bites down on her bottom lip, like she's processing this new development. "When did it happen?"

"She died three years ago. Either I didn't hear her right, or Alison wasn't telling the truth."

"Those ears of yours." She goes to the piano, sits down on the bench, eyes the keys, raises her hands like she wants to play something, but then decides against it, settling the palms of her hands on her thighs.

"I know, they can't be trusted. In any case, she died in a boiler explosion in her home. It was followed by a very bad fire. I guess we missed it in the papers."

"Oh, poor, poor Patty," she says, slowly shaking her head in both disgust and sadness. "I never read the obits. You know that. Now I feel even worse for Alison. I should have said something. Patty and I were as close as friends can be at one time."

She looks out the big window on her left onto the darkness, as if seeing herself comforting Alison.

"Why were you sleeping?" I say after a beat.

She perks up at the question. "After we got home and brought our bags upstairs, Alison suggested a drink of some cold lemonade. She mixed it for us while we sat out on the porch and enjoyed the rest of the beautiful afternoon. After a little while, I got sleepy, and so did Henry, so we decided to take a nap." Shaking her head, her smooth dark hair veiling her sweet face. "I never realized how much vacation can be exhausting."

Alison, mixing them some lemonade. Alison slipping them a mickey.

"How long were you out?"

"Believe it or not, about three full, restful hours."

"You never nap, El. Henry might nap a lot because of his condition, but I can't imagine him not spending two or three hours playing Nintendo right off the bat after having been deprived of his fix all week."

"Crazy, I know, right? But there you have it." She stands. "Course, now we'll probably be up all night."

"Let's hope not."

She fingers a couple of piano keys. Even standing she makes beautiful music. As she stares down at the keyboard, a sour grin now suddenly replaces the happy face.

"For some reason," she mumbles, "the C-minor key is sticking. Must be the humidity, or wear and tear. The piano is almost as old as I am."

I'm not sure why, but it strikes me as odd that she's complaining about keys that stick. Maybe I'm being paranoid.

"Listen," she goes on, "have you eaten? Henry and I slept through dinner. We were thinking of ordering a pizza."

I glance at my watch. "It's almost ten."

"It's still summer." She smiles, like vacation hasn't ended. "'Sides, Smith's Tavern is still delivering."

Smith's is the only pizza joint that delivers in the mostly rural area. Otherwise, you have to call a joint in the city and that can take an hour and cost a fortune. I don't make nearly the cash sniffing out bombs in Albany that I did shooting buildings.

"I'm in if you're in," I say. Cocking my head over my shoulder. "I'll go check on Henry."

But before all that, I head back into the kitchen, take a look around the brightly lit room, half expecting Alison to jump out of the closet. I go to the fridge, open it, grab a cold beer. Popping the tab, some of the foam oozes out the opening, drips onto my hand. I shift over to the sink, turn on the water, wash the foam from my hand. It's then I notice the two drinking glasses set in the sink.

Alison made Ellen and Henry lemonade. They then fell asleep for several hours. Just doesn't sound right to me. It's one thing to offer my family a ride home. But to then hang around and make lemonade, and at the same time, text me from Ellen's phone. I stare down at the now empty glasses in the sink and my mind spins.

A realization sinks in.

I lift the glass out of the sink, run my finger around the interior, bring it to my nose. Nothing but the smell of lemons. But that doesn't mean Alison didn't purposely try to knock Ellen and Henry out while she did something inside the house. Maybe she searched the place. Stole something. Took pictures. Who knows what the hell she could be up to.

The front doorbell rings. At the same time, the swinging door that separates the kitchen from the TV room/den opens.

"Hey, Dad, you're home," Henry says. Then, "Who's that at

the door?"

"Pizza guy," I say. But then, I'm not even sure Ellen has had time to order the pizza yet.

"You stay here," I say, pulling a steak knife from out of the drawer, sliding it into my back pocket.

Heading out of the kitchen, I go to the front door.

CHAPTER 25

I breathe easy. Because the person at the door is not a stranger. It's not Alison either. It's Homicide Detective Nick Miller.

"Hope I'm not interrupting," he says, stepping into the vestibule.

"You might have called first," I say, feeling for the knife in my back jeans pocket. I pull it out.

"Sorry to rattle the cage," he says, not without a smile on his face. Looking at the knife. "Jesus, I didn't think explosive junkies were that jumpy."

He's wearing a blue blazer, white button-down, and a red-and-black-striped Repp tie, the ball knot of which is neatly tied. His slacks are tan, and his shoes are brown polished cordovans. If it weren't ten at night, I'd say he was on his way to work.

Ellen comes in. I hide the knife by inverting it in my hand, the blade now pressing against the interior of my forearm.

"Hi, Nick," she says, pleasantly. "You're just in time for some pizza. Smith's. The best."

"I'm not staying," he says. "I was in the neighborhood, so thought I'd stop by and see Ike real quick now that your vacation is over."

Ellen does her best not to look cross-eyed at him. He's a downtown homicide detective. Our farmhouse is located way out in the country. Not exactly in Miller's neighborhood.

"Well, if you change your mind," she says, "the pizza will be here any minute."

She leaves us alone.

"Get rid of that thing," he once again insists, staring down at the hand that holds the knife. "You want, I can provide you with a service weapon. I can have someone drop it off for you. I seem to recall your having been approved for a carry/conceal permit."

My initial reaction is to deny the offer, because the first image that blasts through my brain is shoving the barrel of my semi-automatic into my mouth while sitting inside my truck in the Port of Albany. But under the very real and present dangerous circumstances what harm can having a piece to defend myself and my family do?

"That would be good," I say.

He looks at me for a beat. Then, "I looked into that blown boiler at Patty Darling's house back in 2012. It was quite the explosion. Quite the fire. As I was looking into it, it all started coming back to me. How unusual it is for a boiler to blow and for it to result in a fire."

"Arson?"

"They didn't find any problem with the scene. Investigation showed nothing unusual for an old boiler that built up too much pressure and blew its lid, literally."

"What about an autopsy?"

"Body was pretty badly burned. The entire house went up. It was a natural gas boiler after all, and I'm told the line was severed. But from what the report says, death was consistent with the blunt force trauma from an explosion. Her bedroom was located directly above the boiler room. It took the full force of the mostly vertical explosion. Like it had been directed to blow that way. She died instantly."

In my head I see the Patty Darling I conjured up in my head while making the drive back to Albany. The cracked skull, the blood leaking from her nostril, the pink cotton T-shirt, the black panties, the mussed up dirty-blonde hair, the burnt-to-a-crisp skin.

I pull the receipt from my pocket, hand it to him.

"You might want to hang onto this, Nick. You ask me, Alison rigged some sort of timed fuse IED to the boiler that not only blew it sky high, but also ignited a bucket full of napalm. Stuff would have burned so hot when combined with a natural gas fire, there wouldn't be much trace evidence of it left. Residue might have gotten picked up by the vacuum, the sifting kits or even the sifters. But they'd have to be looking for something out of the ordinary to notice anything other than a blown boiler and a resulting severed gas line, which is exactly what it looked like. This is small-time Albany after all. Not uptown Manhattan."

"You weren't there, last I heard."

"Hey, all I know is she told me her mother was dying of cancer and now I find out she was killed in an explosion. Something's not adding up with my former partner's daughter."

"She's mad. She's angry over what happened to her mother and how badly it all turned out for her family. Once she gets it out of her system, you won't hear from her again."

"That so. You believe that?"

"She's a successful young woman, Singer. A doctor of nano-thermites. She's a professional, with contracts all over the country. Not a sadistic madwoman, Ike."

"So what are you saying, Nick?"

"What I'm saying is, she doesn't exactly fit the profile of a stalker bent on doing physical harm. It just doesn't add up."

I nod. "Wish I could believe you."

A voice explodes over the radio stored inside Miller's car. Something about the downtown Albany Wellington Hotel.

"Jesus, they're driving me nuts about that implosion tomorrow."

"Let's hope it has nothing to do with homicide."

His eyes go wide. "Chief wants everyone on deck case anything goes wrong. You planning on being there?"

"I'm technically working for arson. I'll be on call."

He grins. "You wish it was Master Blasters taking down that building, don't you?"

"How's that?"

"You wish it was you blowing the Wellington. Or, what do you call it… Shooting."

"Had crossed my mind."

"One day, Singer," he says. "One day you'll get that license back. What happened to you all those years ago wasn't your fault."

"Tell that to the judge who revoked my license. A dozen people were injured in a blast that occurred without warning. If we hadn't had most people behind the exclusion zone already, there would have been deaths and I'd be doing fifteen to twenty for involuntary manslaughter. There's a cut-rate demo guy in Philly doing twenty years for manslaughter after the tower he was taking down fell onto some innocent passersby."

"Life and death ain't fair. You ask me your partner was trying to kill you."

His words are enough to make me become conscious of the big purple scar that runs the length of my back. Where a piece of hot steel cut me.

"You know that. I know that. Maybe God knows that. But try convincing the judge."

Just then, two white headlights cut through the darkness of the long, tree-lined driveway. Someone pulling up. The car stops and a kid gets out, a pizza in hand.

"Looks like your dinner has arrived," Miller says. "I'll take off."

"Okay," I say, as the kid approaches the open door.

"You order a pizza?" the skinny boy says to the detective.

"Not me," Miller says. "I was just leaving."

Making his way across the porch floor, the detective descends the steps. Before taking the gravel path back to his ride, he turns.

"I won't forget about sending over the you-know-what along with the proper paperwork."

He makes like a pistol with his right hand, brings his thumb down slow.

"Thanks," I say. Then, to the kid. "Pizza belongs to me."

I dig for some cash, hand him a twenty.

"Keep the change," I offer.

He thanks me, takes off. That's when something occurs to me. I set the pizza onto the small table that collects keys, cell phones, and sunglasses. I run back out onto the porch.

"Nick," I bark. "Hold on." Descending the steps, I go to the Suburban, open up the back, grab the damaged rim, carry it back to his unmarked cruiser. "Do me a favor," I say, opening the back door, setting the rim inside. "Lay that on Pendergast's desk, will you?" I say, referring to the young cop assigned to me in bomb squad. "Put a note on it asking him to have it tested for any foreign elements. There's more where this came from, he needs it."

"What kind of foreign elements?"

"Anything not already visible to the naked eye that shouldn't be there."

He furrows his brow. "Thought you had a simple flat."

"Blowout, which the mechanic suggested wasn't all that simple."

"I'll see that it gets done."

I shut the door.

"Sure you don't want a slice for the road?" I say through the open window.

"And risk getting sauce on my tie? Thought you knew me better than that. 'Sides, at my age, a chef salad and a plain yogurt will suffice for dinner." Grinning. "Washed down with some Jack Daniel's, of course."

I step back and away from the cruiser. He takes off, the gravel crunching under his wheels. I climb the steps back up to the house. For a time I stand out on the porch in the darkness, listening for anything unusual. Staring out onto the woods that take up the entire front perimeter of my property.

Alison.

Maybe she's out there. Or maybe she's not. The fact that I don't hear anything other than crickets doesn't mean something bad isn't out there waiting for me. Waiting for me and Ellen and sweet old Henry.

A quick glance over my shoulder. I imagine Patty seated on the porch swing, bleeding, smiling, rocking slowly fore and aft. Her head is cracked like an egg and the skin on the entire right half of her body is burnt and blackened to the bone. It makes my back teeth hurt just to look at her, and it breaks my heart knowing how beautiful she was in real life.

"Hey, Ike baby, two starving people in here," Ellen shouts.

I shake the image from my brain, head back inside, lock the door behind me. Already the pizza is getting cold.

CHAPTER 26

After the two cars leave the driveway, she emerges from the trees located at the front of the property, only a couple of dozen feet from the farmhouse. She's dressed entirely in black. Black acrylic leggings, rubber-soled tactical boots, long-sleeved Under Armour tee that fits her body like a second skin. Plus black tactical gloves, black kerchief wrapped around her light hair, and black NATO camo face-paint. Mounted to her skull is an Armasight Vega Gen 1+ Night Vision Goggle armed with a built-in infrared illuminator. She can see in the dark. See her prey running for its life.

A chrome-plated, 5-shot, Smith & Wesson 460XVR, long-barreled, .460 caliber revolver—the only revolver that will accommodate the experimental thermite loads without its alloy metal composite construction breaking down—rests on her right hip directly beside an eight-inch fighting knife, while her military grade–encased smartphone is carried in a nylon holster on her left hip. Fully charged for the night's festivities, it will not only serve as her life-and-death line with Ike Singer and his perfect family, but the keypad will also provide her with the electronic means for creating the night's program of pyrotechnics and fiery brilliance.

Her body trembles with an excitement so profound, it's a wonder the whole world can't hear her heart pounding. Once tonight's mission is accomplished, she will oversee the true implosion of the Wellington Hotel. The explosion and the dust cloud will provide the perfect distraction for her getaway. The chopper will pick her up and carry her away from Albany for the rest of her days.

Albany. The city that abused her, betrayed her. The city where all her hopes and dreams imploded. Her memories of this place are dismal. How she looks forward to her new life and new identity, free from the Darling family that was anything but. Free from the soon to be destroyed Ike Singer.

If only she could get the show on the road and prove to her father's old back-stabbing partner and best friend that one must pay for one's choices in life.

Putting some distance between herself and the trees, she darts up the length of the gravel driveway, careful not to step on anything that might blow her legs clean off.

CHAPTER 27

Ellen carries the pizza into the TV room along with some paper plates, bottles of spring water for her and Henry, a brand new beer for me. At Henry's direct request, we've decided to make a party of it.

"End of the vacation," the young man says. "It deserves a party."

He's laid out on the couch, shoes off, feet up, a blanket covering his legs. He's got the clicker in hand and he's rifling through the stations like it's more entertaining to watch two or three seconds of a few dozen shows at a time than one program for its entirety. Part of me can't help but think that his attention deficit has more to do with his limited time left than it does an inability to concentrate on any one program. Perhaps he feels that by speeding through one program after the other, he'll at least get a small taste of everything before the time comes when he won't be getting a taste of anything whatsoever.

Or maybe I'm just overthinking it all. But my God, how I wish he were healthy.

"Henry," Ellen says, sitting herself down by his feet, "I'm going to have a seizure if you keep changing the channel like that." She picks out a big triangular slice of the cheese pizza for the boy, sets it on a paper plate, and places it on the coffee table within his reach.

I crack open my beer, take a deep drink of the cold, effervescent liquid, feel the immediate calming effect of the alcohol. Picking up another empty plate, Ellen sets another slice onto it, then looks up at me.

"Babe?" she says.

"I'll wait a minute. Let me enjoy my beer, catch my breath."

Catch a buzz, I should say. Turn my brain off.

"It's been quite the busy day and night for you, Singer." She grabs her own slice, sits back on the couch. "A busy day for us all."

"At least Professor Alison was there for us," Henry interjects, his eyes now focused on the television. "I can't believe how much she's grown up. And not a single bad knock-knock joke."

For the time being, he's settled on a pre-season football game. The NY Giants versus the Washington Redskins. Henry loves football. Sometimes, when he's watching it, I'll see his eyes light up at the action. The running, the hitting, the throws, the kickoffs. Maybe, if God had had something different in store for him…something more normal, or even something uniquely gifted rather than uniquely deadly, he might have made one hell of a football player, with a shelf full of trophies to show for it. It's something I would have wanted him to have for himself. Not for me. Me and my pride. Okay, that's not entirely true. I would have been super proud to be the dad of an All State football player.

Eyes on the wall-mounted flat-screen.

The New York Giants kick off from their own thirty to start the fourth quarter of the game. A stocky Redskin whose thighs look like two big hams catches the ball, then speeds and plows through the Giant defenders like a triple-crown winner through a racecourse filled with deadbeat horses. The only one left to stop him is the kicker, who is about half his size. Still, the little guy shows some spunk and guts when he lowers his head, rams it into the ball carrier's mid-section, thrusting him out of bounds, saving a sure six points. The crowd in New York explodes in cheers. The kicker's teammates punch his shoulder pads and slap his helmet. Even I feel a wave of warm pride fill my veins for the little guy.

"Way to go," I whisper under my breath. "That's showing them."

"Way to go what?" Ellen says.

I sip my beer, turn to her.

"I was just commenting on the football, El." My eyes shifting back to Henry, who is taking a small bite of his pizza. I recall what happened after lunch due to his sensitive digestive tract and pray that it doesn't happen again tonight. He needs his rest.

My cell chimes and vibrates like an oversized hornet, startling me. It's the APD. I press the phone to my ear.

"Singer."

"Mr. Singer," speaks the agitated voice of Jack at the switchboard. "We got a live 10-89 in progress in West Albany along with a live hostage. This is no joke. A live 10-89. In progress."

Pulse rises. Throat closes up.

"Who called it in?"

"Uniformed patrol in the area. I'm calling it in direct because you don't have a scanner."

Adrenaline shooting into my brain.

"What are we looking at?" I say, my eyes now wide and concentrating on Ellen, whose eyes are just as wide.

"Mailbox bomb. Judge John Bescher's house. Lennox Avenue."

"The judge…Judge Bescher…is the hostage? You're sure about that?"

"Affirmative, Ike. SWAT is notified and en route."

"Have the area secured, evacuate every house within a thousand feet of the mailbox. Call in Homeland Security and Staties. I'm on my way."

I cut the connection. "Guys, I have to go."

"What is it?" Ellen says. "What's happened?"

"Explosive device reported inside a mailbox at Judge Bescher's house."

"Who's Judge Bescher?" Henry says.

"Old state appellate judge who put a lot of bad guys behind bars," I say. "Works at family court in his spare time, putting away deadbeat dads, defending foster parents, among other things."

"The very same judge who took Daddy's blasting license away," Ellen adds. Then, not without disdain. "How, ummmm, ironic."

"I seem to remember you applauding his decision to shut me down," I point out, as I head into the kitchen, grab my keys.

Ellen is right behind me. "But you haven't been called in to investigate an emergency in nearly a year and tonight you just happen to get a call for the real thing. And Judge Bescher of all people. My heart is pounding."

"Don't worry," I say, taking her in my arms. "I'll be extremely careful. Besides..."

"Besides what?"

"Besides, Rob will do all the dirty work."

"Let's hope Robot Rob is in proper working order tonight."

I kiss her on the forehead, go for the back door. "Don't wait up, El."

"Are you kidding?" she says. "I'll be watching the live news."

"I'll toss you a wave."

As I open the door, step out onto the back porch, closing the door behind me, I can't help but feel that the judge's bomb isn't meant for him and him alone.

CHAPTER 28

What my wife was referring to were the legal charges I faced after Brian had shot the Alphabet City warehouse after illegally detonating the charges with a secondary electronic control box. Maybe the site had already been secured prior to our original shooting schedule. But once the call had gone out for everyone to stand down, people--workers, security, media, and innocent bystanders--started to relax. It was one of those situations where you smoked 'em if you had 'em on you.

So when Brian pressed the black and red triggers on the remote control device and the blasting caps started exploding, and the timed charges began their detonation sequence from Stage 1 at the way-back of the warehouse, all the way to Stage 3 at the warehouse's front, people were caught unawares. We were lucky no one lost their lives (including myself). But unlucky in that some of the shrapnel from the exploded concrete managed to connect with two or three of the bystanders who had drifted outside the exclusion zone.

Master Blasters was sued, of course, and brought up on charges, including negligence. Our bonding company dropped us, and after fighting a prolonged but losing battle in District Court, the New York State Appellate Court, presided over by the Honorable Judge Bescher, didn't feel the need to indict me as the lone surviving partner of Master Blasters, Inc. He did however, lift my license and insist I pay a considerable fine, which just about wiped out the remainder of the business's accounts. In the end, I was lucky to keep my farmhouse and the property it sits on.

Naturally my lawyer tried to convey my innocence to the judge. Brian's plan to shoot the building with me inside wasn't my fault, after all. But he saw it another way. My partner and I shared in the responsibility for the timed implosion, just like we shared in the profits. I should have been aware of his actions, plain and simple. Safety first and last.

"'You're dealing with hundreds of pounds of explosives here,' I believe were the judge's exact words. "'Not cheeseburgers.'"

I was allowed to work for another outfit if I chose to do so, but only operating manual demolition equipment and not explosives. So much for my career blasting big high-rises. So much for my dream of a true implosion. So, if I was banned from explosives, why would the police take me on as their sole bomb disposal expert? First of all, it was a job nobody wanted. Second of all, maybe I couldn't legally set a charge, but they sure as shit didn't mind if I took a chance on disarming one. What was the worst thing that could happen after all? My flesh, bones, and brains blasted all over the city?

I arrive at Judge Bescher's residence on Lennox Avenue, in the upscale section of the West Albany suburbs. I'm greeted by my support staff, if you want to call it that. It consists of one man, a dog, and a robot. The young man is assigned to me not because of his expertise in bomb disposal, or his crime-fighting skills, or his uncanny ability to profile those individuals, like those radical Islamic creeps, the Tsarnaev brothers, for instance, who planted a couple pressure cooker bombs in the middle of the Boston Marathon.

Instead, he's assigned to me because he's a young rookie and therefore no one else wants or feels safe enough to work with him. His name is Ted Pendergast and he's a wiry man of medium height with thick black hair cut regulation short. He's a little on the nervous side, which is always a cause of concern when it comes to dealing with explosive devices and their disposal. But then, we've never had to deal with a hot situation of this magnitude (or apparent magnitude) until now.

Lucky me. Lucky Ted.

We shove through the throngs of reporters, bystanders, EMTs, cops, and television reporters, slip on past the fire trucks and squad cars. A SWAT team member dressed in full riot gear pulls aside the barricade for us. That's when I spot the mailbox. And something else. A man duct-taped to the mailbox post.

It's the judge.

He's dressed only in a pair of baby blue boxer shorts and a wife-beater T-shirt. His mouth is covered with a duct tape gag, but his eyes are wide open and pleading for someone or something to save his life.

"Holy shit," I whisper. "Didn't any of the neighbors see what was happening? Or were they too petrified to step outside their protective walls?"

For a brief moment, I feel like the earth is about to shift right out from under my feet. It's one thing to be employed in a job where you spend twenty-four-seven anticipating something that rarely, if ever, happens. But then, it's another thing altogether when that something happens, and the something in question is a bomb and there's a man attached to it.

SWAT Man is saying something to me, but it sounds like a near silent mumble. A quick shove against my shoulder.

"You with me, man?" SWAT Man barks.

"Yeah," I say, nodding, trying to clear my head.

"Miller is waiting for you by your van," he says, cocking his head. "Go, now, go."

I turn to Ted.

"What about Nemo?" I say. Our bomb sniffing German shepherd, Nemo. "He get a whiff? Could be that mailbox is stuffed with a bunch of newspaper for all we know."

Ted shakes his head rapidly.

"No such luck, boss," he says, his tone high-pitched, voice trembling. "It's the real deal. Nemo nearly pissed on the judge he was so excited."

Over my right shoulder, I spot Miller standing before the open back doors of the bomb disposal van.

"Follow me, Ted," I say, before approaching Miller.

"There's nobody dead yet," I say to the homicide dick while Ted jumps into the van where Nemo is pacing nervously in his oversized crate.

"Let's hope it stays that way, Singer," he says. "I'm here because we need to talk."

"Last I heard, there's a bomb to defuse in that mailbox behind me. For all we know it could be on a timer and set to detonate at any second. I gotta get in there now."

I cock my head in the direction of a large brick ranch probably built in the 1950s. The lawn is lush and green in the mobile LED lamps and the headlights from the cruisers, EMT vans, and fire trucks. At the bottom of the drive is a standard aluminum mailbox mounted to a wood 4X4 post that's been painted black. The same post the portly, balding judge has been duct-taped to.

Ted sticks his head out. "You wanna use the shotgun?"

I shake my head. "Jesus, Ted. There's a man attached to the bomb. Guess what happens I shoot the bomb?"

He bites down on his bottom lip, raises his hand up, slaps his forehead.

"Stupid," he says. "So...fucking...stupid."

"We were all stupid and young once, Ted. You're just nerved up. Happens to the best of us. Don't take it too personally."

"Better get the suit," he says.

"Now you're cooking with natural gas, Ted. And get set to power up Rob."

Ted pulls the explosive ordinance disposal, or blast, suit from the van sets it onto the edge of the van floor.

Miller says, "The judge is a little bit upset."

"I would be too, somebody taped me to a mailbox that's about to blow."

The detective runs his hand over his mouth, crosses his arms.

"There's a little more to it than that."

"And that's why you're here, Nick?"

"God, pal, so perceptive for a guy who isn't really a cop."

Pulling off my cowboy boots, I slip into the blast suit, legs first. Then, with Miller's help, slip into the arms. I zip it up and put on the ballistic gloves.

"A note came with the mailbox setup," Miller adds. He digs around in his pocket, pulls out a white index card with some typing on it. "'Master Blasters says Hello!' It was taped to the judge's forehead when we arrived."

All oxygen exits my lungs.

"Now, I feel quite certain you had nothing to do with this," Miller says. "But it might not be easy convincing Judge Bescher of that. That is, if we're not peeling what's left of him off the neighbor's garage door. He is the judge who pulled your license after all, if I recall. He's well aware you have a hard-on for him."

"Not stiff enough to kill him, for Christ sakes, Nick. Come on."

He nods, pockets the note. "I'll put somebody on this note right away. Might require a visit to your house. You own any typewriters?"

I picture the one in my basement office.

"Affirmative. It was my grandfather's during the Second World War. A Remington. Weighs about fifty pounds. So what?"

"Should be no problem making a check on the typescript then."

"That makes my night complete, Miller." I pop the helmet onto my head, while the sound of a motorized tracked vehicle pulls up behind me. Robert, the autonomously remote-controlled bomb disposal robot. The rookie cop hands me the combination remote control/video display. "Mind if I do my job, Detective Miller?"

"Not at all," he says. Then, setting his hand on my shoulder. "Be careful, Singer."

I smile at him through the helmet safety glass. "You kidding?

This is the most fun you can have next to shooting a ten-story tower."

CHAPTER 29

You're young.

Young and stupid. Definitely old enough to know better. Maybe ten or eleven years old. But that doesn't stop you from what you're about to accomplish. You're outside in the backyard of the aluminum-sided, two-story split-level you grew up in, inside the cookie-cutter suburbs. Your mother and father have no idea you're out there and what it is you're doing, because the old man is at work, and mom is upstairs ironing clothes in front of the television.

The blood runs fast through your veins, your pulse pounds in your head, because what you're about to do is so insanely cool, so incredibly destructive and explosive, so fucking radical, you can feel the anticipation in the pit of your stomach. It must be what it's like just before you have sex with some hot girl, or so you tell yourself. Sex with the older girls with real boobs, like from the seventh or eighth grade.

In the box you hauled up from the basement are stored the dozen Revell plastic model kits you've spent the better part of a year constructing. There's six German World War II–era planes. Two Stukas and four Messerschmitt ME-109s. The six tanks consist of three Tiger tanks, an American Half-track, and a Sherman tank.

In your pocket is a fresh pack of firecrackers and three M-80s, or what collectively amounts to three-quarters of a stick of dynamite, all of which were acquired rather illegally from your best pal in the sixth grade, the red-haired and freckled Patrick Daly, who spends his summer down south where recreational explosives are legal. Amazing how much firepower five bucks and an old dog-eared copy of Penthouse can buy.

You spend the better part of a half hour fixing the explosives to the planes with black electrical tape you stole from the kitchen junk drawer. Going for realism, you then hang the planes on the clothesline with fishing line. When the planes are airborne, you proceed to get started on the ground war. You tape the three M-80s to the three Tiger tanks while the remaining tanks get firecrackers. For the final touch, you position three dozen green plastic toy soldiers all around the tanks.

With everything wired to blow and the foot soldiers in position, you stand back and admire your handiwork. The planes appear to be flying above the tanks. The German armament appears to be honing in on the Allied tanks. It's like a scene out of one of your History of World War Two magazines set on the nightstand beside your bed, or even something out of Patton, the CBS Saturday Night Late Movie you watched in your bedroom on your black-and-white Sylvania portable just two weeks ago.

"So...fucking...radical," you whisper to yourself.

You reach into your pocket, pull out the Bic lighter you lifted from your mom's purse. You look one way, then the other. You peer up at a blue sky and you gaze down at the dry, mid-summer brown grass.

"Sit rep perfect, HQ," you say aloud in your best GI Joe commando voice. "Proceeding with the operation."

Bending at the knees, you begin lighting the fuses. You start with the tank-mounted M-80s first since they have the longest fuses, and then move on to the firecrackers. Standing up straight, you light the firecrackers attached to the bellies of the planes. You hear the alive, crackling hiss of the burning fuses and you feel the urgency in your body telling you to run.

Run very far away.

But for some odd reason, you feel like you're at home with the explosives. You feel almost calm in the brief moments leading up to what will surely be the first in a sequence of spectacular explosions and blasts. In a word, you feel happier than you've ever felt in your short life.

A smile beaming on your face, you see the first of the M-80 fuses disappear as the sliding glass door opens and your father comes storming out of the house…

The rapid-fire explosions were spectacular enough to blow the model tanks and planes to tiny bits. It blew the toy soldiers into the neighbors' yards. They were also violent enough to instinctively send your Korean War veteran dad down on his belly, as if the Chinese were finally bombing upstate New York.

The grass caught on fire, engulfing the two wood, cross-like clothesline posts, the scene reminiscent of a KKK rally gone bad. A fusillade of sparks landed in your thick black hair, burning a hockey puck–sized patch all the way down to your scalp. The fire department came, put out the grass and clothesline fire with their hoses, and lectured your parents on the evils of unsupervised adolescents who have a penchant for pyrotechnics.

You were grounded, of course, for the rest of the summer, while you worked off the $500 Albany Police Department fine by mowing as many lawns as you possibly could fit in.

But it was all worth it.

The radicalness of those M-80s and firecrackers was worth every blade of grass you had no choice but to cut. You had found something near and dear to your heart. That summer was the summer you discovered explosives. That was the summer you became the detonator.

The pyrotechnic excitement hasn't waned in the years and decades since I blew up those models. It's only grown more intense. I might not be blowing anything up right now (quite the opposite in fact), but I feel the intensity in the pit of my stomach as I position my thumbs on the video game–like controller's double joysticks. Taking it slow and easy, I maneuver the small tracked robot into the center of the now abandoned street.

Keeping a distance of maybe twenty feet between myself and

the mobile disposal machine, I can both hear and feel the anxiety coming from the crowd that's built up behind me. Or, what I can only hope is a safe enough distance behind and away from me.

I'm not going to lie. I feed off the energy of it all. Like knowing that my every step is being recorded for several live news feeds. Maybe even a national news feed. Maybe my brain is filled with adrenaline right now, but I can't help picturing Ellen and Henry watching me from the couch, their eyes wide, white knuckles stuffed between their teeth. Maybe, just maybe, even Alison is somehow watching.

Bomb disposal doesn't have the same rush as blowing a massive building up, but it comes close, let me tell you. As Robot Rob closes in on the mailbox and Judge Bescher, I follow, maintaining what I estimate to be a safe enough distance while protected in my blast suit.

When the crowd issues a collective gasp, I know for certain the show is about to begin.

Positioning Rob's arm directly underneath the mailbox, I extend it so that the combination video cam and claw can easily access the narrow opening. The controller comes equipped with a small, smartphone-sized live video feed. My eyes are focused on the feed as the claw's LED lamp shines into the box.

"Take it easy, Judge," I say, my voice amplified electronically by a device installed inside the big bulky helmet. "I'll have you out of here and back in your bed in just a few minutes. I promise."

I can't help but wonder if he has any clue whatsoever as to the identity of the man disguised in the bulky blast suit. I must admit, despite the dog, and his built-in-no-bullshit-explosive-detecting nose, I nonetheless half expect to see a dummy bomb or no bomb at all when the door opens. Just a bunch of rocks or something like that. But what I see dissolves every bit of moisture from my mouth.

It's a pipe bomb.

But a pipe bomb like no other I've witnessed in my time

training for bomb disposal. What I'm looking at is a shiny, metallic e-cig device. Most pipe bombs are anywhere from ten inches to sixteen inches in length, the aluminum or metal tubing being about one inch in diameter. But this device is only about four inches long, and maybe several centimeters wide. What do the kids call them? E-Go cigs? It's similar to what Alison was smoking at the outside bar in the Cape.

Alison, is this your handiwork?

The e-cig devices are about the size of your average adult male index finger. I'm guessing there's no need for an external battery because e-cigs contain an internal battery and the low-voltage wiring to go with it. But the small metal capsule, if you want to call it that, is wired to a timer, making it an official timed-improvised explosive device. A Timex watch head. And from what I can see via the red-numeral digital display, there's only two minutes left on the watch.

Why the hell not trigger it remotely with a cell phone like the roadside bombs you commonly find in Iraq, Syria, and Afghanistan? Because I can bet the farmhouse mortgage that Alison, if she is indeed responsible for this, is not to be found within a radius of one mile.

Pressing the monitor on my chest-mounted radio.

"IED," I whisper into the radio. "Miniature pipe bomb. A bomb stuffed into an e-cigarette. An e-Go." In my mind, visions of the explosive that took out my tire, warped the tire rim, shattered the brake drum. "Experimental explosive, I'm guessing. Maybe enough to vaporize the judge and blow a six-foot-deep hole in the driveway. Maybe enough to take out the house and the whole block. I won't really know until we detonate it. Make sure nobody gets through, understand?"

"Roger that," comes Ted's tinny voice over the speaker. "Jesus, an e-cig? Never heard of that before."

"This is a first for me too, Ted."

Thumbing the controllers, I open Rob's claw and extend the arm just enough so that the first of two wires is caught in the center of the now V-like claw. That's when I finger the command for the claw to close and for the wire to be cut by the attachment's interior blades.

But something's wrong. The claw isn't closing.

I finger the controller, shifting the joystick back and forth, thumbing the action triggers. But there's no response. It's as if Rob suddenly ran out of batteries.

"How much we pay for this junk, Ted? Over."

"It was a secondhand model, remember? Over."

"Fucking garage sale."

"It's Albany, Ike. Money's tight. So they tell me."

Time check. One minute, forty seconds. Pressing the radio transmitter.

"No time," I transmit. "I'm going in on my own."

"I don't have to tell you to be careful. Over."

And I don't have to see Ted's hands to know they're shaking.

My breath warm and stale inside the oversized helmet, my soundtrack is the thump, thump, thump of pulse pulsating, drumming. Some blast suits are equipped with a digitally enhanced sight device which allows for a close-up examination of an IED from a relatively long distance. But due to the aforementioned APD budget constraints, I must rely only on my eyes. The APD paid me for my six months of Improvised Explosive Device Disposal (IEDD) and Public Safety Bomb Disposal (PSBD) which resulted in my being fully certified for both. But in terms of equipment, I'm a hurting unit. I don't have access to portable X-ray systems, projected water disrupters, or a laser ordinance neutralization system. I do, however, enjoy the use of one slightly used and therefore inexpensive portable bomb containment chamber, numerous disruption charges which I prefer not to utilize (what's the point of planting an unstable bomb on top of another unstable bomb?), and even the use of a good old-fashioned shotgun if worse comes to worst.

I pull the pliers from my utility belt and, despite the cumbersome suit, speed-walk my way across the street to the mailbox. The judge is looking up at me, his eyes bloodshot and full of panic. He's shouting but the gag is doing its job, making his words indiscernible. I could remove it, but better that he's not screaming in my ear while I try to defuse this bomb before we run out of time.

Maybe the bomb material itself is something new, if not out of this world. But the setup is a classic timed IED. There are two wires connecting the timer to the fuse, which in turn is connected to the interior of the little pipe. Inside the pipe you'll more than likely find a detonator, a battery, and an explosive that may turn out to be of the thermite or super nano-thermite variety. Something I and Rob the Robot have never before encountered. Unlike my previous occupation, the problem with bomb disposal is this: if at first I don't succeed and this sucker detonates in my face, I don't get to try, try again.

I examine the two wires leading into the e-Go pipe bomb.

This isn't like the movies. The wires are not color coded. There's no red wire and blue wire. The wires are both coated with black plastic and one of them is connected to the battery, the other to the detonator. The odds here are not fifty/fifty. There is no right or wrong wire to cut. They are both the wrong wires. But then, they are also the right wires. What I mean is, I will either blow the place sky high…and myself and the judge along with it…by cutting one of the wires. Or nothing will happen at all.

One thing is for certain. If I do nothing, this bomb explodes in less than twenty seconds. I could try to remove the bomb itself from the mailbox. But there's too much tape. It connects the bomb to the mailbox, and the judge is connected to the mailbox. That means the judge is connected directly to the bomb, which I suppose is the point. No choice but to attempt a disarming on the spot. Attempt it now.

The pliers gripped in my dominant hand, I open them, bring them to the wire closest to me, press the cutters against the wire.

I stare into the judge's eyes. A drop of warm sweat drips into my eye. I feel the burn. It tells me I'm still alive. That this thing hasn't yet detonated and I'm now dreaming or living some sort of grand illusion.

"Here goes nothing, Judge."

I press the pliers tight.

The wire cuts.

We're still here.

I look at the Timex watch timer. Fucker is still ticking. I bring the pliers to the second wire, inhale a breath, hold it.

I cut the wire.

The clock stops.

So what's it like to narrowly escape being plastered all over a serene neighborhood street? You might not believe this, but the sensation is not all bad. The adrenaline that pours into your blood and speeds throughout veins and capillaries is like a drug. A sedative. You feel euphoric, alive, and lighter than air, even if the blast suit is weighing you down like a suit of cement. In that slight moment of time when the final wire is cut and nothing happens, you are as happy as you will ever be.

Pulling the knife from my utility belt, I proceed to cut the judge from the post. It takes a full two minutes for me to get through the bulk of the tape. As a final gesture, I pull the gag from his mouth. He never flinches at the pain that must surely come from having tape ripped from his mouth. He never lets on for a moment that he recognizes me. He just stands, wobbly, out of balance, makes a run in his underwear for the EMT van parked one thousand feet down Elmhurst Avenue.

As for me, I'm left with a bomb to dispose of.

I call for Ted over the radio. Tell him to dress himself in the second blast suit, and to bring the bomb container.

"You want me to come to you, Ike? Over."

"Yes, I want you to come to me, kid."

"Don't forget to say, over, Ike. Over."

"Yeah, over," I say, annoyed. "Over and Roger Wilco and out."

He comes to me as soon as he's dressed in the suit, the heavy, cumbersome container gripped in both his hands. We get to work right away. Ten minutes later, the container now houses the mini-IED which we have no choice but to explode in the middle of the street. Maybe the bomb is small. Tiny even. But the blast it produces is far more powerful than I anticipated. It not only lights up the darkness in a brilliant flash of white/red light, it nearly destroys the container. The crowd roars with enthusiasm, as if this were the pre-show to the big show tomorrow morning at the Wellington Hotel. They clap, as if bomb disposal were pure entertainment.

That's when Miller comes up on me from behind, grabs my arm.

"You're not going to fucking believe this," he says. "But we got a second confirmed 10-89."

CHAPTER 30

"Who is it this time?" I say, running my forearm over my sweat-soaked forehead. Now appearing in my brain, the agonized faces of my wife and sick child.

The thoughts burning through my brain: Please God. I'm not much for praying. But please, if you're out there and you can hear this, don't let it be them.

"It's a priest," he says, his face unusually pale in the white artificial light. "Same deal. But he's not duct-taped to a mailbox. This one is taped to the altar inside his church."

I feel a sense of relief pour over me, knowing the next victim is not Ellen or Henry. But the realization is beginning to sink in. The mailbox bomb, the explosion that destroyed my back wheel, and Dr. Alison Darling, an explosives expert reentering my life is no coincidence.

It's exactly how I put it to Miller.

"I hear you," he says. "Maybe it's time I paid a little visit to the doctor." Then, looking over his shoulder at the bomb disposal van and the German shepherd pacing in circles inside its crate. "But I gotta tell you, there's another note. Like the last one, it was stuck to priest's forehead."

I might be sweating, but my body grows cold.

"A note," I repeat, as if saying it makes it more believable.

He consults his smartphone. "It says, 'Father, forgive me for I have sinned. I have fathered a child who is now lost forever to the angels.' And it's once more signed, if you wanna call it that, with Master Blasters."

The words haunt me…"I have fathered a child who is now lost forever to the angels…"

Is it possible Patty truly was pregnant with my child after just one night together? Of course it's possible. Biologically speaking. But if she was, then why not tell me about it? Why not at least give me the chance to be responsible? Because I refused to answer her calls. Refused to see her under any circumstances. That's why.

"We gotta get over to St. Patrick's downtown," Miller insists.

"Listen," I say, grabbing hold of his sleeve, "there was a timer on this device. Chances are this one will have one too."

"How long did we have for this one?"

"Thirty minutes."

"The report came in five minutes ago."

"If the anonymous caller is also our bomber, he or she is staging the blast sequence. Tops we have twenty-five minutes."

"Let's move," he says.

It's like a train moving down the center of Central Avenue on the way to the city's downtown. Miller's cruiser leading the way, a blue uniform behind the wheel, flashers reflecting red, white, and blue LED lights against the empty storefronts that line both sides of Central Avenue, the main east-west artery that runs through the heart of the city. Behind Miller, my van follows, the rookie doing the driving, his young face intense and filled with anxiety. Behind us, an EMT van, the fire trucks, the media onsite camera trucks, plus more than a few bystanders who take to a crisis like fish take to water.

What's better than reality TV? Reality as it blows up in your face.

In my head I see Alison smoking an e-cig while she sat directly across from me at the beachside bar, only yesterday afternoon. She was taunting me, playing with me. Daring me. She was shoving her power in my face, like an enemy combatant that test fires a missile capable of carrying a nuclear warhead.

I steal a quick minute to text Ellen, make sure everything is safe on the homefront. How can I be sure the promised cop check on my property is happening now that the bomb crises have raised their ugly heads?

I receive a near immediate response.

All okay. Watching you on TV. Worried.):

I text, I'm safe. Make sure doors locked. Be home ASAP. Love you. XXX

Come back in one piece. I mean it. Henry and I will be waiting. Love U. XOX

I know I should be careful and turn the phone off. Static electricity and IEDs don't mix for obvious reasons. Especially an IED with a built-in battery and wiring system. But I pocket the phone, leave it operational. Maybe I should feel reassured that my family is okay. But I can't be sure it will last. It's imperative I'm in communication at all times.

We enter into the center of the city, the modern tall towers now replacing the four- and five-story century old brick storefronts. As Central Avenue turns into State Street, we pass by the long colonnade of marble pilasters that belong to the old New York State Museum and on the right, the massive stone-fronted, State Capitol building that tops off the crest of the State Street Hill. The capitol that Teddy Roosevelt built.

We tear down the hill, the late night traffic pulling off to the sides to let us past, until we come to the bottom, where the sprawling, 1920s-era New York State Education building resides along what used to be the banks of the Hudson River, until Governor Rockefeller decided to build a riverside arterial connecting Albany with its smaller sister cities to the north. Cohoes, Watervliet, and Troy.

My phone rings as we pull a right turn and the steeple of St Patrick's church comes into view on Green Street inside the old Pastures, an area consisting of two- and three-story century and a half old, brick and wood townhouses that once upon a time housed the city's red light district. That is, until the police cleaned the place up in the 1960s and '70s.

I peer down at my phone.

Miller.

"Yeah," I bark.

"You ready for this?"

My heart sinks. "Probably not."

"We got a third 10-89, just called in. Same non-traceable, anonymous source. Up on Lark Street. Planned Parenthood. Similar deal. But a woman, apparently the boss, duct-taped to her desk chair, and a miniature pipe bomb duct-taped to her abdomen. An electronic cigarette device, just like the judge."

Heart sinks, stomach collapses, Alison's presence taking up more and more space in my brain.

"See if you can't get the State Police to start on it. Or Homeland Security."

"They're on it. But they're slow. Too fucking slow. And way too fucking cautious."

Or too fucking afraid.

We pull around the corner onto Green Street, pull up to within five hundred or so feet of the old stone church.

"Stop, stop!" I shout, not bothering with my helmet or gloves, just making sure my utility belt is securely buckled to my waist.

I jump out, bark at everyone to stand back.

"Go!" I shout. "Go! Go!"

Miller jumps out of his cruiser, runs to me.

"Are you crazy?" I bark. "Get back."

But the tall, white-haired man approaches me anyway, with all the calm, cool, collectedness of a man who believes he is already dead.

"I need to know how you want to handle the Planned Parenthood bomb."

I pull my helmet back on.

"One at a time," I say into the slightly fogged up safety glass. Turning, I begin climbing the steps in my bulky blast suit until I come to the big wood doors. Opening the door to my right-hand side, I take my first look inside at the church. There are two long rows of empty pews and beyond them, what appears to be a black man bound to the far left leg of the altar with gray duct tape, the same tape also extending overhead to the gold-plated tabernacle where, I'm guessing, the IED is stored.

As I begin moving toward him, I can see that his mouth is covered with tape, just like the judge before him. Unlike the judge, however, this man seems to be at peace with himself and his salvation, however it should turn out. When I'm within a few feet of him, he looks up at me with deep, bloodshot, but somehow caring eyes. If he could speak to me, I imagine he might say something like, Just do your best, son. That's all you can do.

If only he knew my real talent lies in blowing things up, not defusing them, he might sing a different holy tune.

Footsteps coming from behind me. I turn.

Miller.

"Fuck you doing in here?" I shout, my voice reverberating off the stone walls. Then, cocking my head in the direction of the priest. "Forgive me, Father."

"Can the kid do it?" Miller says.

"What are you talking about?" I say, turning back to him, the weight of the helmet pressing down on my trapezius muscles.

He says, "Can the rookie, Ted, neutralize that Planned Parenthood bomb?"

Shaking my head inside my helmet.

"He can take it out," I say. "But he'll end up taking out that woman and himself along with it. Just make sure the perimeter on Lark Street is secured. Light a damn fire under SWAT."

Miller bites down on his bottom lip. "How much time do you think we have?"

"How the hell should I know?" Then, "Excuse me again, Padre."

"How...much...time?" Miller, pressing me hard.

"I don't even know how much time I have on this one."

The sweat is pouring off my forehead into my eyes. Miller is standing stone stiff behind me, refusing to leave. For all I know, the IED is about to detonate while we stand there doing nothing. If it blows, then for certain, Planned Parenthood on Lark Street will follow.

"Screw it," I say, knowing I'm not about to apologize to the priest or God for a third time. Pulling off my helmet, I drop it to the floor. I'd remove the blast suit's top and bottom too if it wouldn't take so long. I step up onto the altar, the pliers already gripped in one hand, the Maglite in the other.

"Won't be long now, Father," I say. But I don't tell him precisely what won't be long. Detonation or disposal.

He looks up at me with exhausted eyes, while I gently open the tabernacle door, shining the bright white LED Maglite inside. It's an identical bomb to the one I tackled at the judge's house. A blue-light activated e-cig device about the size of an index finger, the two wires extending from it attached to a Timex digital wristwatch head.

I feel Miller behind me, more than I hear him.

"How…much…time?" he again presses.

I read the time on the watch head. Ten seconds. My heart sinks to somewhere around my ankles.

I scream, "Miller, get the hell out!!!"

Raising up the pliers, I squeeze my eyes closed, sever the wires.

CHAPTER 31

The good news: we're still alive.

The bad news: if we only had ten seconds to disarm this bomb, then we have maybe three or four minutes tops to get up to Lark Street and attempt to defuse that one.

I speak into my chest-mounted radio, give the all-clear, instruct Ted to get in here immediately to clean up the bomb and dispose of it.

"You're safe now, Padre," I say. "My people will cut you out of this and get you away from here." Turning, I start jogging for the door. But jogging in a blast suit is like running in a suit of armor. "Miller, come with me."

Together we shuffle past a blast-suited Ted. Coming up on him fast from behind, two SWAT cops who sprint past us, automatic rifles gripped at the ready.

"As soon as you're done here, Ted, get your ass up to Lark Street."

"Roger that," Ted shouts over his shoulder.

We head toward Miller's unmarked cruiser.

"You're driving, Nick." I open the passenger's side door, shove my bulky body inside by sheer force of will.

Miller opens the door, gets behind the wheel, fires the engine up. Stomping down on the gas, he makes an abrupt three-point turn, tires spinning on the macadam, spitting gravel. Shifting into drive, he floors it, heading directly into the crowd of gawkers and news media. They've got no choice but to jump out of the way or get run down.

"Goddamn young cops can't keep the crowd off the road,"

Miller grouses, turning off of Green, onto Broadway.

"We've got to calm the hell down."

"I don't wanna calm down," he says. "I work better when I'm not calm."

"Albany's never been so explosive. They find another note with this bomb?"

"Affirmative. Says 'My child's life ends here…' or something to that effect. Signed Master Blasters, just like the others."

I make a fist. Slam it against the dash.

"Easy," Miller warns. "We don't need that airbag exploding in your puss."

"Don't you see what she's doing, Nick?"

"What's she doing, Ike?"

"She's going after me, trying to pin these bombs on me."

He's quiet for a weighted beat. Just the noise from the over-strained engine loud in my ears.

"Your company was Master Blasters, Incorporated. You were the Master Blaster."

"Easy for her to say."

"How do you think she managed it? That is, she is the one responsible for this. How did she manage to plant three bombs in three separate areas of Albany? And at the same time, manage to apprehend and tie up two grown men and one woman?"

I cock my head over my left shoulder. "Who knows? Maybe she had help." I see Patty. Her memory, her face, her ghost, in my head. "Help from the great big beyond."

"Master Blaster help?"

"Thanks for that. I appreciate your confidence."

"Just messing with you," he says, painting a grin on his face. But there's an air of seriousness in his joking and it makes me more uncomfortable than I already feel in this sweltering blast suit. Then, "Hold on," he insists.

He hooks an abrupt left onto State Street, the back end fish-tailing, tires spinning. We speed up the hill under an army of fluorescent city lights, the mirage-like glare illuminating the empty road. On our left is the Wellington Hotel. It's surrounded with bright orange storm fencing, while the demolition crews who have no doubt worked well into the night setting their det cord and C-4, Nitro, and Symtex charges are doing their best to get some sleep before the morning's scheduled nine AM implosion. But it will be a night with no sleep, take it from me.

"Maybe you should shut that implosion down," I say, my voice loud and terse over the straining six-cylinder. "Postpone it."

Miller gives me a quick look. "You think that tonight's IED festivities and the Wellington explosion have something in common other than explosives?"

"The contractor hired Alison to work on it," I confirm. "I'm not sure in what capacity. Maybe she's just a consultant. But if my gut serves me right, she's responsible for all this tonight. Doesn't matter how complicated or impossible it seems, she's the one who planted these three bombs. Those experimental IEDs."

We shoot past the state capitol, back toward the center of the city.

"You think that young woman would go to these lengths to exact her revenge on someone who slept with her mother? Doesn't make sense to me, Singer."

"People thought those Oklahoma City bombers, Tim McVeigh and Terry Nichols, were happy-go-lucky too."

"You may be right," he says. "When we're done here, we're gonna find a way to take her in, and grab up a bench warrant while we're at it."

"You got a judge who will play ball on something that's essentially my word against hers, at least for now?"

Another quick look, a smile on his face. "I got a few judges in my back pocket, you know what I mean."

I picture my family watching all this unfold on the couch in our home sweet home. I know how much they like the adult Alison, how much they trust her, even after knowing her for what amounts to a period of only hours. It dawns on me how sad, if not angry with me, they will be when they hear I'm directly responsible for her arrest. But then, how relieved they will be when they also discover what a psycho she is. A psycho explosive killer.

"Can't this thing go any faster, Miller?"

"I'm giving it all she's got now," he stresses above the noise of the straining engine. Glancing at his watch. "How much time you think we got?"

"Fuck, man, wish I knew." I grab hold of the handlebar mounted to the cruiser's frame above the door. What do they call it? The "Jeez bar." As in Jesus, let me out of this thing!

The blast that rocks the city catches even a Master Blaster like me by surprise.

CHAPTER 32

Miller hits the brakes, comes to a skidding stop in the middle of the road. Out the windshield, we can make out the small fireball that boils up into the night sky. Car alarms blare. A scattering of people come rushing out of the surrounding buildings, terrified.

We both get out, our eyes attracted to the now dissolving orange ball in the sky.

"We're too late," Miller says, forcing the words from the back of his throat.

Heart sinks, aches, bleeds.

Behind us, fire truck sirens growing louder and louder.

We both get back into the car. He jams the column-mounted transmission into drive.

"Now," he says from deep inside his throat. "Now we've got our homicide."

CHAPTER 33

The train of emergency services, SWAT, Homeland Security, and local media junkies converge on the blast site all at once. So it seems. But it's too little too late. The entire front portion of the brick, block, and glass Planned Parenthood building is gone, leaving only a bombed out, smoldering shell. The blast was big enough…expansive enough…that it not only evaporated the woman who was attached to it, but it was enough to suck the oxygen from any fire that had started from its white heat.

The bomber is no amateur. The bomber is an artist. The bomber is a doctor. The bomber is an expert. Alison.

"She's going to pay," I whisper under my breath. "Alison is going to pay dearly."

I hear Patty's voice. I know what she would say if she were standing in front of me right now.

But this is all your fault, don't you see, Ike? All your fault.

I would respond, "Even if it is my fault for loving and leaving you, Patty, the punishment doesn't fit the damn crime. The punishment has been a little excessive, to say the least."

But then, maybe Alison is just getting started. Maybe she's not just angry at me, but angry at the city that turned its back on her, angry at the world, angry at God.

There's a crater so wide and so deep, extending to the middle of Lark Street, you can drive a tractor trailer into it. Many of the windows on the brick townhouses that line each side of the historic old Albany street have been shattered by the blast. Onlookers who surround the site are horrified and saddened. Many of them, dressed in their pajamas and robes, weep at the sight of the blasted out building facade.

Uniformed cops make a check up and down the block. To make sure no further bombs have been planted, to interview witnesses, to maintain order. Since nothing else is coming over the scanners or Miller's cell phone, it's not impossible to assume the worst is over for the night.

"I've got an address for Dr. Alison Darling," he says. Then, looking at his wristwatch. "It's midnight. You want to come with me? Or you want to get back to your family?"

Ellen and Henry. In all the commotion, I forgot about them. I pull out my smartphone. There's at least five calls from Ellen, and just as many texts. I click on the latter.

R U OK????

The other messages are just another version of this one.

I type, Yes Yes Yes All OK. Home soon.

We're still up

"Did you get the warrant?" I say, turning to Miller.

He purses his lips. "Not exactly."

"What's that mean? Back pocket judges not cooperating?"

"They saw what happened to Judge Bescher. They want real evidence before we take somebody in before a grand jury."

"Let me guess, Miller. If she's the one…if Alison is the bitch responsible for all this…they don't want her getting away on a technicality."

"Doesn't mean we still can't make a fly-by. Gather up that evidence."

"And if she's not home, sound asleep in her feather bed like Little Red Riding Hood?"

"Well then, that's just the kind of thing that makes an old cop like me even more suspicious."

CHAPTER 34

I remove what's left of my blast suit, toss it into the back of the van. I feed the dog a bacon treat from out the palm of my hand, then give him a quick belly rub. After that, I ask Ted to run back to headquarters, fill out the necessary paperwork, and from there head back home for some sleep. I also remind him to meet me at the Wellington tomorrow morning an hour before the scheduled implosion.

"Thought we didn't have to show up for that," he says, like he's disappointed over having to get up for work in the morning.

"Considering tonight's events, I can't think of anywhere else Albany's only bomb disposal unit should be."

Miller and I climb back into his cruiser, pull away from the Lark Street blast site. He stops for a crew of blue-windbreak-er-wearing Department of Homeland Security officials who are now stationed at the end of the road behind a series of yellow barricades. One of the agents pulls the barricades open for us. We drive on out, back into the city.

"They think this could be a terrorist act?"

"You mean like radical Islamists making a lone wolf statement?" he says. "I sort of ruled that out right away with the typed Master Blasters index cards that accompanied each bomb. Hardly a call to jihad, you know?"

I nod. "A judge duct-taped to a mailbox containing a bomb…a priest duct-taped to the altar that supports a tabernacle filled with the Body of Christ and a pipe bomb….the boss of the local Planned Parenthood duct-taped to her desk chair, a pipe bomb taped to her mid-section…her fucking uterus. What we have here is a bomber who thinks and acts in metaphorical terms."

"You happen to know where the suspected metaphorical bomber resides?" Miller poses.

Turning to him quick. "Why would I know that? I didn't even know she still existed until a couple of days ago when she found me on the beach in Cape Cod."

"Well," he says, "GPS gave me an address for a townhouse over in New Scotland Woods. It's on the way to your house, to be honest."

"If you know where she lives, why ask me anything at all? Maybe you should order SWAT to sweep the place right now."

He looks at me, smiles unhappily. "Just seeing how you'd respond. It's the old cop in me. And to answer your question, this isn't Hollywood. It's Albany, New York. You don't just cut to the scene where SWAT knocks the door down with one of those metal battering rams while the bad guy or gal sleeps in her bed, even if it does make for good drama. We need that warrant and in order to get it and make it stick, we need solid evidence tying Miss Metaphorical e-cig bomber to tonight's downtown bombings."

"You don't trust me, do you, Nick?"

"Hey," he exhales, "I thought we were friends."

"That's what I thought…pal."

"I need to make sure no stone goes unturned. A woman died tonight in a blast that almost surely would have taken out a lot more people had it occurred during the day. I need answers. We need answers. We need evidence."

"Not for nothing," I say, "but a place to start is one of those vape stores like Vapor Geek. Alison probably bought dozens of those little smoking devices. Maybe we got her face captured on CCTV."

"Already thought of that, already got somebody on it. But that can take time. Or, who the hell knows, maybe she ordered them off of Amazon."

It dawns on me that a woman as sharp as Alison wouldn't be stupid enough to buy an unusually large number of e-cig devices at a traditional store. She purchased them online, no doubt about it, and it's exactly how I put it to Miller.

I add, "We're going to have to find a way to snatch up her computer, Nick."

"Good luck with that," he says. "We need the warrant."

We head out of the city and into the West Albany suburbs. One- and two-story clapboard bungalows for as far as the eye can see. Which isn't very far in the deep night.

"Who was she?" I say after a time.

"Who was who?" Miller answers.

"The woman who died."

"Woman named Pat Mahoney. Fifty-eight, married. Two kids, both out of college. She's been running the Lark Street Planned Parenthood office for nearly thirty years. Major league advocate for safe sex and contraception. Very much against some of these women…young women most of them…who use the Planned Parenthood system as a means of contraception. I'm told she was planning on retiring this year." He shakes his head, sighs. "Damn shame you ask me."

I pull out my phone, type in the name Pat Mahoney. Already, the online version of the Times Union newspaper has run a story about her on the website, along with a photo. She's got short red hair, a smooth face, bright green, optimistic eyes even for someone who's been at the same job for so long. In the picture she's wearing a white turtleneck sweater, and her face bears a smile that seems neither forced nor coerced by the photographer. In other words, the smile is genuine.

Now the forensics experts will have no choice but to identify her by salvaging whatever teeth they might find from the rubble.

I pocket the phone, stare out the window, as Miller hops on the short highway extension that will take us to the village of New Scotland, which is located due west of the Albany city limits.

"You get Patty Darling pregnant that night inside the hotel

room?" Miller says after a time.

His words are soft-spoken, but they hit me like a brick.

"Listen, Miller," I say, "I'm telling you the truth when I say, if she did get pregnant, and she did….how do I say this…get rid of the baby, then I had no clue. No clue in the world."

God forgive me. I know how much of an absolute jerk I must sound like right now. I'm also wondering if Patty ever actually met with the now deceased Pat Mahoney. If she in fact did, the first time must have occurred not long after our little tryst in the motel. Patty would have visited the clinic only after much soul searching. She wouldn't have taken a procedure like abortion lightly. Patty was the sensitive type. Even after a few days she would have felt the baby growing inside her body, its tiny heart beating. You don't just destroy something like that on a whim. For Patty, making a baby with me might have been the most wonderful thing in the world, until I ruined it for her.

"You never spoke afterwards?" Miller asks.

Shaking my head, not in response to him necessarily. But because I can't believe how much I hate myself right now.

Patty's face stares back at me from the side-view mirror. *Coward. The Master Blaster is a coward. Come on, admit it…*

"Not once," I say. "Not even at Brian's funeral."

"But she called you, didn't she, Singer?"

"Yes."

"She called you again, and again, and again. And you never once answered her or called her back. That right?"

"Patty, shut…" I catch myself.

"What?" Miller says.

"Nothing. Just thinking out loud."

My entire blood supply feels like it's spilling out my feet.

He goes on, "Even when she was at her most desperate, maybe leaving you messages that were tear-filled, frantic. Even when she said she might kill herself if you didn't call back, you chose to ignore her. How's the picture I'm painting here?"

"What's your point?" I say, voice raised, tone angry.

"My point is that we all make mistakes, Ike. You made one that didn't have to be so painful or hurtful, had you called her back. Just once."

"Lesson learned."

"Is it? All it takes is one night…one single night…to ruin a woman's life, Ike. Take it from me. I watched my wife die on an operating table from an aneurysm that could have been repaired had the surgeon not been drunk when he cut into her head."

"That what this is all about? You lost your wife one night and now you're taking it out on me because I spent one night with a woman and never called her back?"

"Maybe," he says. "Maybe not. But think about this: I'm guessing she never once called or approached your wife about the situation. Even if and when she got pregnant." He shoots me a look. One eye on the road, one on me. "You know what that means?"

Me, staring down into my lap, wishing the roof would somehow open up and I could just fly away. "What's it mean?"

"Means she cared enough about you not to ruin things for you, Singer. Even if she couldn't have you, she took the high road and refused to hurt you. Hurt your family."

Glancing into the side-view, I once more see Patty's face, a tear falling from her eye, combining with the blood that drips from the crack in her skin and skull.

I exhale, my stomach feeling like it's been sucker punched.

"Let me ask you something else," he adds. "Then I'll shut up."

Me, shifting my gaze from the side-view, out the window onto the far edge of the Albany suburbs. The edge of darkness.

"That time in the motel back in 1999…was it the only time you slept with her?"

Turning back to him, glaring at him. For so long, and so coldly, I know he can feel it. Read it. Taste it. Hear it.

"That's what I thought," he says, after a weighted beat. "Maybe it was only once, but once was enough. I know now why you're so desperate to keep it from Ellen."

"Anything else, Miller?"

"What I know for certain is that all actions have consequences whether we want to believe it or not. No one gets off scot-free in this life. No one is exempt from the push and pull of the cosmos. No one. Not even God."

"Thought you said you were gonna shut up."

Looking one final time into the side-view mirror, I watch Patty's face slowly disappear like a tear in the rain.

We make the turn onto New Scotland Avenue, the night growing darker as Albany County's urban infrastructure transitions to the rural countryside. After a couple of miles, we turn onto Woodside Drive and enter into one of those townhouse developments that were so popular back in the 1980s and '90s as a less expensive housing alternative for the young urban professionals graduating from law and business school.

The buildings contain two separate living units apiece and if not for the black numbers tacked to the plain, egg yolk–colored aluminum siding, they would all be identical. The road dips for a while, then levels off. As we approach number 32, Miller douses the cruiser headlights, pulls over onto the soft shoulder, kills the engine.

"This is where we get out," he says, lifting up the center console, pulling out a small plastic box.

"What's that?"

"You'll see."

He tells me to follow him, like fire follows a lit fuse. Like either one of us has a choice in the matter.

CHAPTER 35

We walk quietly in the darkness, the lights in the townhouses all extinguished while the residents sleep, oblivious to an explosion that rattled the downtown and took the life and body of an innocent woman. Slowing, we approach unit 32, which is on the left-hand side of a two-unit complex.

There's a car parked out front. A four-door silver BMW.

"That her car?" Miller asks.

"Looks like it," I whisper. "I never did get a chance to memorize the plate."

"Could be she's home or trying to make it look like she's home." Foraging into his jacket pocket, he pulls out a pair of light blue latex gloves, slips them on. Then, opening the small box he retrieved from the cruiser console, he pulls out a small aerosol can and what looks like a paintbrush.

"I'm guessing we're not just gonna knock on the front door."

"Not without a warrant. However, we can check the car for any residue it might contain."

"Residue. What kind of residue?"

"You gotta ask, pal? Are you or are you not the APD's only official bomb sniffer?"

"That would be the dog."

"Okay, in human terms."

"So I'm guessing we're checking for explosive residue. But she works with explosives all the time. There's probably residue all over the place."

He stops as we come to the top of the shared driveway. "I

realize that. But in this case, if there's residue that matches the residue from the bombs planted downtown tonight, we at least have reasonable suspicion, and reasonable suspicion backed up by solid evidence will be exactly what one of my pocket judges will be requiring when he finally gives us his blessing on a bench warrant. Any further questions then?"

I shake my head. "But aren't we trespassing? Judge gonna allow you to submit evidence lifted off her property more or less illegally?"

"You let me worry about the details," he answers. "You stay here and watch and learn."

He walks so softly and carefully up the driveway, it's like he's tiptoeing in ballerina slippers. Taking a knee outside the BMW's driver's side door, he sprays some of the aerosol on the door opener and swipes the brush over it. When he's done, he wipes the brush onto a pad, which is stored at the bottom of the small box. He performs the same process on all three of the remaining door openers on the car. Then, standing up straight, he goes to the front door and brushes the doorknob. About-facing, he quickly but stealthily makes his way back down the driveway.

"You get what you need?" I ask. "That paintbrush really pick up residue that small?"

"A modern collection kit...you know, from like the twenty-first century...would include a mini electron scanning microscope. But I'm strictly old-school."

"Let me guess. APD budget."

"Double cliché for you, Ike. You work with what you got, and you do what you have to do."

"Especially when it comes to murder, the worst cliché of them all."

"Let's go," he says, "before she wakes up and calls the cops."

"I thought you were the cops."

"That's beside the point."

CHAPTER 36

Of course, they'll wonder how such a small, fragile young woman like Alison Darling was able to plant those three bombs, and more astonishingly, subdue three grown people.

It wasn't hard getting the people to cooperate, once a gun armed with super-thermite rounds was pointed in their faces (not that they had any idea of the thermite rounds; but then they weren't exactly in a position to debate their existence either). Easy-peasy, in fact.

The judge, he's old and lives alone.

The priest, he's old, lives alone inside a giant rectory, and can barely walk, much less lift a finger to stop her.

And as for Planned Parenthood Pat, she was caught just before turning out the shop lights for the night. What better way to earn the birth control professional's trust than to engage in some friendly chitchat about contraceptive responsibility and freedom of choice? In the end, however, Pat couldn't resist the gun when the barrel stared her down and those thermite rounds were poised to take away her life and her soul. Most women hate guns. Pat was no exception.

But these three bomb situations went down precisely as planned. At least, she knew full well that it would be nearly impossible for even a master blaster like Ike Singer to defuse that last bomb. Not with such an incredibly short detonation time. And so what if that woman died in the blast? What was her full Christian name? Pat Mahoney? Didn't she kill little babies and then sell their organs for profit? Is that what happened to her little brother back in '99? Isn't that what happened to her own child just a few years later?

A woman like that deserves to be wiped off the face of the earth. A woman like that is a co-conspirator in a murder. A long string of murders.

Now, Alison stands on the edge of Singer property, watching mother and son from outside the living room window, their faces glued to the big high-def flat-screen television and the fine job the man of the house is doing saving humanity. She knows that in a matter of minutes, the time will come when he will pay for the sins he committed not only against God, but worse, against her mother, her father, herself, and two unborn children. All because Ike Singer wouldn't admit the truth to himself. That the married woman he slept with one night in a sleazy motel room loved him with all her heart. That he broke her heart when the next morning, he left the hotel room without ever speaking to her again....Wham Bam Thank You Ma'am...Don't let the door slap you in the ass on the way out.

"Knock knock," she whispers to herself, as she takes hold of the detonation controller, her thumbs tickling the two triggers. "Who's there? Opportunity. Opportunity who? The opportunity to blast away Ike Singer's life forever only knocks once."

CHAPTER 37

Pulling out of Woodside Drive, Miller hooks a right back onto New Scotland Avenue.

"You're going the wrong way," I say.

"Listen, it's going on midnight. You have got to be tired after all the shit that went down tonight. Take a look at your hands."

I peer down at my hands in my lap. My fingers are trembling.

Jesus, when did that begin?

"If you were a real cop, Ike," he goes on, "I'd make you take the rest of the week off and visit the shrink. You hear what I'm saying?"

"I'm fine. My first time under battle conditions, so to speak. True battle conditions."

We drive for a while as the country that surrounds us thickens. The sky is clear tonight, with a full moon. The light from the moon makes the tops of the Helderberg Mountains visible eleven miles to the west. You can almost pinpoint the cliff top of Thatcher Mountain, its three-mile-long cliff face a gift from an ancient glacier that carved its way northward as temperatures heated up at the end of the last ice age.

Another peek at my hands.

Still trembling.

I see the darkness but I also see my future. My family's future. If Alison was able to pull off what she did tonight, and do so alone, she is far more formidable an enemy than I could have ever imagined. It's not the sheer physical and emotional strength it must have taken to abduct those three adult human beings, duct-tape them to their respective IEDs. It's not even the knowledge of lethal explosives she displayed and the ease with which she fabricated her improvised e-cig device time bombs. It's her fearlessness. If the only thing to fear is fear itself, then you bet your ass, I'm afraid. Afraid for me and my family.

I look up as we approach the extended driveway to my farmhouse.

"Nick," I say, "you mentioned a gun. For me."

He turns onto the driveway. He doesn't respond until we come to the top of the drive and the front of my farmhouse and the red barn beside it, both of which are still lit up in white spotlight. Lights that will stay on all night long.

He drives onto the front circle which surrounds a small green, the center of which sports a white flagpole, the stars and stripes adorning the top of the poll, full mast. In the stillness of the warm night, the flag isn't moving at all.

The detective throws the transmission into park, then leans over me, opening the glove box. There's a gun inside. A semiautomatic. He pulls it out, closing the glove box at the same time.

"What you see here is an oldie but a killer. A Colt .45 Model 1911." He thumbs the magazine release, examines the load, slaps it back home. Thumbs on the safety. "There's eight rounds in there and one already in the chamber. All it takes is one to stop a charging rhino."

"It's not rhinos I'm worried about."

He hands over the gun, grip first. In my head I not only see Patty and what's now become her persistent presence in my life. But I see myself sitting behind the wheel of my pickup truck back in 1999, a gun barrel stuffed in my mouth.

"You sure you're comfortable with a 1911, Singer?"

I nod. "I'm no stranger to the range. You know that. Got my permit years ago when we started carrying around a lot of explosives. You can imagine the problems should we get hijacked and that stuff ends up in the wrong hands."

"Why no guns of your own?"

"I said I have my permit to carry and conceal. I didn't say I was a gun guy. Not anymore."

He grins. "I understand. But tonight you are a gun guy."

Reaching into his jacket pocket, he pulls out a sheaf of paper, tells me to sign where indicated by the Xs he's scratched in blue ballpoint. He informs me that he already has a photocopy of my permit on file, so I don't need to produce my original.

I pull back the slide, just enough to inspect the chambered round. I open the door, step on out.

"Let's just hope I don't have to use it."

"I'll pick you up in the morning for the Wellington show. Seven AM good?"

"I'll be up."

He pulls away.

Shoving the Colt into my pant waist, the barrel cold and hard beside my spine, I somehow get the feeling I'll be up all night.

CHAPTER 38

Ellen and Henry are waiting for me when I come in. Rather, Henry is fast asleep on the couch, while Ellen is waiting up. She wraps her arms around me like I've just come home from the wars.

"Still think the job is boring?" she whispers, voice gravelly and spent. It's been a hell of a long night for my family too.

"I take it all back," I say, holding her tightly. So tightly I think I might break her.

A voice sounds off in my head then. A voice separate from Patty's and my own. A loud voice belonging to me, but that is not entirely my own. It tells me to confess. Tell her everything that happened between Patty and me all those years ago. The affair, the heartbreak, the destruction of the marriage, and now, quite possibly a baby who never had a chance to be born. Admit how wrong I was not to come clean about the brief affair in the first place, but also to have so abruptly broken off communications with Patty, as if she'd been there to be used and then discarded at my whim.

But then another voice sounds off.

It tells me I've kept the secret silent for this long already. That what Ellen doesn't know won't kill her. That the last thing Henry needs while he spends his final months on this earth is to think of his dad as a cheater. A liar. A baby killer.

Releasing Ellen, I remember the pistol stuffed in my pants. Pulling out the tails on my shirt, I conceal it, knowing how much Ellen despises guns, as if they are capable of loading themselves, aiming themselves, triggering themselves.

"I have some pizza I can heat up for you," she says.

"That would be great. But right now I want a beer."

"Can't blame you."

Heading into the brightly lit kitchen, I go to the refrigerator, pull out a cold beer, pop the top. Meanwhile, Ellen turns on the oven, places two slices onto a cookie sheet, slides it onto the rack. Closing the oven door, she turns to me.

"That poor woman at the Planned Parenthood," she says, her face taking on a frightened, tight-lipped expression. "How on earth could someone do such a horrible, unspeakable thing to another human being?"

I steal a long drink of the cold beer, feel it soothe the back of my parched throat. I'm tasting the beer, but I'm still smelling the results of the explosion on Lark Street. The acrid smell of blasted concrete, brick, and granite.

"There's real evil in the world," I say. "I've seen it in action." Heading to the opposite end of the white kitchen, I gently push the swinging door open, catch a glimpse of Henry on the couch. Ellen joins me, sets her hands on my shoulder, cranes her neck to get a look.

We're both thinking the same thing. Henry's ultimate passing. With that heavy burden always on my mind, how could I ever lay the truth about Patty and me on her? Or perhaps I am a coward, plain and simple. A coward who can't admit to the truth for fear it will be far too painful, not for my wife or dying son, but for me.

"It's going to be hard when he finally leaves us." She sighs heavily. "It's going to be so very hard."

I allow the door to close. There's been too much talk about Henry's death as of late. Way too much talk.

"We don't have a choice," I say. "Henry doesn't have a choice. It's up to God now."

She takes hold of my hand, squeezes it desperately.

"Do you wish we had terminated the pregnancy, Ike?" she

asks. "Back when we had the chance."

Cold air slices through me like broken glass.

"For God sakes, El. Never. I can't imagine what life would be…will be…without our baby boy."

She sniffles, wipes her eyes. "It's just that, we gave him this life, and now it's being stolen from him. He had nothing to do with it. It wasn't his fault. It was our fault for bringing him into this world in the first place. It just doesn't seem fair."

"I know it's a raw deal. You know it's a raw deal. He, of all people, knows it's a raw deal. He's in pain, and he's dying. But somehow, that still doesn't mean he's not happy or that he's not enjoying what little life he's got left."

She wipes her eyes again and goes quiet for a few beats.

Then, "We'll be there for one another, won't we? We'll be one another's steadfast pillars of support. One another's rock. It won't be like when he was born and you got very angry and retreated from me. We trust one another now. Rely on one another. More than the average couple. We don't just love one another. We have a common bond like no other, and he's asleep on the couch."

I see my son…our only child…lying on the couch, his face looking old and decrepit, his hair thin and receding more and more each day, his body beginning to fail him. But then I also see my little boy…my toddler…who only yesterday I held in my arms while I rocked him to sleep inside his nursery. How in the world can I possibly admit to an affair with Patty at this point? How can I do it when Ellen's heart is already breaking a little bit more each and every day in direct proportion to Henry's deteriorating health? That the reason for all the destruction in Albany is partly my fault?

"We've been blessed to know him, El," I say. "To love him. For now, let's not talk about it anymore. Let's just enjoy the time we have left with him."

The smell of pizza begins to fill the kitchen.

Ellen crosses to the other side, pulls the pan out, slides the slices onto a dinner plate. I drink down the rest of my beer, grab another.

"You mind if I eat in bed?" I say, not without a sly smile on my face.

"It's late, cowboy." She's smiling, but I can tell she's forcing the smile. Forcing an attitude adjustment. A very necessary attitude adjustment. It's the same adjustment I'm forcing upon myself. I need to be close to my wife right now. I feel the sudden, almost panicked urge to be as physically close as we can get.

"It's not that late," I say. "Besides, I need to make up for that less than stellar performance in the shower at the Cape."

"Wow, how can a girl refuse an offer like that?" She giggles while she wipes her eyes with her fingers. "Just remember. Making love isn't about performance. It's about trust and security and, well, love." Smiling warmly. "See you upstairs, lover boy."

The fine hairs on the back of my neck stand at attention. Patty used to call me lover boy.

"What did you just call me?" I say.

She furrows her brow. "Lover boy. You got a problem with that?"

"No." I smile. "Not at all. Just don't think I've ever heard you use that term before."

"Now you have," she says, giving my arm a squeeze. She turns. Heads out of the kitchen, toward the stairs.

Lifting one of the slices from the plate, I take a bite. The pizza is hot and delicious. Smith's. Good choice. The only choice out here in the country. Grabbing hold of the can of beer, I drink it down in one, long pull. Tossing the can into the recyclables under the sink, I grab another from the fridge, pop the tab. I keep drinking like this, I'll grow a beer belly in no time.

She's sitting on the counter beside the sink. Rather, I can't help but imagine her sitting on the counter. Just like she were alive and well.

You're right, Patty says in my head. *I used to call you lover boy, even as far back as college, when we weren't even lovers.*

And yes, keep on drinking and you'll get fat…

Stealing a sip of the new beer, I feel it going to work on me. Calming me. But thus far, I've had only one can. Not nearly enough to cause hallucinations. But then, I don't need to be drinking to see Patty in my head, or out of it.

"It would tear her apart," I say silently. "And you know it. What the hell do you want me to do? March upstairs after disarming explosive devices that your own daughter set tonight, and calmly tell my wife that I not only cheated on her sixteen years ago, but that it resulted in my having a child that was aborted? And that the woman who died tonight at the Planned Parenthood can be directly traced back to my bad decision?"

She's still dressed in the black panties and pink T-shirt she wore during our one night together. Her hair mussed up, the blood leaking out of both nostrils now, the crack along her forehead more visible, the skin purple and swelled in the bright overhead light. Her condition is deteriorating. At least, that's the way I'm creating it in my brain.

You're going to have to tell her sooner or later. You know that, don't you?

"Sure," I say, sipping some more beer.

Alison is one very determined young lady. You know I never saw the psychosis in her. Never thought for a minute she would be capable of killing me, not to mention the antics of this evening. She makes like a pistol with her right hand, brings the thumb down like it's a pistol hammer. I were you, Ike, I'd watch my back…

"The police are onto her. Her best bet is to turn herself in now while only one person is dead."

Patty laughs.

The long and winding road, she sings, mimicking the old Beatles song. *You remember that one, Ike? It was our song.*

"It was never our song," I say. "We weren't a couple in the first place."

Oh, but it was. We listened to it how many times that night?

That lovely night? The night I'd been hoping for for so very long. But a night that turned out to be so tragic and so deadly. I wonder how we choose the songs we love. The songs that mean so much to us. Must be something ingrained in us. Something deep and indescribable. Something in our genes. Something truly emotional. Like the will to kill. Who knows why Brian wanted to kill you. Making a time-out T with her hands. Well, hold the phone on that one. I know very well why Brian wanted to kill you. You fucked his wife three or four times inside that motel room. And it was a very fun three or four times let me tell you. You never lost your hard-on. Not even once. But as for Alison, who knows what her motivation is other than bitterness. Because who doesn't want a real family growing up? Who doesn't want Leave It to Beaver? Instead, all she got was torture and a city that shuttled her from one foster home to another.

"She got a shit sandwich after Brian died. I get it. But that's no excuse for murder. She's going to be arrested and nailed with murder one. How's them apples?"

She smiles.

Alison has already exacted her revenge on me. You're next, Ike. So yes, how's about them apples?

Then, coming from upstairs. "Singer, you coming?"

I shake my head, stare down at the beer in my hand.

"Yeah, be right up," I bark, loud enough for her to hear me.

I glance at the counter. Patty is gone because she was never there in the first place. There's nothing supernatural about her death, but there's something very real in the guilt I feel now, and have felt for years. Patty's presence is still somehow being felt in my bones. And it is a bitter cold sensation.

I grab hold of my plate, set my beer onto it beside the slices of pizza. Turning out the kitchen light, I slip into the den and, for a brief moment, consider moving Henry. But he's so caught up in a deep sleep, I don't dare move him. Turning off the light, I whisper, "Love you, son."

He mumbles something under his breath. It tells me he's

dreaming. Sweet dreams I pray. Before heading back out of the room, to the center hallway, I take one last look outside the picture window, and the spotlight-lit yard. A wave of ice cold washes over me.

Something's out there, and it's not good. Or perhaps I'm being paranoid.

The weight of the semiautomatic presses against my backbone.

Inhaling a breath, I turn, go to the stairs.

CHAPTER 39

Alone inside the bedroom, I place the pizza and the beer on the nightstand. Opening the drawer, I carefully, quietly, set the pistol inside. Then undressing, I slip under the covers. Ellen occupies the sink in the bathroom, directly across the room from me. She's wearing red and green lace panties and a tight, white, muscle-beater T-shirt that shows off her pert breasts. Her entire body is as fit as it was the day I met her in college at a Halloween party during our sophomore year. Her creative costume made it appear like she was in bed with her nightgown on, cold cream on her face, hair in curlers, and a mattress strapped to her back.

She looked absolutely beautiful to me.

I'd decided that year to purchase a rubber scalp so that I appeared entirely bald. I bought a pair of round metal-framed granny glasses, and wrapped a white bedsheet around my midsection. Add to that a pair of sandals, a walking stick, and I was now an oversized Gandhi. We spent our first five minutes of getting acquainted laughing aloud at one another. It certainly beat trying to come up with small talk.

We both drank too many cheap draft beers from a keg and ended up walking to the all night food truck which was parked on the road that separated the upper campus from lower. We shared a cheeseburger sub and talked about what we wanted out of the life that lay ahead of us like a long and winding road. I already knew how much I wanted to work in the commercial construction industry, but not building things. Rather, tearing them down…blasting them to smithereens.

She wanted to be a concert pianist.

I made a joke about how loud we would be if we ever got married. Her eyes went wide and she barked, "Loud residence!!!" mimicking the old Saturday Night Live skit from the late 1970s back when we were still in grammar school.

I walked her back home that night and ventured a kiss. She gladly reciprocated. After that, we became inseparable for the remainder of our academic stay. We graduated, moved to Albany, began our respective careers. Mine by having already partnered up with Brian Darling to form Master Blasters, Inc., a firm that was financed by Ellen's attorney dad. And she by taking on a job as a piano teacher at the Jewish Community Center. First to get married were Brian and Patty, who were still our best friends, and then we tied the knot a few years later. When Ellen found out she was pregnant with a boy, we thought nothing could invade the wonderful life we'd built for ourselves. In a word, I'd found true happiness, even if my career centered around destruction (what I called "Construction Destruction"). Happiness was all any man could ask for.

Until Henry was born an old man, and I lost it. Until despair invaded the life we'd built, and I sought the love of a woman who, it turns out, never stopped loving me even from a distance. The foundation cracked then, but somehow, our marriage still stood. I've always believed it stood then and it stands now because Ellen knows nothing about the truth behind what happened.

Ellen shuts the light off in the bathroom, comes back in, and slips into bed. I've eaten my pizza, but I'm still sitting up drinking my beer. The time on the clock says two AM. But my heart is beating. Pounding.

"You gonna stay up all night drinking beers?" Ellen says quietly. "Or are you going to have dessert?"

I feel myself smiling because she is clearly feeling better. Setting the beer can on the nightstand, I turn over, set my eyes on her. I can smell her clean rose petal scent as I bring my face to hers, kiss her gently on the mouth. She wraps her arms around me, digs her fingernails into the flesh on my back. Rolling her over onto her back, I press myself against her and run my hands through her thick, long hair. That's when we begin to slowly slip one another's clothing off, our mouths never disconnecting, and bodies never separating.

When she parts her legs, I enter her, and I listen to deep passionate moans, and her sweet voice whispering, "Don't stop… Don't stop, Ike." My mind spins but it also plays tricks on me. In my head I see Patty's face. I see the blood running from her nostrils, down her lips, and I see the crack in her skull. I hear the sound of her voice just like we were back inside the motel room, the neon lights flashing on and off the ceiling. *Ike, I love you…I love you so much…I always have…and now that you're here with me, it's like a dream.*

I begin to lose it. Physically lose it.

Ellen whispers, "You okay?"

I try to shake the image and voice of Patty from my head, but it's like she's standing inside our bedroom watching us. Standing in the corner by the door in her panties and T-shirt examining our every move. Like she's following us, stalking us.

It takes everything I have left. All my strength. I keep my eyes open so that all I see is Ellen, her beautiful face, her deep brown eyes, her tan skin. I see her in the white exterior spotlight that manages to spill in through the windows. I don't dare look in the corner, don't dare give in to Patty's presence, and despite her, I feel myself growing rock hard again. As hard as I can possibly get. Ellen's voice grows louder, her movements faster, more forceful, and soon we both come to that place where we can't possibly love one another more than we do at this moment in time.

When it's over, we both roll onto our backs and inhale the fresh night air.

"Patty," I whisper, as if I'm not in control of the words leaving my lips.

"Singer," Ellen says, her eyes suddenly wide. "Did you hear

yourself?"

"Hear what?"

"You just called me Patty."

I feel the weight of this night now resting on my chest like pile of hardening concrete.

"Why would I do that?" I say. But I know precisely the reason why.

"What's wrong?" Ellen says after a time. She gently sets her hand on mine.

"Nothing's wrong."

"Liar," she giggles. "I know when you're having trouble concentrating. Like something else is on your mind. Something was definitely bothering you last night when we took a shower together."

"Lots on my mind. Then and now."

She rolls over, faces me, while I stare up at a blank ceiling.

"Is it the three bombs? The poor woman who died? It couldn't have been bothering you last night, because it hadn't all happened yet."

Should I tell her now? Maybe my obsession with Patty's memory won't go away until I come clean. Or maybe I should continue to hold off.

"Could be I was somehow anticipating the bombs, El. Like a psychic."

"Okay, Mr. Psychic," she says, squeezing my hand. "It's not another woman, is it?" Her tone is faux angry and concerned because she firmly believes I'd never cheat on her. Trust was always a part of our bond. Our unbreakable trust.

If only she knew the truth. It might kill me...kill our marriage. But at least I would be forever free of it. Even God might forgive me.

"Of course it's not another woman," I utter. I lie because like all liars, I'm weak, and I don't want to risk losing what I have by stating the truth. "I think I just need to get some rest. Tomorrow is going to be a big day. I need to be at the Wellington at eight

AM."

She removes her hand. "So you are going to the Wellington shoot after all."

"APD wants me there in light of tonight's explosive festivities."

"Does Nick Miller think there could be a connection between the three downtown bombings and the hotel implosion?"

"You mean like someone who's working the demo job perhaps being responsible?"

"That's precisely what I mean, Singer."

"You never know. Awfully coincidental that the three charges were set tonight before the morning's big bang, when we haven't had a bombing in Albany in what I'm guessing is forever."

"Maybe they should cancel it."

"Take it from me, that would cost hundreds of thousands of dollars. They need to carry on with the implosion, that is, the demo outfit doesn't want to face hefty daily fines by the property owners."

"Alison," she says, after a beat. "You think she might know who could be the culprit? The murderer? Maybe you should call her, Ike."

My body tenses up at the sound of the name. "Let's just get some sleep, babe."

I turn over, kiss her tender lips once more.

"Good night," she says. "I love you, Ike. Always have."

"Good night, baby," I say. "Love you more. Always have."

My head hasn't yet settled into the pillow when the detonation rattles the property.

CHAPTER 40

The exterior lights go out. A fireball rises up from the depths. Lights up the darkness, fills the night sky like a miniature sun.

Ellen screams.

I sit up straight, my backbone a heavy-duty coiled spring.

Henry is down in the den. Kid has got to be scared to death. Why isn't he screaming? No way he could sleep through that blast. That flash of brilliant firelight and white hot heat.

"Mom! Dad! Mom!"

I throw on my clothes, my entire body trembling. Pulling open the drawer, I retrieve the semiautomatic, shove the barrel into my pant waist. I also retrieve the mini-Maglite which I keep by the side of the bed, thumb the latex-covered trigger.

"Where the hell did you get a fucking gun?" Ellen cries, jumping out of bed.

"Never mind that." Grabbing my cell phone. "Let's just get downstairs. Go see to Henry."

She tosses on a pair of brown Ugg boots, exits the bedroom, heads out into the hall. I hear her bounding down the wood staircase before I even get around the bed. I'm thumbing the phone application to dial 911 when the text message comes through from Dr. Alison Darling.

Stopping dead in my tracks, I click on the text.

Knock Knock

I text, You bitch. I will get you for this.

Knock Knock...Play right. Do it. Or old man Henry dies before his time is up...DO IT

Fuck! You!

An MSS comes through. I open it.

It's a photo of Henry lying on his back on the couch. A mini pipe bomb fashioned from an e-cig device is attached to his chest via two separate strips of duct tape. The blue light radiating from the pipe shines against the boy's petrified face.

"Singer!" Ellen shrieks. "Get down here now!"

CHAPTER 41

Handing the Maglite to Ellen, I instruct her to aim the bright white LED light onto the thermite pipe bomb. The timer is set to detonate in two minutes. How long it's been taped to his body I have no idea. How she managed to sneak in here without us hearing her I have no idea. How Henry managed not to make a sound I have no idea. The only thing I do know is this: if I don't stop this bomb from detonating, my son…all of us…will die in two minutes.

Less than two minutes.

My phone chimes again.

Knock Knock

My eyes go from the phone to Henry to a weeping Ellen back to the phone again.

Who's there?

Glancing at the Timex watch. One minute thirty.

"Ellen, get it together," I say in as calm and steady a tone as I can possibly muster. "Go into the kitchen, grab me a pair of scissors. Now."

One minute fifteen.

Imagonna

Fuck me, this isn't happening.

"Am I going to die, Dad? Are we going to die?"

"Hang in there, son. I'll get you out of this…Ellen!"

Imagonna who?

"Why are you texting, Dad?"

Imagonna huff and puff and blow your stupid house up!

One minute five seconds.

Ellen comes running back in, a pair of scissors gripped in her hand.

"How in Christ's name do you turn an e-cigarette device into a fucking bomb?!" she cries.

I steal the scissors from her. Yank them right out of her hand. Opening the blades I clip the first wire. Don't even think about it. Just cut.

Ellen places one hand gently beneath Henry's chin, while stroking what's left of his hair with the other. He's crying, but doing his best to hold it in.

I open the scissors once more, position them to cut the second wire. But before I clamp them shut, I look up into Ellen's eyes.

"Anything can happen, El," I say. "When I cut this second wire, anything can and will happen."

She nods. She understands me perfectly.

"I'm ready," she says. "What choice do we have?"

"I'm ready," Henry says. "Maybe this way I can beat the damn reaper."

But they're not ready for me to cut, so much as they are ready to leave this earth. Ready to see God. I suppose I am too, so long as we all go together.

Closing my eyes, I snip the second wire.

CHAPTER 42

The clock stops.

I breathe. We all breathe. A sigh of relief which turns out to be short-lived when my phone chimes again.

Another text from Alison.

"Who the hell is that?" Ellen asks, tone verging on panic.

"Hang on, babe. Please."

Maybe I stopped the timer on the IED, but my son is still wearing it on his chest. Nothing will be right until I safely remove it from his body, dispose of it out in the backyard.

Knock Knock

Oh for fuck's sake…

Who's there? I text.

Stupid.

Stupid who?

Stupid thinks the bomb is defused. This one goes boom by remote control.

Meaning what?

It means try and remove it and it's BOOM BOOM Out Go the Lights!

Remote control. It means that currently Alison is positioned within a one-mile radius of the house. She's got to be observing us, perhaps with a night vision device, or maybe she's standing right outside the window looking in. Or, what the hell, for all I know she installed a series of cable-wire cameras in the wall while we were on vacation.

"Who on earth is that, Ike?"

Looking up at my wife. "It's Alison."

"Alison." Shaking her head, confused, scared. "But why?"

Typing a new text, What do you want from us?

Alison responds, Gee let me think. I know…I'd like wifey to play me a song on the piano. The Long and Winding Road. The Beatles. Remember how much mom loved the Beatles?

That one night flashes into my brain. Lying in bed in a hotel room lit only with the exterior lamp light that bled in through the narrow vertical openings in the drapes. Patty had brought along a small CD player on which she constantly played the Beatles. Especially "The Long and Winding Road." A song that stabs my guts every time I hear it.

Time to get the show on the road, lover boy.

Lover boy…Just like Patty would say.

Peering into Ellen's wide, frightened eyes.

"I need you to play a song for me on the piano," I say.

CHAPTER 43

"Now?!" she screams. "You want me to play the piano now? Have you noticed that a bomb is strapped to our son's chest? That our barn just blew up? That's it's burning the fuck down? That somebody obviously wants us dead?" She's shaking her head, her face pale and sickly. "Ike, for the love of God, tell me what the hell is going on."

"I can't," I say, shifting my eyes to Henry, lying stone stiff on the couch, his wrinkled old face now just as pale as his mother's. "Not now anyway. Please just do as I tell you. Go to the piano and play."

She nods, a single tear falling down her cheek.

While she slowly walks out of the den, into the center corridor, and into the living room, I take my first good look out the picture window, onto what's left of the still burning barn. That's when I see a shadowy figure dashing past the flame. A dark silhouette racing before the bright orange dry-wood-fed flames.

Alison. She's out there. She's in control. I can't remove that bomb from Henry's chest without her detonating it. Without my detonating it. I can't help but wonder if the fire department knows of the barn explosion, the flames that have followed. If anyone heard the blasts. We're far enough out in the open country that the fire would have to be reported. Even with the blast having shot across the valley, the area is still sparsely populated. Anyone who might have heard it, or placed any importance on it, would be fast asleep. They would attribute it to a bad dream. Or maybe not. Maybe someone did hear it. Maybe someone noticed the fire and called the fire department and the police.

But then, Alison would have figured that out. She would have planned on the police and the emergency services discovering the explosion and resulting fire right away. She would have planned for that eventuality. But how? Is she somehow in communication with both departments? Will she insist that nothing's wrong out here in the sleepy countryside? But then, why would they believe her for even an instant?

That's when it dawns on me with all the cold reality of sharp steel. She's wired the place to blow. Not just the house, but the perimeter. It's a guess on my part, but an educated guess. A guess I can rationalize because my entire adult life has been all about explosives and their living, breathing power. It's how I would do it. I'd wire the entire perimeter up. I'd make sure that whoever breached it was destroyed. Violently.

Music coming from down the hall.

The cell phone chimes.

You will now retire to the music room

I look down at Henry. "We have to get up, son."

He starts to cry again. He's afraid. Of course he's afraid. Me too. I have no choice but to bend at the knees, help him up off the couch.

"Easy, buddy," I say. "Take it easy. No rush."

That's when he does something that takes me by surprise. He starts to laugh.

"Will you look at how strange this picture is, Dad?" he says, laughing through his tears. "You're helping an old man of nineteen years old who's got a fat-batt bomb strapped to his chest into Mom's music room so he can listen to her put on a Beatles concert in the middle of the night, while our barn burns down. And you can't stop texting."

I too laugh.

"You got a point there, kid," I say, as he gets to his feet, his right arm wrapped around my shoulder. "It is pretty surreal to say the least."

He stops.

"Dad," he says, under his breath. "Alison...What the hell happened between you two? I always remembered Alison as a nice girl. Bad knock-knock jokes, but still pretty cool."

"It's complicated, Hank."

We walk, his almost feather weight bearing on my shoulders.

"I'm an old man now," he says. "Older than you even. I'd understand."

"I promise I'll explain it later. Right now, let's get through this night."

We enter into the living room, where Ellen is already playing the piano.

"The Long and Winding Road," as requested.

My phone chimes again.

Alison. Another text.

Take a video of the wifey playing piano. Do it now. No arguments. The whole song from beginning to end.

Heart in my throat, I set the phone up to record a video.

"Ellen," I say. "Start from the beginning."

She looks at me, not with fear in her eyes so much as distrust.

"Please," I say, setting Henry on the piano stool beside her. "Just do it. Let's get out of this alive."

I start filming and she starts playing. Something's happening when she presses one of the black keys near the center of the keyboard. It gives off a sour note, and the key sticks. It's the key Ellen has been complaining about all along.

C-minor.

I keep filming.

Ellen keeps playing, until she hits the key once more and this time it doesn't rise back up. The music stops. She's starts pounding with frustration on the key. With extended index finger, she comes down on it, like she's trying to put her hand through the piano, tears falling from her eyes, her weeping audible and pained.

And that's when it dawns on me. The key is no longer just a key. The key has become a detonator. A rack-bar detonator.

Shoving the phone in my pocket, I grab both Henry and Ellen by their arms. I yank them back onto the floor as the piano erupts.

CHAPTER 44

The blast was small and contained. Designed to shoot out vertically from the piano's interior workings, rather than peripherally. But I could be wrong about that. This wasn't C-4. It was something else. Something more volatile. More unstable. Not nitro, but nano-thermite. Super nano-thermite. Just like the bomb that killed Pat from Planned Parenthood. Just like the other two bombs which I defused. Just like the bomb strapped to my son's chest. Enough to destroy the interior of the piano, shattering its insides. Enough to frighten and knock the daylights out of us. If I had to guess, no more than a drop or two. About the same amount used to blow out the Suburban tire.

Ellen is lying on her back, her face covered in dust, eyes wide and angry.

"Who is doing this?!" she screams. "Are we going to die now?"

"No." Rolling over, taking her in my arms, squeezing her. "You did good."

There's a ringing in my right ear. It's so loud it feels like it's piercing my brain. I bring my fingers to my ear, feel for the Miracle Ear. It's popped out of its place in the canal. I shove it back into the correct position, and the ringing stops.

Ellen sits up.

"What the hell is happening?" she begs. "And why are you texting Alison?" Then, her eyes wide, her face tight and pale. "Where the hell is Henry?"

I shake my head, free of the cobwebs. In all the confusion, I just assumed he was lying right beside me. I look around but he's nowhere to be found.

"He's not here. The blast must have knocked us out."

"Henry!" Ellen screams. "Henry! Henry!"

I shout for him.

My phone chimes.

Down on my knees, I find it on the floor. It's covered in dust and the glass screen is cracked and chipped in the corner. But it still works.

Knock Knock

My stomach sinks. Index finger trembles as I tap the screen.

Who's there? I text.

Henryis

Pulse pounding, head aching, heart breaking.

Henryis who?

Henryis with me now say buh bye asshole

Another chime and another text.

It's a picture.

I see Henry, on his knees, mouth covered in duct tape, hands taped at the wrists behind his back, that mini pipe bomb still strapped to his chest. He's bathed in white flashlight.

"She's got him," I say, the words tearing themselves from the back of my throat. "Alison has taken our boy."

CHAPTER 45

Text: What do you want Alison?

Revenge.

Your mother…she knew what she was doing.

A pause in the communication. Like she's mulling over her mother's responsibility in the affair in her warped brain. Like maybe there remains the possibility that she'll call this whole thing off, return Henry to us unharmed, turn herself in to Detective Miller and the APD.

The phone chimes, vibrates. Another Alison text.

No police. If I see police, Henry dies. If I see the army, Henry dies. If I see FBI, Henry dies. If I see Home Sec, Henry dies. If I see Santa Claus, or Jesus, or Elvis, Henry dies…Tonight I'm going to test you, push you to your limits. See for realz just how good the bomb sniffer really is…We're going to prove to Ellen and Henry and the world, just how frail and weak and afraid is the Master Blaster. The coward who ran away from my mother. The coward who killed my father and my brother and my child

I text, Tell me where you are

Knock Knock

The words, like a swift kick in the gut.

Who's there? I answer.

Waitforfur

Waitforfur who?

Waitforfurtherinstructions dummy

I stand, go for my gun. But it's gone. She must have taken it when she nabbed Henry.

Ellen stands. Wipes tears from her eyes. "Please tell me what's happening and why Alison Darling is torturing us."

I look her in the eye.

"Ellen." I swallow. "I haven't been entirely truthful."

CHAPTER 46

It only takes a few minutes to spill the truth.

An old, rotting, festering truth…

But when I'm done telling her everything, she drops to her knees, raises her hands to her face, begins to weep far harder than before.

"How could you?" Her voice deep, guttural, hateful. "How could you do this to me? Do this shit to us?"

My heart sinks. So low that if I were to take a step forward, I would stomp all over it, like a gut-shot deer trampling all over its own intestines.

"It was a long time ago, El. Right after Henry was born. Immediately after. You know the effect it had on me…on us…I was in a dark place. A place so dark I couldn't see my own hand in front of my face."

She wipes her eyes, raises herself up slowly. Painfully.

"You're not reading me," she says, her voice wavering between a whisper and an almost all-out scream. "What I'm trying to get through to you is this: How could you have known that Alison was out to get us, and not be honest with me? Get us for your mistake. Now look at what's happened. Our son is abducted. There's a bomb strapped to his chest, Ike. A fucking bomb. For all we know there are bombs planted all over the house. All over the yard. That as soon as she's a safe enough distance away, Alison is going to flick a switch and blow the place to bits with us inside it. And all because you had to put your dick inside her mother during one of the most difficult times of our lives."

She raises her hand, slaps me. Hard. I feel the pain, but it doesn't seem to register. Like my nerve endings are no longer operable. Coming from outside the house, the sounds of the barn collapsing under the weight of the now charred wood. The crash resonates in my ears, my head, my heart.

"I didn't want to alarm you. I thought I could handle the situation all by myself. Take control of it."

"Tell that to the poor woman she killed outside the Planned Parenthood office. Tell that to the other two men who were nearly killed." She slaps me again. This time, I don't feel it at all. "Tell that to Henry, you son of a bitch."

Sadness and anger mix like a lethal soup. I grab her by the shoulders.

"Look it, Ellen. What I did...not telling you about Alison, about her mother and what happened all those years ago...I did out of concern for our safety. I love you. I love Henry. I'd never do anything to put you at risk. You have to know that."

Her eyes wide. Teeth clenched. If her frustration and anger were daggers I'd be bleeding out all over the wood floorboards.

Cell phone chimes inside my pocket.

"No, I don't know that," she goes on. "You didn't say anything about Alison not because you wanted to keep us safe, but because you were afraid of my reaction. You were afraid I would kick you out for cheating on me. For living a lie for as long as we have. That's why you didn't say anything. So don't pretend I don't know what your motives are. And do not, above all else, make it sound like you're playing the martyr, the hero, the knight in shining armor trying to take the bullet for the family." She inhales, exhales. "I will do everything in my power to help you find our son. But from this moment forward, you are nothing to me."

The blood in my veins feel like it's been replaced with embalming fluid. It is cold realization. My wife is absolutely right. I release her shoulders, stare down at the tops of my boots.

The phone chimes again. I pull it out with a trembling hand. A missed call from Miller. He's left a voice message. I dial in the code that will retrieve it.

"Ike. There's been an explosion reported near your address. We sent out a squad car. Everything all right out there? Check in, pal. Check in ASAP."

If I see police, Henry dies...Alison's exact words.

"Who was it? Was it the police?" Ellen begs, her voice softer somehow. Perhaps more accepting of our situation. However bleak.

"Miller. He's sent a squad car."

Her eyes go wide. "That a good thing, right, Ike? We need the police."

Heart pounding, pulse drumming.

"Listen, El. All it will take is a quick text and the police and SWAT will be on this place like flies on the dead. But we just can't take the chance."

"Why the hell not?"

"Because Alison explicitly said no police or Henry dies. We just can't risk it. She's psychotic. We have no choice but to go after him on our own."

"And why should I trust you?"

Looking her in the eyes. "Because I'm all you've got."

My focus drifts to the burning barn. A series of sparks fly out from it as the flames begin to burn out, now that the old dry wood is all but consumed.

"You need to put some clothes on," I add. "We need to do something. We need to go find Henry now."

She bites down on her bottom lip, brushes past me with cold contempt, and heads back upstairs to get dressed.

CHAPTER 47

She stares up at a brilliant night sky made more brilliant by the crisp, cool country air. The kind of clear sky you look for on the eve of destruction. Or, in this case, the implosion of a ten-story building like the Wellington Hotel. It's also the kind of night that makes her think. Reminisce. About the things she'd rather forget. But at the same time, things she wants never to forget.

Her foster father.

The first one. The one who went after her. The short, stocky, solidly built man with the bald head and the small brown eyes. The one who always smelled of body odor morning until night when he drank himself to sleep. The one who impregnated her.

What was his name?

How could she ever forget his name?

David. Such a plain name for such an evil man.

She looks up at the sky. She doesn't want to remember, but she can't help but remember.

David taking long walks with her in the woods. By the light of the moon, or so he would say. A night just like this one. A bright round white illuminating moon with which you could see in the dark of night, even inside the thick tree cover. David was a bit of a prankster. An evil prankster. Because after he'd walk her out into the woods back behind their house across the river in Chatham, he'd begin to lay his hands on her. Naturally she'd resist. But this made David mad. Happy too. Mad and happy. Judging by the smile on his round, scruffy face and the big purple vein that popped out of his neck like he swallowed a live snake.

He'd grab her arm, run his tongue up and down the smooth

white skin. Then, letting her go, he'd tell her to run.

"Run, rabbit," he'd say. "Run rabbit run, like your life depends upon it."

Of course, she'd run. And soon, when she'd hear him howling at the bright night moon, she'd feel a cold shiver run up and down her backbone, and she'd run even faster.

"The big bad wolf is coming!" David would shout. "The big bad wolf is going rabbit hunting. And tonight, you—you little succulent creamy cunt—you are the furry rabbit."

CHAPTER 48

To be on the safe side, I wait for her at the bottom of the stairs, Maglite in hand. Maybe Alison has wired the house to blow or maybe she hasn't. But her last text tells me she is not about to blow Ellen or me up anytime soon. She's got something far more creative in store for us. But all we need to be concerned about is getting our son back. Then, and only then, can we get the hell out of here.

God willing.

When Ellen comes back down a couple minutes later, she's wearing jeans, a long-sleeved denim shirt, and a pair of tan lace-up boots. Her long hair is pulled back in a ponytail.

"What's the next move?" she says, acid in her voice. "This is your show, right, Singer?"

"We need to figure out a way to leave the house and search for Henry."

"So why don't we just leave through the front door?"

"No," I insist. "You said it yourself, there could be charges set all over the house. Chances are the house is booby-trapped. At the very least, we can only assume she's watching us, a remote detonator gripped in her claw."

"What if we take a chance and call Miller back?"

"Alison insisted no cops. How many times I gotta tell you that? The first sign of a cop car, or a cop, Henry will die."

"You don't know that."

"She's already committed murder tonight. The first one is always the hardest."

"She's not the only one who's killed something tonight. Murdered something special."

"Okay," I say, "fair enough, El. But we cannot take a chance on calling Miller into this. As it is, he's already sent out a cruiser."

I go to the far window on the opposite side of the stone fireplace, look out on the fire. Alison is nowhere to be found. What the hell are we going to do? We can't just stay in here knowing the place could erupt at any second. My poor sickly son. He hasn't got long to go as it is, and now his mother and father can't even decide on a plan.

Sirens. Coming from the direction of the city.

Ellen and I turn to one another. Lock eyes.

"Police," I say.

"Alison will hear them, Ike."

"Gotta find a way to turn them back."

I go to the front door, put my hand on the closer.

"Singer," Ellen says, "what happens to Henry if the police get too close?"

Then, a brilliant flash followed by a short, sharp blast. It's the tragic answer to Ellen's question.

CHAPTER 49

Another fireball. This one coming from the opposite side of the property. By the looks of it, at the start of the long driveway. The entire house shudders.

My phone chimes, vibrates.

I pull it from my pocket. Open the text.

Knock Knock

Who's there?

Crispybacon

Crispybacon who?

Crispybacon smells like dead cops

I didn't call them

Lover boy gets a mulligan. But I see another cop, Henry smells like crispybacon. What's left of him. Get it?

Hands shaking, phone about to slip through my fingers.

I gaze at Miller's missed call, thumb the text option, type in All good here. No explosions. Trying to get some sleep. See you in the morning.

Maybe the homicide detective will buy my lie. Maybe he won't. But I have to at least try. Anything else is just too risky.

The phone chimes again. I expect a reply from Miller, but I get something else instead. A series of photos. Photos of Henry. One snapped with him facing the camera. Another from the side, and yet another from the back. I can't tell where he is, because the background is almost entirely blacked out, like Alison hung up a black bed sheet for a background. His hands are still taped behind his back, his legs taped at the ankles. There's a piece of tape covering his mouth. The super nano-thermite explosive device is also still strapped to his chest.

I'm not sure the purpose of the photos, other than to torture Ellen and me.

Another photo arrives. This one a close-up of the IED's digital timing device. 4:00. Glance at my wristwatch. 2:30 in the AM.

I do the math.

"She's giving us one and a half hours," I say.

"One and a half hours for what, Singer?"

"To find Henry."

"And if we don't make it in time?"

The oxygen escapes my lungs. My throat constricts suddenly, like I swallowed something I'm deathly allergic to.

"You're not going to answer me, are you?" she adds.

"Do I need to?" Me, forcing the words.

The phone chiming again. Vibrating. Tormenting.

I open the text.

Knock Knock

I want to throw the phone against the wall, shatter it. As if the action will crush Alison's slim little body, make her bleed to death.

Who's there? I text.

Karmais

Karmais who?

Karmais a bitch. But revenge is sweet

"What is she saying?"

"It's one of her knock-knock jokes."

Ellen exhales. I can feel the anger building up in her. Anger at me, at Alison. The need for her own brand of revenge.

I text, When I find you I will kill you

Alison: Sticks and stones

Me: As God is my judge

Her response: Time is ticking. Let's see how good you are bomb disposal man. Let's see if the Master Blaster is a Master Life Saver. But be careful where you step. Who knows the dangers that lurk in these woods

I finger the green phone-shaped symbol that will allow me to call her directly. I do it. But all I get is a computerized answering service.

Shove the phone back into my pocket. "We have to go get him, El. We have to find Henry before she does something bad. Worse than she's already done."

"But how? What if the house is rigged to blow the second we begin to step outside the door?"

"We have no other options. We have to do something or for certain he'll die."

"Where do we begin to look?"

"She said in her text that danger lurks in the woods."

"The woods between here and Thatcher Park, Ike?" It's a question.

"Only makes sense for her to take him there. That's why it's so black in the photos."

"But if we have to watch our every step, we won't get three feet before we both die."

"It's amazing we're not dead already."

"Singer, what the hell do we do?" Ellen shouting, her hands clenched into fists.

Glancing over my shoulder, I spot my Suburban outside. It doesn't look any worse for wear even with the barn having been torched.

"I have an idea," I say.

CHAPTER 50

Ellen follows me down into the basement. There's a long counter pressed up against the far wall, and above it, a peg board where my tools are hung. Set out on the counter is my typewriter. The old World War Two–era Remington manual handed down to me by my late grandfather. Placed beside it, a stack of index cards. The cards Alison used to plant on the three bomb victims earlier tonight.

At the far end of the wall to my right, directly under the den, is a new, rust-colored Bilco door with a small wood staircase in front of it that leads up to the house exterior.

"We need those metal doors, El. Grab the hacksaw on the wall over the tool counter."

She does it. I grab the hacksaw, set it onto the first of the wood steps leading up to the Bilco doors. Pulling the Maglite from my pocket, I shine the white beam onto the doors, concentrating on the narrow spaces that exist between the edges of the doors and the box frame. Since the farmhouse is old, and no longer entirely level, the fit of the doors was never entirely airtight, which means I can see through the narrow cracks by shining the LED light on them.

"Ellen," I say. "On the counter, you'll find a Leatherman. Can you get it for me?"

She goes to the counter, comes back with the Leatherman.

"Open up the blade."

"Please," she says, agitated.

"Pretty please."

She opens the blade, then hands it to me. Sticking the blade slowly, gently, almost surgically into the separation between door panel and frame, I'm able to feel the wire.

I pull the knife back out.

"The doors are wired to blow if we open them," I point out.

Her eyes blink rapidly. "It's like I said, isn't it? Alison must have set the whole house to blow."

"But if I can defuse this charge, we can use this opening to exit the joint."

"But you can't see the bomb," she says. "How are you going to defuse a bomb you can't see?"

I cock my head over my shoulder. "With a little luck. And some divine Providence."

I ask Ellen to shift her position all the way to the opposite corner of the basement.

"If this charge ignites," I add, "the blast will go outward, but it will still be pretty bad inside this stairwell."

"Be careful," she says, setting her hand on my shoulder, then sliding it off before retreating to the opposite side of the old, dimly lit basement. Her touch sends a shockwave through my system. A good, welcome shock. Something only Ellen is capable of producing inside me. It means she still cares, regardless of what's happened. Regardless of my meaning nothing to her.

Using my knuckles, I begin to tap the underside of the steel panel, the noise sounding hollow, indicating to me that no obstructions are pressing down on it from the opposite side. I keep on tapping until I come to the center where both panels join together to form a joint. That's when the hollow sound disappears and the tapping becomes muted.

"That's it," I say. "That's where the mini pipe bomb is. A small metallic electronic cigarette device filled with nano-thermite charge, just like the ones I defused in Albany. Christ, she could have carried a bunch of these e-Go sticks around undetected in her purse and still leave room for her wallet and makeup."

Shifting myself to the far right of the Bilco doors, I once more shine the Maglite up through the crack between door and frame, spot the first wire. I slip the blade once more through the slit-like opening, search for a second fuse wire. Starting at the bottom, I slide the knife upward, careful not to cut anything unnecessarily...something that might accidentally trip the detonator.

When I find the second wire, I shine the light on it. Then, opening up the small scissors on the Leatherman, I poke them through the opening, find the first wire, and cut it. Without hesitation, I once more find the second wire, and cut that too.

Sweat runs down my brow, into my eyes.

Shooting a look at Ellen, I can see that both her hands cover her face, only her wide, stressed out eyes visible.

"So far so good," I say. "I'm gonna open the door now."

Unlatching the interior opener, I push up on the right-hand metal panel, and rise up out of the basement.

CHAPTER 51

A small strip of duct tape secures the mini but lethal e-cig pipe bomb to the left-hand panel. There's a remote control fuse still attached to it. If Alison is watching me right this second, she could easily evaporate me with the simple flip of a switch. But she's either not watching me, or she's not ready to kill me yet.

If I were a betting man, I'd go with the latter.

Carefully pulling the taped bomb off the door, I cradle it in both my hands as if it were as precious and fragile as an injured chick, and sprint toward the tree line one hundred feet or so across the flat back lawn. I set the charge down in front of an old oak tree so I'll know where to recover it later, then about-face and make my way back to the doors.

That's when I find Ellen, standing at the landing of the Bilco door staircase.

"What now?" she asks.

"We remove these doors."

She shakes her head. "I'm not following you, Singer."

"You correctly pointed out that we won't get very far going after Henry on foot. That means we have only one other choice."

"We take the Suburban."

"Exactly. But first, we bomb-proof the shit out of it."

Using the hacksaw, I cut the two metal doors at the hinges, carry them to the Suburban, which is still parked by the now smoldering remnants of the old barn. Opening up the trunk, I run a length of common wire from the vehicle's twelve-volt battery to its undercarriage.

"You're building a tank," Ellen says.

"I'm tack welding these plates under the Suburban so that we don't get our asses blown off should we run over a landmine."

"You're serious," she says, her lips parting to make a smirk. "Land...mine."

"Yeah, Ellen, landmines. And we're going to need protection against them."

"Those doors won't attach themselves, Ike."

"Little known fact about car batteries," I say, lying down on my back, the first of the surprisingly light, but full-metal Bilco door resting on my chest. "You can MacGyver them as an impromptu tack welder."

"You're joking."

"Google it sometime, you don't believe me."

I touch the edge of the plate with the wire. It produces a spark and then a constant stream of high energy heat. Enough to weld the corner to the metal undercarriage. Making sure to keep my eyes closed the entire time, or risk burning the retina, I perform the delicate task by touch and feel rather than rely on sight.

Ellen adds, "You really think Alison has managed to plant landmines around the house...out in those woods even?"

"We heard that cop cruiser until we didn't hear it anymore. That means it pulled into the driveway and came into contact with something that blew it away without warning. My guess is a landmine. An IED of some kind that was hidden from view. Ergo, a landmine...homemade, of course."

"When the hell would she have time to plant mines?"

"My theory is this, El. She's been keeping tabs on me for a long, long time. Maybe for more than a decade. She's always wanted to exact her revenge. But just a simple stab in the back, or maybe a bullet to the head, wasn't going to be enough for her. She wants drama. High drama. Something not too far gone from the napalm-furnace explosion and fire she rigged to kill Patty. Her own mother. Something that maybe even mimics some kind of trauma she endured as a kid way back when. Who the hell knows what motivates a psycho killer? And when she got involved in high explosives, especially super nano-thermite technology, she figured she finally had access to the resources that could create the supercharged high drama she wants. No more messing around with burning old garden variety materials like C-4. No more screwing around with implosions that offer up some drama, like light shows, rock 'n' roll music blasted over huge speakers. Christ, even crazy daredevils walking tightropes over an imploding tower. No, this is different. In terms of high drama explosive scripts, this one could very well win an Oscar."

"High explosive excitement," Ellen says. "Is that it? Sounds like the tag line to a cheap B movie. And it also reminds me that you really fucked up big time when you decided to fuck the woman whom I once called my best friend."

Me, tacking the other end of the panel, then starting on the other corners.

"If only I could take it back. But I can't. And remember, Alison obviously knew we'd be away all last week, not to mention precisely where we were going. So my guess is she had the run of the place, inside and out, for an entire seven days and seven nights. So who knows what the hell is buried all around the house. Who knows the hell that's about to blow up in our faces. This is a long planned murder and she holds the upper hand."

I start on the second plate, positioning it under the middle of the vehicle, and the gas tank.

"Why would she go through all this?" Ellen says. "Why take this kind of chance? Doesn't make sense to me unless she wants to die herself."

"I really don't know, other than she feels confident enough to pull it off. And maybe she does want to die. But one thing is for certain."

I slide out from under the Suburban, stand, pull the wire off the battery, close the hood.

"What's for certain, Singer, aside from my broken heart?"

"She doesn't want us dead yet. Because if she did, we'd be

dead already."

"That's encouraging." Then, extending her arm, pointing at the Suburban's undercarriage. "So that's it? That's our bomb-proofing?"

"It's enough to deflect the blast from something conventional, like C-4. But if she comes after us with thermite charges, which she's sure to do, we're doomed even if we're riding inside an Abrams tank. Still, at least the Bilco doors will provide some semblance of nominal protection." My eyes peering out beyond the smoldering barn into the dark woods. "But then, we're not quite done yet, either."

I head around the back of the house, go down into the basement where I grab two sets of tire chains from two separate six-penny nails pounded into a four-by-four post. I carry them out to the driveway with me. Setting each section of chain in back of each of the four tires, I then get behind the wheel of the Suburban, fire it up, and back the tires onto them. Exiting the vehicle, I fix each of the chains around the tires.

"Now," I say, "we need to pay a visit to the cruiser that was blown up in the driveway. There will be some tactical gear stored inside it that will offer us protection."

"On a road that could be mined."

"But at least we're somewhat protected now, if it is." A glance at my watch. "We're down to one hour. We need to go."

She nods, climbs into the passenger seat of the Suburban.

I slip behind the wheel, shift the tranny in reverse. Then, shifting it into drive, I motor around the farmhouse turn-around and, while keeping the speed at an even ten mph, traverse the dark driveway in search of whatever died out there earlier.

THIRD STAGE

CHAPTER 52

She's wearing violent death. It's wrapped around her narrow waist in the form of a utility belt, while crisscrossing her chest are two black leather bandoliers. The belt supports a fighting knife and other necessary tools for fighting a war. It's also able to hold one dozen thermite rounds while the bandoliers hold one dozen rounds apiece, making for a total of thirty-six lethal super nano-thermobaric pistol cartridges. Experimental prototypes which (when in a lab-controlled setting) are capable of generating a concentrated high-temperature explosion not found in any other short-barrel compatible round on the face of the earth. A round topped off with a bullet that, because of its atmospheric-air-triggered explosive, creates its own blast wave.

The bullets are the first of their kind and a tribute to the possibilities of nanotechnology. Big bangs can now come in very small packages. Something she has already demonstrated to downtown Albany with something as silly and trendy as an e-cig, and something she fully intends on demonstrating to Ike Singer tonight while he attempts to rescue his old boy.

She sits atop the Polaris all-wheel drive Sportsman quad at the edge of the Thatcher State Park cliff edge, feeling the thunderous vibrations of its idling 78 HP high-performance engine (an engine powerful enough to tow a railroad car) throbbing up through her sex, past her flat stomach, and into her chest cavity. Just one more inch forward, and she would most certainly drop the three hundred feet to the jagged rocks below.

But she feels no fear. She feels only an energy she hasn't felt before in her young life. Explosives are not about destruction.

They are all about control. A person who can harness hell-on-earth at will, will ultimately make any man or woman her slave. Tonight, Ike Singer will most certainly become her slave. Her bitch.

Right now, however, Ike will assert his own control. He will fight back against the terror. He will fight to win. That's the kind of man he is. It's one of the reasons why her mother loved him for as long as she did. But he's climbing an uphill battle and surely he knows this. As she folds the night vision scope over her left eye, she spots the burned out barn, and something just beyond it that's moving away from the farmhouse.

"Where are you going, Ike?" she says, pushing the scope up and away from her eye. "Don't you know there's no escape? Don't you realize that no police or emergency medical technicians or even Pope Francis himself will be coming for you tonight? You see, they will be way too busy. Way too panicked. Way too overwhelmed with the explosive calamity that is about to tear through this city of thieves." She giggles happily, proudly. "If they thought those three little nano-thermite IEDs were a major problem tonight, imagine the heartbreak when they discover they were only an appetizer to the main meal."

The explosions will be like nothing they've ever scene or heard. They will come from an explosive that in some cases, is smaller than the circumference and thickness of a George Washington quarter. The explosive is odorless, undetectable, and entirely untraceable prior to its detonation by remote control. If Albany believes the morning's implosion of the Wellington Hotel is going to be the biggest, loudest, most pyromaniacal display of fireworks ever to grace the city, they will want to be awake for tonight's festivities. One major explosion for the next couple of hours. With the new technology at her disposal, she need not be located within a mile of the IED like she would if dealing with the average IED set to explode inside an Afghan market or a crowded street corner in Paris. Now she can detonate the charge from a comfortable distance of ten miles if necessary.

Pulling her smartphone from its nylon holster, she selects the dial application, thumbs the nine-digit number that will initiate the timed explosions, the first one to commence in exactly ten minutes. The location of the explosion will be discriminate (nothing carefully planned or designed is ever indiscriminate), and it will shatter the security and pride of the Empire State capital. The white marble that makes up the Family Court building constructed over a century ago is about to go BOOM BOOM, Out Go the Lights!

In her head, it's 2001 again. She sees foster father David coming for her through the woods. She sees he's got his gun gripped in his hand. She sees the flash of the muzzle before she hears the shot. She senses the bullet whizzing past her head. Somehow, he knows exactly where to aim the gun, shooting not to kill, but to frighten. Picking up a rock from out of the soft earth, she awaits him…

"Stop," she says aloud, trying to transport herself back to the present. "Concentrate, woman."

Clearing her head of her memories, she turns the quad around, cocks her left wrist, giving it the gas. Rear tires spitting dirt, she speeds in the direction of the Thatcher State Park entrance, and the cross-country trail that leads through the apple orchard, over the rushing white water of the Vly Kill, and eventually to the Singer property.

A property set to blow as soon as she issues the command.

"But not yet."

She is God. She is the devil. She is an explosive force like no other.

"Let the detonation games begin," she says aloud. "Let them begin not with a whimper, but with a bang."

CHAPTER 53

I don't turn on the headlights until the tall stands of trees block us on both sides. The white LED headlamps light up the gravel as it passes under the chassis. Something on the surface of the road sticks out at me. Something that might not have registered if I wasn't looking for it.

"You see the discoloration there in the headlights." Arm and index finger extended like a pointer. "That pale, egg-shaped coloration in the dirt. I'll bet dollars to donuts that it's a buried IED."

"You mean another e-cigarette vaporizer filled with explosive?"

"Maybe. Or maybe just the naked explosive applied to the gravel. Come into direct contact with it, and it blows. That's how unstable it is."

Braking the vehicle, I pull around onto the shoulder and up onto a short berm-like bank of vegetation-covered gravel. The big vehicle bucks and sways, but I'm able to get around the discolored spot.

I take it slow, eyes focused on the road immediately ahead of me. Road showered in LED light, every stone and every pebble suddenly taking on new meaning. I can almost hear Ellen's heart beating in her chest. Her bruised heart. She sits stiffly, slightly forward, her hands clenched in white-knuckled fists, her big brown eyes peeled to the road along with mine.

"There," she shouts. "You see it. Another circle of white dirt."

I'll be damned, because she's absolutely right. This section of gravel is located closer to the left shoulder of the long driveway, which means I turn the wheel to the right. I take it slow, hands tightly gripping the wheel, finger bones feeling like they're about to burst out of the skin. Every inch of ground covered making my pulse beat faster, my breathing more shallow. I'm used to explosive devices and what it takes to control them. But what I'm not so used to is their having total control over me. It's as if my nerves are rubber bands stretched to the breaking point. At any given second they will snap, and the entire world around me will go up in white-hot flame.

Turning the wheel to the left, I enter back onto the road. I catch my first glimpse of the police cruiser then, its engine block blown out along with its windows and windshield, its doors blasted wide open. It looks like it's been hit by a tank round.

There's a body lying a few feet away from the passenger's side door, my headlights shining on the uniformed officer's legs which are twisted and pretzeled in ways God and nature never intended. From where I'm standing, he looks more like a broken doll than a human being.

I can't help but pick up a little speed as I cover the remaining twenty or so feet to the vehicle. When I'm within a few feet of the cruiser, I stop, throw the tranny in park, leave the engine idling.

"Wait here, El. If something happens to me, take the wheel, turn the truck around, go back home. Get in through the basement. Don't touch anything in the house. Just wait for help to arrive. You understand? After a while, the cops are going to come after their missing cruiser and the cop it belonged to."

"But Henry," she says.

"Just do what I say…I'm begging you."

She nods.

Reaching out, I give her hand a squeeze. "Nothing's going to happen to me." I'm not sure how she's going to react to my touching her, showing her my love. But she doesn't pull away. It's a good sign. A hopeful sign.

"How about them apples, Patty Cakes?" I say internally, seeing her face in my head, and her mussed up hair.

"Promise me," Ellen presses.

"I promise."

But in the back and front of my mind, I know that my wife no longer trusts me like she did once upon a time. She can't possibly trust me after discovering the truth about Patty and me. After discovering that I kept the truth from her for so very long. Because of one bad decision, I've placed the lives of my family at risk. The inevitable conflict that is sure to come is, for now, placed on hold, like a fuse cut off in the middle of its burn. But soon, the fuse will be relit, and the resulting explosiveness will cause a firestorm that will be difficult if not impossible to extinguish. That is, if we live through this night.

If Henry lives.

I open the door, slip out of the vehicle, step down gently onto the gravel road. Leaving the door open, I take a few steps forward, careful not to step onto any portion of the drive where the gravel appears paler or recently disturbed.

It takes maybe a full half minute for me to cover just a few feet where the officer lies on his side, his legs nearly blown off, his arms stretched over his head, his eyes still wide open, as though staring directly into the eyes of his maker. Any food that's in my system comes up on me then and, bending at the waist, I retch a throat-stinging mixture of bile and half-digested pizza.

When it's finished, I wipe my mouth. For a brief moment, I consider reaching for the officer's neck, placing two fingers against his jugular. But let's face it, he's dead. Poor, poor bastard never knew what hit him. The power unleashed directly underneath him.

I steal the service weapon and the two extra magazines attached to his utility belt, shove the former into my pant waist and the latter into my right-hand pocket. Then, straightening myself up, I back away from the body with all the trepidation of a man who's looking at his own death.

Bathed in the white LED headlights, I peer into the cruiser.

Although the odor is that of smoldering plastic and metal, the explosion did not cause a fire. As if the explosion caused the air to be robbed of its oxygen for enough time to prevent a fire from kindling.

Super thermite bomb. Nano-scale. Something Alison would have access to. Something unstable in the wrong hands, but also something that in the right hands…her hands…can be manipulated entirely.

I look for anything useful. Something defensive. Something to give us an edge against a maniac like Alison. I spot the riot shotgun, still fixed to the center console, six buckshot shells attached to a stock-mounted carrier. I pull it out. Then, yanking the key from the ignition, I search for the button that will unlock the trunk. I thumb it, and the trunk opens. Thank Christ the front end took the brunt of the blast.

I go around the cruiser to the now open trunk, peek inside. Two black ballistic body armor vests laid out beside two black riot helmets. Pay dirt. Leaving the trunk open, I carry the vests, the helmets, and the shotgun with me back over the section of open driveway leading to the Suburban. Before getting in, I set the shotgun and the two helmets onto the seat, along with the service weapon and the extra mags.

"Take this," I say, handing Ellen the first ballistic jacket. "Put it on, same way you would a down vest."

She takes hold of it.

"It's heavy," she says.

"It will protect you from shrapnel if there's a blast." Handing her a helmet. "This too, El."

"My God," she says, "I feel like we're in a war."

"We are in a war. Henry is the prisoner-of-war and the enemy executes its prisoners."

Slip on my ballistic vest. Put on the helmet, adjust the chin strap. Picking up the 9mm off the seat, I pull back the slide, chamber a round, thumb the safety on. I set the pistol barrel-first into the console cup holder along with the two extra mags. Grabbing hold of the shotgun from off the seat, I load it with the rounds, hand it to Ellen.

She grips it with all the enthusiasm of my handing over a live snake.

"What the hell do you want me to do with this, Singer?"

"Listen very carefully, Ellen. If we happen to come upon Alison, I want you to shoot her in the face. Do not hesitate. Do you understand me?"

She looks like she's going to be sick.

I get in, feeling the extra weight of the vest and helmet.

"Seatbelts," I say, strapping myself in.

"Safety first and last, Master Blaster," Ellen says, her voice laced with sarcasm, the shotgun now placed between her legs, barrel facing up at heaven. She straps herself in as best she can considering the bulkiness of the body armor vest.

Taking it inch by inch, foot by foot, I manage to turn the long Suburban around, head back in the direction we came, following precisely the two almost indiscernible tire tracks we created in the dusty gravel-covered road.

What remains of the burning barn is in our sights when the distant eruption rattles the vehicle.

CHAPTER 54

Fuck the landmines.

I floor it. To the top of the driveway, then slam on the brakes. Opening the door, I jump out, focus my gaze in the direction of the city. When Ellen does the same, something besides the obvious captures my attention. Staring into her eyes, I see the reflection of the red-orange ball in stereo, as it rises up to the dark heavens. Stepping forward, I turn to it, as if drawn to the light of a sun that's suddenly appeared in the middle of the night. And it has.

It's not a nuclear detonation. But that's precisely what it reminds me of.

"There goes an entire downtown city block," I whisper, gravel in my throat. "Maybe more."

Glancing down at my watch. "Three o'clock. On the money."

"Alison," Ellen says.

"Alison." Exhaling, stomach tightening, eyes filling.

I think, You're on your own, Albany. I cannot help you now. Not when Henry is out there all alone, a bomb strapped to his chest. You are without your one-man bomb disposal unit.

About-facing, I look beyond what's left of the barn, into the darkness made all the darker by the trees, and beyond that the orchard, and beyond that the river, and beyond that, the long, tall cliff face of Thatcher Mountain. Where the Indians punished their sinners by tossing them over the side to their deaths onto the rocks below. My boy Henry is out there somewhere, and Alison Darling, who is anything but, wants us to come after him.

If it's war she wants, it's war she's gonna get. Nuclear war.

"Ellen," I say. "Get in."

I slip back behind the wheel, buckle in. My wife does the same. Taking hold of the riot shotgun, she pumps a round into the chamber. Throwing the transmission into drive, I motor across the back lawn, and into the trees.

CHAPTER 55

Once more she pulls the smartphone from her belt, opens the app that allows her access to the CCTV cameras mounted to numerous telephone poles around the perimeter grounds of the Family Court building. The poles that surround the blast site, that is. The fire trucks are just arriving, along with a police van out of which emerges a SWAT team, their frames suited from head to toe in black tactical clothing, AR15s gripped at the ready, night vision goggles masking their faces. Behind them comes the regular APD, who also don tactical vests and helmets. Behind them the state troopers, and behind them, Department of Homeland Security.

The action never wanes tonight in sleepy old Albany while the first third of the marble Family Court building now sits in ruins. While severed live electrical wires spark uncontrollably like snakes cut in half but somehow still alive. Still slithering. While broken water pipes spew hot and cold water, and natural gas lines leak enough gas to spark another explosion perhaps even larger than the one just detonated by remote device.

No one is really prepared for a bomb, much less believes in the presence and the possibility and the power of a bomb, until it goes boom, right in front of their faces. Even those e-cigarette devices have been known to blow up in the faces of the nicotine starved now and again, without being armed with explosives. But when a bomb does go off, there is plenty of blame to go around, along with many severed limbs and smeared brain matter. In Albany's case, the man who would be in charge of defusing the bombs before they detonate is presently indisposed while he attempts to rescue his very old boy.

It's all going according to plan.

One last glance at the digital screen. Another car pulls up. This one an unmarked police cruiser. A tall, plainclothes cop whom she recognizes as the very same detective who assisted Ike Singer earlier in the evening. A lonely middle-aged officer whom she knows as Miller.

Nick Miller.

Miller suspects her in the earlier bombings and he will no doubt suspect her in the Capitol bombing. He will attempt to contact Ike Singer but he will get nowhere. Nor will he be able to leave the scene of the Family Court bombing and the many homicides that surely litter the smoldering ruins. Not yet anyway. By the time he does, he will once more find himself occupied with more explosiveness. More death.

She holsters the phone, brings the scope to her left eye.

Out there, in the near distance, headlights.

Just like Foster Father David came after her through the woods, Ike is coming for her. Only this time, she is the Big Bad Wolf, and Ike Singer is Little Red Riding Hood.

She peers up at the bright white moon, and she hears David's gun once more, shooting round after round that speed past her head or land near her feet, embedding themselves into the soft dirt. Shooting live rounds at his foster child. It's how David has fun.

But he doesn't want to shoot her. He wants to touch her where touching is forbidden. Do unspeakable things to her. Do things that would not have been possible if Ike Singer hadn't raped her mother inside that lonely motel room.

She's watching the light of the moon, but in her mind, she sees the rock coming down on Foster Father's skull, the bone cracking open, the blood spilling out, but somehow, his eyes wide and alive as he looked up at her from down on the forest floor. She remembers the feel of the gun as she took hold of it, pressed the barrel right between his eyes, just like they do in the movies. She can still hear the sound of his words, exiting his mouth.

"Don't. Please. Don't."

To this day she feels the pull of the trigger, the kick of the pistol, the louder than loud crack of the round as the bullet left the chamber and buried itself into David's brains. That was a good day. A day for awakenings. The day her universe was created. Her own personal big bang.

CHAPTER 56

Plowing through the thick woods that surround the back of my property, the going is slow. But at the same time, the Suburban is also a tank, and the chains on the tires help with cutting through the wet, soft, slippery soil. The truck bucks and bounces over ruts and roots, some of the natural obstacles slamming against the metal Bilco doors, the noise abrupt and deafening.

My heart stops when Ellen shrieks at a deer that jumps out of nowhere, leaping across a berm, its six-point rack extending outward and defensively, almost like a bull in the bullring. Instinctually I tap the brakes, but then realizing what I'm doing and where I'm doing it, and that there's the possibility of my sinking into the muck, I hit the gas once more. I continue to bushwhack through the swampy woods, knowing that on the other side is the more navigable apple orchard, and beyond that, the open valley that extends all the way beyond the Vly Kill and its rushing white water, to the cliff wall.

It takes maybe another five minutes of stop and go, up and down, side to side driving until we break out of the woods onto the relatively smooth terra firma of the orchard.

Cell phone chimes, vibrates. Shifting myself in my seat, I yank up the tactical vest, pull it out of my pants pocket.

Knock Knock

I should have known she'd be out there watching us. Watching our every move. Now typing with the thumb on my dominant hand. Not able to make it grammatically correct. But who gives a fuck at this point?

Who there? I text.

Ima

Ima who asshole

Ima your worst nightmare

It comes at us like a flare from the direction of the cliff face. A red-white streak that shoots across the black sky and slams into the earth only inches before the front grille. The explosion that follows doesn't just send dirt and gravel up against the windshield, it blows the glass out, sucks the oxygen from our lungs, and leaves us punch drunk for what seems to be hours, but for what I quickly realize is only a minute or so.

The phone chimes again. It's fallen between my legs onto the seat. I pick it up, thumb what is a surly text from Alison.

I purposely missed

Reaching out, I take hold of Ellen's forearm.

"You okay, El?"

"Yes, I think so." She shakes her head under the too big black helmet. "What the hell was that?"

"I can't be entirely sure, but I think it was a very small nano-thermite charge. Probably a super-thermite round."

"A round," she repeats, disbelieving. "As in a bullet. Like from a gun."

"Like I said, I can't be sure. But I think it's what Alison was describing during lunch yesterday. She drew a diagram of it on a napkin, remember? A brand new kind of bullet that doesn't just stop an enemy combatant, but annihilates him. Obliterates him. Erases him. Just pick an adjective. The bullet can stop an armored Humvee, or a Suburban four-by-four if the shooter so chooses."

"So we're toast?"

I throw the tranny into drive, hit the gas, pull out of the woods and onto the solid orchard ground.

"Not if we keep moving," I say, brushing away the window glass from my lap. "If we keep moving, we have a shot."

This time the phone rings instead of chiming.

"Need you to get that," I say, both hands on the wheel. "My hands are kinda full."

She picks it up, looks down at the digital face.

"Miller," she says.

"I was expecting him. Something just blew sky-high in Albany. Judging from the size of the explosion, the casualties could be horrific. He needs me to do my job. To inspect the site, to determine if any more charges are set to explode. But I can't do it. I need to find Henry. We have less than an hour to find him. Or she'll kill him. That sick little bitch will kill him."

Ellen's face goes pale under the black helmet.

"What time it is, El?"

Glancing at her watch. "Three twenty."

"Forty minutes to find Henry, to be precise."

I speed between the apple trees like a rocket ship between asteroids, the chains on the tires making a metal on metal racket. I push the engine to its breaking point, the RPMs going through the roof.

"Where exactly are we going, Singer?" Ellen says, voice raised above the roar of the engine.

"If I can get us over the bridge, we'll be close to Henry."

"How do you know? He could be anywhere."

"Look at the pictures Alison sent. What I was confusing for the plain dark of night is actually a rock face. Dollars to donuts it's the cliff."

She opens the pictures, runs through them. "I think I see it." But she doesn't sound convinced.

I swerve to avoid another tree, turn the wheel sharply to avoid another one, then sideswipe a third. The humid night air pelts our face. We rock back and forth in our seats like rag dolls with helmets on. No choice but to press on.

Up ahead is the Vly Kill, the Thatcher Mountain–fed river that runs through the state park and that also runs smack dab through the center of the orchard, providing the tree farm with its almost never-ending supply of fresh water. I'm inhaling its metallic smell. If I can get us through the trees and over the bridge, we'll be that much closer to Henry. Once we retrieve him, we can then hook up with the road outside the state park and head directly for the city and Miller.

I catch something scooting through the trees maybe ten or fifteen feet away. A quad 4X4. The rider is dressed in black.

"What the hell is that?!" Ellen screams.

"Shotgun!" I shout.

She raises it up off her lap, presses the stock against the shoulder, short barrel poking out of the busted windshield. I grab hold of the semiautomatic with my shooting hand.

"Wait till she makes another pass."

I make out the sound of the quad now coming at us from the opposite direction.

"Get ready!"

Alison speeds past, her image visible for only a split second at a time as she navigates between the thick apple trees. I squeeze off three rounds in between the trees. Ellen shoots.

I hit the brakes. Breathing, I listen carefully.

"Did we hit her?" Ellen asks.

"Quiet," I whisper. "Just listen."

There's only the sound of the idling Suburban engine combined with the hum of cicadas and other insects. Is it possible we managed to kill Alison? I shift the vehicle back into drive, tap the gas, slowly pull forward. That's when I hear the sound of a quad engine being kick-started only a beat before a white-hot beam shoots across the sky.

"Incoming!" I cry, a half second before the round makes a direct hit on our tail end.

CHAPTER 57

The shock wave lifts the Suburban up like the hand of God, drops it back down onto its wheels. The oxygen is sucked out of my lungs. I struggle to regain my breath. My head rings, hands tremble. I try to speak. But the words come out like I'm talking through a tube. That's when I realize my already fragile eardrums have once more been bruised. Bringing my hands up, I feel for my hearing aid. It's still there, stuffed into the ear canal. If I didn't know any better, I would say my brains dropped out of my ear canal along with it.

If not for the vests and helmets, we'd be dead.

I reach out to touch Ellen. "You okay, El? You all right?"

Turning to look at her, I see that her face has turned pale white. A trickle of blood is running out of her nostril, onto her lips, just like I imagined Patty's post-boiler explosion corpse. Sensing the blood on her mouth…tasting it…she wipes it away with her hand.

"Are we dead?" she asks.

"Not exactly. Alison is saving the best for last."

"Why not just kill us all now? Get it over with?"

"Because revenge is a dish better served cold."

"What?" she whispers. "What's that even mean?"

"You don't exact your revenge while you're angry. While you're hot. You give it its own sweet time, stretch it out."

She looks up at me, her face a mask of pain, confusion, and desperation beneath the oversized black helmet.

"I feel it," she says. "I feel it. Alison's vengeance. Her fucking psychosis. It's so cold it makes me shiver."

Another glance at my watch. Twenty minutes until four. At least my watch is still working. You can always trust a Timex. How did the old commercial go? It takes a licking, and keeps on ticking. Just like the Singer family.

I turn the engine over, tap the gas. It starts.

I'll be damned.

I pull out, the two front tires now flat, but able to gain traction from the chains still attached to the damaged wheels. Up ahead is the bridge. If only we can get beyond the bridge and the Vly Kill, we can ditch the vehicle altogether and proceed on foot under the cover of darkness. I'm not sure if that's a good plan, but it's as good a plan as any.

One hand on the wheel, the other gripping the automatic, I drive, knowing full well that we're not out of the damned woods yet, and that another thermite blast awaits us.

CHAPTER 58

The Suburban creaks and strains, the engine spewing black smoke, the interior filling with a toxic gas that smells like a combination burning rubber and oil. But still, she runs.

Up ahead, the wood bridge that spans a river, or kill, that flows heavily in the recent summer afternoon storm-driven downpours running off the mountain. Driving up onto the one-hundred-foot-long bridge, I feel the give of the wood planks beneath us and the sway of the less than solid timber supports. Driving slowly or else risk running the less-than-stable damaged vehicle off the bridge altogether, I concentrate only on the end of its wood span and the flat farmland that awaits us.

"Hurry," Ellen says, her voice slow and slurred, as though she suffered a concussion. "Hurry…Hurry."

"It's all about the control right now, babe," I say, the flat front tires feeling more like metal tank tracks as the chains gouge the wood.

The water runs fast beneath us, the spray rising up and entering the truck through the broken windows, coating our faces, combining with our sweat. I feel the constant bucking of the bridge against the current, and I feel the strain of the overstressed engine as much as I hear it. Shooting a glance at Ellen, I see that her face is still pale, her lower jaw locked tightly against the upper jaw, the stress taking its own special toll on her. No choice but to concentrate on getting across this bridge and onto the flat land and from there, the Thatcher Mountain cliff face where we'll find our boy, Henry. Find him alive.

I make it to the center of the bridge when the supports beneath us ignite.

CHAPTER 59

The blasts are muffled by the heavy stream current, but their effect on the pilasters is immediately felt loud and all too clear.

"She had them rigged the whole time!" I shout. "She must have gambled on our taking the Suburban into the woods. She knew we'd have no choice but to head for the bridge."

The Suburban spins a full ninety degrees in the two separate blasts, its front end hanging off a bridge that is now swaying from the damaged piers, and the white water that's pounding against them.

"Oh, sweet Jesus!" Ellen shrieks. "We're going over!"

I try to speak, but my throat has closed up on itself. Quickly, I store the semiautomatic in my pant waist. I'm reach for the smartphone, but not before the piers snap in two and the bridge collapses out from under us.

CHAPTER 60

We hit the water hard, the jolt shooting up my spine and into my head.

Ellen screams, both her hands gripping the Jeez bar mounted to the vehicle's frame above her head. In a word, she is petrified.

The truck begins to speed down the rapids toward the rocks. At the same time, it takes on cold water. We slam into a boulder and my forehead pounds the steering column while Ellen is thrust forward. My head spins. I know that if I close my eyes, the world around me will go black, and I may never wake up again. We will all die.

But I do my best to stay alert, to make a decisive move that will save us.

This is what I know from fly fishing the river: two hundred feet due north is a series of falls. One big falls of about fifty vertical feet and beyond those, two shorter falls of maybe twenty feet apiece. I also know this: Ellen and I don't stand a chance if we take on those falls in the wrecked Suburban that will surely fill with water.

Here's what I do: I unbuckle my seatbelt. Then, reaching around her, I unbuckle hers.

"What are you doing?" she shouts, the water splashing in through the busted windshield and passenger windows.

"We're getting out of this thing while we can. Remember, you've got to swim for the Thatcher Park side bank on our left. Don't forget that."

Up ahead, I can make out the drop-off of the first big fall. We're approaching it far faster than I anticipated. I look at the floor. My feet are covered in water. In a matter of seconds it will be up to my shins. We hit another boulder, careen off of it, while I struggle to open the center console. Inside it, I find another Maglite. I shove that into my pants pocket, along with my cell phone.

The drop-off is coming closer.

We have maybe one minute, at best, to exit this vehicle. But we need to ditch the vests and the helmets. It's exactly what I shout out to Ellen.

"Why?" she asks, the anxiety painting her pale face. "If we do that the rocks will break our ribs and crush our skulls."

The drop-off is maybe sixty feet away.

She's got a hell of a point. Only problem is, will the extra weight hold us down like anchors in the swift-moving river? Only one way to find out.

"On three, Ellen. Out the windows!"

Lifting my legs up, I grab onto my Jeez bar and set my feet flat on the seat, thrust my torso out the open window. Ellen pulls her feet up, sticks her head and shoulders out the opening, makes ready to jump.

"Two!"

The mist from the waterfall only a few feet ahead of us coats our faces, clouds our vision.

"Three!"

We jump, the water shockingly cold and frighteningly deep. I turn, search desperately for Ellen. She's swimming as hard as she can in my direction…the direction of the bank we must aim for if we're going to locate Henry. But I can tell that she's losing against the swift current.

Goddamned body armor is too heavy…

My ears fill with two things: the roar of the falls and Ellen's screams. Screams muted by the water that invades her open mouth. Choking her. Drowning her.

My eyes capture what could be her final moments. My wife sinking in the river, her arms slapping at the water, feet kicking.

No matter how hard she tries, she can't prevent the current from pulling her toward the edge of the falls.

No other option but to go to her, try and pull her to the bank.

I swim back into the center of the stream. Reaching out, I grab hold of her vest.

"Swim, Ellen!" I shout above the roar of the falls. "Swim! Swim for Henry!"

But the current is too damn fast. Too damn heavy. Too strong for us both.

I pull her into me as tightly as I can.

"Hold your breath!" I scream, as we arrive at the edge of the falls.

CHAPTER 61

How does one describe what it's like to go over a waterfall?

I could tell you about free-floating in space and time. How my life...surely Ellen's life...passes right before my eyes. From birth to my final breath, which no doubt awaits me on the rocky bottom of this violent waterfall. I could tell you that all fear gives way to a sedate kind of peace. The kind of peace that accompanies realization. When you know for certain these moments are your last and you can rest easy in the solace that you're wrapped in the arms of someone you love very much and very soon you will both be in a far better place for all eternity.

But that's the stuff for television movies and romance novels.

Here's what it's really like to go over a fifty-foot section of waterfall: As soon as you go over the side, your stomach flies up into your mouth, and you drop hard into a deep pool of white water that's churning so rapidly, you have trouble telling which way is up or down. By sheer luck, the stream is still moving swiftly toward a second section of smaller falls, so the pool spits you out all on its own and before you know it, both your helmeted heads are above water, and you're sucking in fresh air like it's the sweet breath of baby Jesus.

By some miracle, you're able to shift yourself toward the riverbank. You're still holding onto one another, but you paddle like hell with your free arms while kicking with all four legs and feet.

Within twenty or thirty seconds of going over the falls, you're hugging the bank, crawling up onto the rocky dry ground and lying on your back while sucking in precious oxygen. You stare up at a night sky filled with brilliant stars and a full moon. You think to yourself, maybe I have died and gone to heaven after all.

But then you realize the time is approaching three o'clock and you're no closer to locating your sick son than you were two hours ago, and you know the bloody horrible truth: I'm alive. I'm on earth. And if I don't do something and do it fast, my son is going to die.

I stand.

Holding my hand out for Ellen, she takes hold of it, and I pull her up.

"You all right, El?" I say. But it's a stupid question. I might as well ask her if she's happy.

"Time," she says.

Hesitantly, I look at my watch. My insides drop.

"One minute until three."

As if on cue, we both gaze at the incline we must climb in order to get back up to level ground. Level ground that extends all the way to the cliff side where we'll find Henry. Without another word, we begin the climb. I'm two or three steps away from the top when the earth quakes beneath our feet and the distant Albany skyline lights up like it's midday. Like it's Hiroshima, August 6, 1945.

CHAPTER 62

The radiant red/orange light from the powerful detonation inside downtown Albany reflects against her face and inside the glass on her night vision scope. She smiles at its brilliance, its thunderous noise and concussive reverberation.

He's a funny man, she thinks, while pulling the quad up to the black Nissan Quest SV minivan. For a man who was all about the control…control of the time-delayed explosion, control of the building collapse, control of the amount of dust and debris that would result from the demolition…he's entirely out of control now. But then, he was out of control the moment his son, Henry, was born. That's when he officially lost it. His pride and joy turned out to be old and gray even before his little head left the birth canal.

Total, fucking, bummer.

The men and women in the explosive demolition business must rely on their sons and daughters to carry the family name on and on and on. They alone teach the children. Not some college or university. Used to be, there was no master's degree in blasting. Academic degrees in explosives did not exist until very, very recently, and even then, there's nothing to match on-the-job experience.

So what are you left with in the end?

There's only the explosive detonator, a fuse, and the men and women who pull the trigger and hope…and she's stressing the HOPE here…that the concrete and steel tower not only falls the way it's supposed to, but that no one gets killed or maimed in the process. Explosives, after all, are like lovers. Beautiful, powerful, but oh so unpredictable.

Approaching the boy who is now lying on his side, fetal position, hands and ankles bound behind his back, eyes bright and wet in the bright light of the fireball that's rising up into the sky like Armageddon, she senses real fear oozing from his pores. But not fear for his life. His life is just about over, after all. The fear he is presently experiencing is for his mom and dad. The boy, who is not really a boy, is more like the parent in this situation. He was born older and he will remain older than his own parents until the moment he breathes his last. No doubt he worries about them, the way a mother and a father worry about their children. He worries for their safety, their well-being, and the last thing he wants is to bury them before they have the chance to bury him.

"Poor, poor Henry," she says, bending at the knees, running her fingers gently through his very fine, thinning hair. "Your short life is one big bitter irony."

The deep, traumatic thunder of the explosion, which has surely taken out most if not all of her intended target, reverberates across the valley, bounces against the rocky cliff face. She stands, folds the night vision scope down over her left eye, spots Ike and Ellen making their way on foot in her direction. They are guided not by maps or GPS, but by instinct and, of course, love. They are determined people who are so desperately out of control.

Raising up the night vision scope, she once more pulls the long-barreled revolver from the holster. Assuming a solid, balanced, modern combat shooter's stance (both hands gripping the weapon), she takes aim.

CHAPTER 63

The laser light streaks across the valley like a white hot spark across a naked wire.

"Down!" I scream, grabbing her vest, yanking her to the earth, face first.

The explosion shatters the ground behind us, the rocky shrapnel slapping the bottoms of our boot soles, pitting our legs and torsos. My head rings from the noise of the concussion. Yanking on Ellen's vest, I manage to climb back up onto my feet, pulling her up along with me. Her nosebleed has resumed, and she is a bit wobbly and out of balance.

Another streak across the sky and this time we don't have a chance to hit the dirt before the blast knocks us onto our backs. Coughing dirt from my mouth, I once more pull Ellen up off the ground and begin to run. Run as fast as possible across the open valley. She's trying her best to keep up with me, and yet I've no choice but to drag her across the dirt while another round detonates to my left. The mini-fireball rises up from it and, at the same time, robs the oxygen from the night air.

Somehow, I manage to maintain my balance while holding Ellen.

"Keep going!" I shout, my voice hoarse, sounding like my throat is filled with mud and stone. "Keep moving!"

Two more blasts, a bit further away, but enough to rattle our bones and slap us with two separate shockwaves. My eyes glued to the cliff side, I feel as if we're two ghost soldiers reliving D-Day at Omaha Beach all over again, explosions raining down on us like hellfire.

Three more streaks lead to three more powerful explosions that tear the ground up maybe a dozen feet in front of us, once more knocking us down, sucking the wind out of our lungs. I roll onto my back and scream into the night.

"Just kill us now! Just kill us all now, you crazy bitch!"

I recall the automatic stuffed in my pants and I pull it out, rolling onto my belly. Taking aim, I blink my eyes, attempt to refocus them. In the light of the moon, I make a quick estimation over which direction the laser streaks came from, and like a soldier taking advantage of the enemy tracer rounds, I set the sights on the dark, humanlike silhouette located maybe two hundred feet ahead of me.

I fire.

Something very interesting happens then.

The silhouette moves. I'm able to make out a figure moving in the pale moon glow that shines against the Thatcher Mountain cliff face. Not much movement, but enough to know that the bullet found its target.

I finger off three more back-to-back rounds, the exchange echoing off the mountain and out across the valley. My eyes concentrated on my target, I see it dropping. I see her dropping.

"Ike," Ellen says, her voice groggy. "Don't shoot. What if you hit Henry? What if you hit the bomb on his chest?"

Her point is well taken.

"I'm not sure I need to shoot at all anymore," I say. Then, raising myself up. "Come on, Ellen. Let's go."

"Go where?"

"I think I've shot Alison. I think I nailed the bitch. Let's go get Henry."

CHAPTER 64

He was lucky.

That's all she can say about the bullet that has cleanly passed through her lower left side. He aimed for a shadow and somehow managed to hit flesh. Had he aimed just a little bit to the left and down a few inches, he would have nailed his son, and perhaps even hit the old boy in the chest. The heat from the bullet would have triggered the device and obliterated both him and her.

Placing her gloved hand to her left side, she feels the warm blood slowly oozing out the wound. The pain hasn't arrived yet, but it will soon. Knowing that time is tight, she approaches the minivan, activates the keyless entry on the hatchback, opens it. Once more approaching Henry, she pulls the fighting knife from its sheath and cuts away the nano-thermite IED, setting it gently to the side. She inhales a deep breath in order to collect her strength. Then, thrusting her hands and forearms under his arms, she drags him to the rear of the van. Fully aware of the agony she is about to cause herself, she exhales and inhales once more, and heaves the boy's shoulders onto the van floor.

She releases a shriek that sounds as if it can cut through rock, but continues with the job unabated, raising up his feet and shoving them in also. She considers herself fortunate that he's so little, so lightweight, so fragile. Once again, she presses her hand to her side, feels the pain that is now beginning to build in direct proportion to the shock that's wearing off.

"I should have blown him up at the designated hour," she mumbles. That would have taught Ike a lesson. I should have blown him up and put him out of his misery. But then the revenge would be over, and all that would be left of the detonation game is to kill off Ike and Ellen. It all would be too soon, too easy. The Big Bad Wolf didn't just attack Little Red Riding Hood in the woods when he had every opportunity. He played her big time. Played her to get to the little girl's sickly grandmother first. Only then, when he'd begun digesting the old lady, was he ready to go to work on Little Red Riding Hood. For the Big Bad Wolf, the fun and excitement was in the challenge, the quest, the payoff.

She goes to the bomb, picks it up, carries it back to the van. Opening the driver's side door, she opens up the center console, sets it inside. Gripping the steering wheel, she pulls herself up, the electric jolts of pain shooting through her torso at lightning speed.

Sometimes the best-laid plans call for change.

Now that she knows Albany is burning, and along with it, the attention of every law enforcement official within a radius of fifty miles, including Detective Miller, she will finish this particular vengeance in a manner befitting the many years of anger she's been forced to swallow.

She will finish it all with a true implosion.

CHAPTER 65

We run as fast as our damaged legs will take us. Our bodies are battered, but we move with renewed confidence, knowing that Alison might be injured or even dead. I can't be sure, but it seems apparent she didn't detonate Henry's bomb. We would have seen the explosion, heard the big bang. We would have felt Henry's death in our hearts.

But then I make out a scream and a few beats later, the sound of a vehicle engine being fired up. I see two headlamps burning holes through the thick dark veil. The vehicle then disappears into a cluster of trees, until moments later, the headlights are once again visible as it climbs the winding Thatcher Mountain road up into the park. Once it gets to the top of the cliff, Alison drives a ways in until she comes to a stop.

"What does she think she's doing?" Ellen says. "I thought you shot her."

"Must be she's only wounded."

There's a slight commotion coming from up on the cliff. A door opening, the shadowy figure getting out, and the hatchback opening. In my mind, I see her doing something to Henry. But I can't see what.

My pulse pounds.

"Shouldn't we be going after her, Singer? Going after Henry?"

"Give a rabbit a chase, a rabbit runs. But in the end, what happens to the rabbit?"

"So we go then?" A question.

"I don't think we have much of a choice," I say, knowing that another trap could be set for us.

The shadowy figure moving once more, her silhouette visible in the moon glow. She comes to the edge of the cliff, extending both her arms, bringing them together at the wrist. There's something gripped in her hands. It can only be one thing.

"Oh shit." I swallow. "Run. Go. Run."

The linear white streak shoots out of her hands a split second before the gunfire. The thermite charge hits the earth a few feet away, explodes. Our bones rattle. Heads ring like bells. Gravel and dirt rain down on us.

"Go for the road!" I shout, not able to hear my own words inside my ringing skull. "Down here we're fish in a barrel."

We run for the safety of the trees.

Even the moonlight is hidden inside this patch of thick woods bookended on one side by a dirt road that leads to the main Thatcher Mountain road, and on the other side, the base of the cliff. Ellen presses up against me. So close I can feel her heart beating.

"Maybe it's time we just called the police," she says, her words weak and strained. The night and the thermite rounds are killing her. "Maybe Henry is already gone."

A wave of anger flashes through me.

"Don't say that. We don't know that."

She's right. Maybe Alison is just trying to lure us up onto the cliff top so she can finish us off once and for all. Enact some kind of grand finale. Everything up until now has been the prep work. The demolition of the bearing beams, the load-bearing walls, the glass and the windows. She's set the fuses, strung out the det cord and the charges. And now she's looking to take down the big tower. It will be the dramatic finish to the game of revenge she's been planning for me…for us…for so very long. It will be her perfect, true implosion.

Still, do we take the bait? Or do we cut bait and call in Miller?

I pull out my cell phone. The face is shattered, the interior waterlogged. I thumb the screen anyway. For a moment, it lights up, but then it quickly dies, as if having exhaled its final breath.

Another flash of rage coursing through veins and capillaries, and I toss the phone against a tree. It shatters into a dozen pieces.

"You didn't happen to bring your phone, Ellen?"

She shakes her head. "Can you believe it kind of slipped my mind?"

In my head, I picture that second explosion coming from downtown. I know that Miller will be up to his eyeballs in death and devastation. Who knows how many people died in the blasts?

So what's left for us to do?

Stand here under a canopy of foliage and hope she goes away? Or do something about her? Maybe she's killed Henry or maybe she hasn't. But as the Albany Police Department's single bomb disposal specialist, there is one thing I, and Ellen, can do not only for him and ourselves, but for the entire city. We can apprehend Alison, bring her in.

Alive.

It's exactly how I relay the plan to Ellen.

She looks up at me. Even though the moonlight is almost entirely blocked by the trees, I know she is biting down on her bottom lip. Something she does when in deep thought, or when nervous, or both.

"I couldn't agree more," she says.

I pull her into me, hold her tightly.

"Will you ever forgive me, El?"

I can feel her tears against the skin on my neck.

"Do I have a choice?" She sniffles.

"Nope. No choice."

I release her.

"Let's go catch that psycho bitch," she says, swallowing her tears.

We slip on out of the woods, head for the dirt road and the mountain.

CHAPTER 66

The night vision scope poised before her eye socket, she watches the Singers begin the climb along the Thatcher Mountain road. The blood is draining from her wound, running down her leg, warm and wet. But she's still strong enough to finish the job she started. The terror she's unleashed. The pain worsens with every passing second. It throbs, electric currents shooting up and down her body. But she's stronger than the pain. Stronger than the wound and the blood loss.

Now, from out of the distance, the sounds of helicopter rotors chopping through the air. She knows that the Department of Homeland Security will be scouring the area for terrorists. The National Guard, the New York State Police, the FBI…all of them will be after her. With the damage she's managed to unleash in the city, they will not be looking for one individual, but an entire terrorist cell. What she's accomplished is a masterpiece, and pales anything that's come before it. Those two creepy kids who blew up the Boston Marathon with pressure cooker bombs was just child's play. The Oklahoma bomber Timothy McVeigh was all about the quantity with that truckload of fertilizer bombs, not quality. No class, no finesse. What she's done will go down in history as magnificent. It will be considered the explosive event they've been waiting for ever since 9/11. They knew it was coming. It was just a matter of when. And months from now, when they discover that she was the bomber and has since disappeared without a trace, she will be remembered throughout history for this specific defining moment in time. People will ask, where were you on the night Albany imploded? What were you doing?

It will be as if they were asking what you were doing when John Lennon was assassinated, or when those planes crashed into the Twin Towers in New York. A moment in time that changes history forever.

Searching the sky through the powerful lens, she spots the chopper coming right for her. It's a gunship. What she recognizes from her military training as a Cobra attack helicopter, probably commandeered from the National Guard base at the Albany International Airport.

Even from a distance of two to three miles out, she's able to make out the two-man crew seated inside the chopper, their bodies glowing green in the night vision along with the eerie green outline of the helicopter fuselage. Maybe she should be afraid. Maybe she should be running…hopping into the van and speeding away. But she knows that it's far too late for that. If she's spotted them, then certainly they've made a positive ID on her.

Pulling the oversized pistol from its custom holster, she loads the five super-thermite charges into the cylinder, closes the breach just like she's closing the cylinder on a six-shooter straight out of the Old West. She will wait for the chopper to close in on her before raising the weapon, taking aim, unleashing hell.

CHAPTER 67

We come to the top of the Thatcher Mountain road, where it curves off to the right to follow the edge of the cliff and to connect with several parking lots that double as observation areas, complete with heavy-duty binocular devices that look like big silver heads shining bright in the light of the moon. For two quarters, the viewer gets a brilliant panoramic view of the valley and the city beyond it.

We spot Alison standing on the edge of the cliff, a black minivan parked behind her. She is no longer searching for us. Instead, she's using both hands to grip what looks to me like a very large pistol, or a delivery device for her super nano-thermite rounds. The pistol is aimed at the sky and a military chopper that's now honing in on her.

Holding out my hand, I signal to Ellen to squat down.

She does.

"They've sent in the cavalry," I whisper. "That's a gunship. Most likely National Guard."

"Are they going to kill her?"

"I'm guessing they suspect she's not acting alone. They'll want to flush her out, take her alive. Just like we want to take her alive."

"How? They're flying a helicopter."

I feel a tinge of sudden optimism. "My guess is there's a ground assault team on their way out here now."

"How did they even know where to look?"

"They might have spotted the thermite explosives. The bursts and flashes will have registered on a satellite feed. A security or weather satellite maybe. Plus there was the cruiser that was blown up at the end of our driveway, and those massive explosions in the city. Put three and three together and you get a terrorist cell that's operating out here in the state park and inside Albany."

"It's a one-woman terrorist cell, Singer. But I guess they have no way of knowing that. No way of imagining it either. Alison would never fit the profile."

The chopper approaches.

"Here's the plan. They're likely to fire a few rounds over her bow, so to speak. Just to scare her. When that happens, she'll hit the dirt. That will be our cue to jump her."

"That's it? That's the plan?"

I look her in the eye. "You got something better, I'm all ears. What's left of them, that is."

A flash captures my attention. I gaze back out over the cliff and into the valley. The flash is now accompanied by a crack.

"Incoming!" I bark under my breath, pulling Ellen and myself face down in the dirt.

The chopper's rockets strike the cliff side. When I look up, I can see that Alison is still standing her ground, unharmed by the missile's blast.

"Correction," I say. "Maybe they are trying to take her out."

The chopper is only about a half mile away at most. In a few seconds it will be directly overhead. She's got that oversized hand cannon aimed at the chopper. She's going to blow it out of the sky.

"Now's our chance, El. While she's not looking. I'll take care of her. You take care of Henry."

"If he's alive," she says, her voice trembling.

"He's alive. I can feel it."

Leaning into Ellen, I kiss her on the cheek.

She bounds up onto her knees, then onto her feet.

"No one dies," she says. "That's all I ask."

"Ask and you shall receive," I say, imaginary fingers crossed behind my back.

CHAPTER 68

Making like a linebacker who's got an unobstructed free shot at the quarterback, I lower my shoulders, take aim for the lower center of Alison's back. While I'm coming up on her from behind, the chopper is approaching her from the front. She's got the gun poised at the chopper as the noise from its rotors and turbine engine shoots across the valley and the cliff top. I'm so close I can make out the crease in her spine when she triggers the nano-thermite round on the oversized revolver. The round shoots across the sky at a sixty-five-degree angle, connecting with the chopper's tail, shattering it in a burst of oxygen-fed charges.

But I don't break stride.

The collision with Alison sends us both onto the gravelly floor. The heavy, chrome-plated pistol is knocked out of her hand, sending it sliding only inches away from the cliff edge. Above us, the chopper is now spinning out of control, the rotors and turbo engine screaming like a wounded bird of prey.

I grab hold of her legs while she claws at the ground, trying desperately to reach for the gun. Her legs are never still, but the wiry strength in them is too much for my grip. She squirms and kicks until free of my hold. I go to grab her again, but all I see is her boot heel coming at my face. When it connects, my world goes in and out of blackness. Until I realize I'm on my back and staring up at a burning, spinning, screaming machine that is about to drop on me.

Rolling onto my side I see her grabbing hold of the revolver where it rests on the cliff edge. I can't help but see the trail of blood she's leaving on the dirt with her every movement.

Grabbing hold of a rock, I bring it down hard on her ankle. She screams and, pistol in hand, turns to me, aiming the long barrel for my head.

There's fire in her eyes, and the anger painted on her face is as explosive as the thermite rounds in her gun. I can't see the chopper right now, but I can hear it coming down, hear it falling, its wounded engine straining, and I know that in a matter of a second or two, I am about to be crushed. Either I die by Alison's bullet or I die when the chopper falls on my head. Either way, I am twice dead.

I have nothing to lose. If I'm going to die, I'm going to take her with me.

"You hear that, Patty Cakes?" I scream inside my head. "Your daughter is coming to see you!"

Springing up to my knees, planting my feet, I lunge, landing directly on top of her. I reach out, grab hold of the hand that grips the gun. That's when the chopper crashes to the earth in an eruption of metal, glass, and ignitable gasoline. And that's when Alison and I go over the side.

CHAPTER 69

I drop onto a pine tree that's growing horizontally from out the cliff face, only a few feet down from its cliff edge.

Alison is saved by the same tree.

Together we hold tight to the extended tree branches with one hand, while clawing at one another with our free hands. But her free hand isn't exactly free since it's still gripping the pistol. She's whipping me with it, slapping it at my face, my consciousness once more coming and going, like a light bulb filament that's in the process of burning out.

We fight for control of the gun, she trying to aim the barrel at my head, as if the explosion from a round coming into contact with my skull won't also result in her own instant death. But maybe that's what she wants. Maybe this is a suicide mission. Maybe this is her scripted ending. An end that doesn't come with a whimper, but a series of big bangs.

We lock eyes, her gray/blue orbs gazing into mine with a hatred that is both pure and frightening. How could I have wronged someone that badly? Or perhaps, my wronging her is just an excuse. Perhaps she was just born angry. Born psychotic. Maybe my family and I are simply the targets of a psycho, and nothing more.

"Knock knock," she says.

"You've got to be fucking kidding me!"

The tree branch cracks, bends. I feel my body about to slip off, tumble the two hundred feet to the rocks below.

"Knock knock," she repeats, our hands still struggling for control of the gun, the other hands holding on to a pine tree that's collapsing under our collective weight.

"Who's…there?"

"Ima."

"Ima who?"

"Ima gonna kill you now, you home-wrecking son of a bitch!"

She puts everything into shifting the pistol barrel toward my face. This isn't brute strength, but something far deeper, far more primal. She is channeling an evil I can't possibly comprehend, and all I can think about is trying to save my life so I can get back to Henry and Ellen. Get them back home. Safe and sound and very much alive.

Sweat drips into my eyes. I feel the welts rising up on my skull and forehead from the pistol whipping. I taste blood on my tongue. I suck in a deep breath as the branch cracks once more, and the muscles in my weight-room-trained arms grow taut, the veins popping out of the skin. Our balancing act becomes near impossible. But the shock I feel in my pounding heart makes me all the more enraged, all the more determined. Pushing back the barrel, I slowly make it shift toward her own face. I see her eyes bulge, like she knows full well her head is about to evaporate.

She screams and pushes back, maneuvering the barrel so that it is suddenly pointed down at the earth below. It's her finger that's wrapped around the trigger, but my finger is pressed against hers. I'm too strong for her. I know that if I press her finger against the trigger, the blast will kill us both. But at this point, I don't care anymore. I just want her dead so that Henry and Ellen will live.

She feels my finger not just pressing against hers, but pumping against it. Like I have every intention of firing not one, but multiple rounds at once. An action that will overheat the barrel and cause the thermite rounds to explode in our faces. Something Alison herself explained just yesterday during lunch at the Mass Pike rest stop.

Alarmed, she turns, eyes wide.

For the first time since Alison Darling has come back into my life, I can taste the fear that oozes off of her.

Slowly, I form a broad, ear-to-ear grin. "Fire in the hole, motherfucker!"

I squeeze her finger against the trigger, three times, rapid-fire, while the grossly overheated chrome-plated barrel explodes and while the tree branch that holds us snaps in two.

CHAPTER 70

I fall upward.

The shockwave and kickback of the exploding gun barrel and the three super nano-thermite rounds exploding in succession at a distance of two hundred vertical feet making us airborne, until a second later, gravity pulls back and we fall once more.

Fall down.

Hard.

CHAPTER 71

When I come to, I see only brilliant sunlight.

A display of radiant orange, yellow, and golden rays that both soothe my soul and warm my entire body. I feel a peace like I have never known before. I am suspended in midair, my body parallel with the ground far below.

I begin to make out a shape.

Arms, legs, torso, and a head. Soon the shapes combine to make a singular soul. Patty Darling. She comes to me from out of the sunset. She looks different from the woman I've become reacquainted with in my brain over the course of two days and nights. Her hair is no longer mussed up, but smooth and clean and freshly brushed. Her forehead no longer bears the fracture, the skin no longer broken or bleeding. The skin, the flesh, is no longer burnt, but milky, smooth, and healthy, just the way it was when I'd happily run into her at our favorite watering hole, the Eagle Park Independence Club, or at the college cafeteria.

"Hey, it's Monday mystery meat, Patty Cakes. Come sit with me and we can figure out what kind of animal they stunned and butchered, together."

She's no longer in her mid- to late forties, but barely cracked her twenties. Like she's got her whole life before her. She floats or glides before me, almost like an angel.

"Patty Darling," I whisper, the words oozing out of my mouth like an exhaled breath.

It's over, Ike, she says, her tone pleasant and smooth as silk. I'm going away now.

"Where are you going?"

Where we all go one day, silly. You know, the place at the end of the long and winding road. Jeez, Singer, do I have to spell everything out for you?

"Am I dead?"

I don't know. Are you?

"Come on, Patty Cakes. Toss me a bone here."

Just know this: It's over.

"What is over?"

It…this…It's all over, and here's the biggie. You ready for it? When she smiles, it's like the sun's radiance is being projected through her entire body. I forgive you. Do you understand me?

I feel my head nodding, as if I'm not the one in control of it.

"I think I do understand."

And with that, her image begins to float back into the sun, becoming one with the light, until it disappears entirely.

I wake.

I breathe in, and my head begins to clear. Maybe I'm in bed and this was all a stunningly bad nightmare. But then I peer over my left shoulder, and my heart sinks. I realize I am not lying in bed, but instead, lying on the hard concrete floor of a high-rise. The top floor maybe. The windows have been pounded out, along with some of the beams. All the interior walls have been knocked out, the material discarded, all the flooring peeled away. All that's left is this empty shell.

It comes to me then. My precise location. The Wellington Hotel.

I crane my neck to the right. My heart sinks further when I spot my family. Henry is located maybe fifteen feet away. He's seated on the floor with his back pressed up against a steel beam that's been wired with detonator cord and a series of blasting caps. I don't see any C-4 but that doesn't mean it's not inserted into the concrete-encased beam on the opposite side. His torso is attached to the beam with heavy-duty duct tape, while his wrists and ankles are also taped together. His mouth is gagged with the same tape. He is fully awake, his eyes locked on me, like he's looking for me to save him.

Located another fifteen feet beyond him is Ellen. She too is duct-taped to a separate beam in an identical manner. Like all the others, the beam is set to blow.

Looking down at my hands, I see they also are taped together at the wrists as are my ankles. I try shifting them from side to side, but there's no give in the layers of tape that bind me to my own steel I-beam.

How the hell did a thin woman like Alison manage to transport us out here? By sheer force of will, she must have found a way to stuff us into her minivan. Even with a bullet wound to contend with, her rage must have been that absolute. Like trying to gun down a crazy man wired out on crystal meth. Or maybe she utilized a piece of equipment like a winch or a come-along.

I want to scream, Get us out of here! But there's not a damn thing God or anyone else can do for us. We are as doomed as this old hotel. Doomed as the concrete, brick, and mortar that is about to implode under the destructive force of hundreds of pounds of TNT, C-4, and nitroglycerin charge.

I make out footsteps, then the figure of someone exiting a stairwell.

Alison.

She makes her way slowly past Ellen, offering my wife a casual if not friendly smile. Then offering the same smile to Henry while bending at the waist, she gently, almost lovingly, kisses him on his balding head. It's like she's the sister he never had.

Finally she makes her way to me. When she reaches for the gag on my mouth with both her hands, I can see that the thumb and index finger on her dominant hand have been blown away, leaving only bloody stumps. For certain, she took the brunt of the exploding revolver. Using both her hands, regardless of the severe injury to her fingers, she somehow manages to take hold of both ends of my gag, ripping it away.

I don't feel the sting of the pulled away tape. I only feel the desire in my soul which screams at me to kill this woman and save my family.

"Now, is this the perfect ending for Ike Singer, Master Blaster, or what?" she asks, her eyes wide and bright. She's still dressed in that tight black outfit, her left side bleeding through a thick bandage cobbed from a formerly white towel and some of the same gray duct tape. She's trying her best to appear happy, but I can see that her face is chalky pale and that she's lost enough blood to cut her life short by sixty or seventy years. But that does nothing to stem the hatred I have for her right now.

One thing is for certain. Alison, wounded or not, is resourceful. Getting us into the van is one thing. But how the hell did she manage to drag us all the way up here?

Out the corner of my eye, through one of the wide window openings, I see that she used the temporary construction elevator, which has yet to be removed from the building, telling me the morning's scheduled detonation has indeed been postponed in light of the IEDs that have been exploding inside Albany all night long.

"I thought I was already dead," I say, my words feeling like they're tearing themselves from the back of my throat, as if the skin is shredding.

"The explosives saved our lives," she says. "The nano-thermite rounds blasted us back up onto the mountain. Can you imagine our great fortune?"

"The explosives," I say. "They giveth and they taketh away. So how them fingers treating you?"

"Now, for the first time in history, nano-thermite charges will implode this building," she says, ignoring my question. "Perfect really, when you think about it, Ike. Because isn't this what you and my father always desired? To achieve the perfect true implosion?" Raising her hand, she makes a sweeping gesture with her arm, as if bringing attention to the many concrete-covered vertical beams that support the floor. "Take a good look. You see any C-4 or nitro charges strapped to the horizontal and vertical beams?"

I don't want to play her game. But as a Master Blaster, I can't help but look. I'll be damned. She's right. There are no conventional explosives to be found.

"The place is wired with nano-thermites. What used to require hundreds if not thousands of pounds of high-grade explosive now takes just a few ounces of super nano-thermite charge. This will be the first structure in history to undergo a true implosion using the explosive of the future. Too bad you and the fam damily won't be around to witness the future, Ike."

Craning my neck, I'm able to make out Henry, the boy's eyes wide. I see Ellen too. Her wet eyes reflect his same fear.

"Alison," I say. "I know how badly you want your revenge against me. For what happened with your mom. But it has nothing to do with my family. Please do the right thing and let them go."

She winces from the pain in her side, her left hand pressed against it. For a moment, I think she might even pass out. Reaching around back, she unclips something from her utility belt. It's a remote-control electronic detonator box. What I recognize as a "Hot Shot" computerized detonation system. The fire-engine red, heavy-duty plastic controller with its red and black buttons is far different from the one her father utilized when he tried to kill me sixteen years ago, in one important aspect. Rather than rely on the charges to explode at their own, relatively slow pace, the new system is able to minimize the delays between the detonation stages, speeding the entire process up, making it more violent and precise. The "Hot Shot" fits perfectly into the palm of her one good hand.

"You wanted a perfect true implosion," she says, her eyes forlorn, distant. "And all I wanted was the perfect family. But you took that away from me."

What I want to say to her is this: "Fuck you, you no good psychotic bitch…This isn't about me or an affair I conducted over the period of a single night with your mother. This is about your craziness, plain and simple. In your messed up mind, the entire world has screwed you over and now you want to destroy it all. Every damn bit of it."

But considering the lives of my family are at stake, I say this instead: "But look at what you've accomplished, Alison. You're an explosives expert. You're a professor. You're on your way up in the world. You should be proud, not angry or sad."

She nods, staring down at the controller. Appearing now, from out of the rising sun, two helicopters. Both of them black Hueys bearing the red, white, and blue eagle crest logo of the Department of Homeland Security. Their rotors chop intensely through the air. But somehow, Alison doesn't seem to hear them.

"Listen, Alison," I say. "There isn't much time. The police will be here any moment and they're liable to do something bad to you."

She giggles.

"Like kill me?" she says. "Look at me. Look at my side. I'm already dead, Ike."

She raises the controller, places a finger apiece on the two trigger buttons. The black one for charging the detonator cord snaked all over the walls and beams of this old hotel, and the red one for firing off the blasting caps and, ultimately, the main thermite charges.

"You're not dead now. You give up right this second, they will get you to a hospital, and you will have the best help available. Trust me, I work with these people. I can help you. We can help you, Alison."

I watch her hands. She presses the black charge button.

"Oh sweet Jesus no," I whisper.

The charges placed all around us, above us, and beneath us release an ominous hum as they come alive.

"Alison," I say, my mouth having turned so dry I can hardly form the words. "Don't do this."

"It's all that's left to do. It's the way I planned it. The way I wanted to control it."

The two choppers come closer until they begin to hover in place. A siren sounds, indicating the building shoot is about to commence. I look over my shoulder at Henry. He remembers the stages leading up to a blast. The final countdown, the "All Clear" signal, the "Fire in the hole" shout-out, the charging of the detonators, the siren, and finally the blasts in rapid, staged, timed succession. The destruction. The implosion.

Henry knows he's going to die now. Something he has been anticipating for a long time. What he didn't anticipate is his mother and father joining him. What the hell. Maybe in the end it's better that way. That we all go together.

"You can change the plan," I insist. "Just take your finger off the charger. Just remove it, and we can all walk on out of here."

She purses her lips, shakes her head. "You don't understand, Ike. I will be walking out of here. And then they are coming to take me away. To a new country where I will be a new woman, with a new name. I will be looked upon as a hero."

I have no idea what she's talking about, or what she means when she says she will be walking away a hero. Only moments ago she said she was already dead. The blood that seeps out from multiple wounds is the proof.

All I know is that the hum from the charging detonators is getting louder with each passing second. I also know this: there's a beam of red laser light originating inside the closest chopper. The laser light comes from a high-powered rifle that is now aimed at her back.

"Alison," I say, knowing that if they start shooting and fail to kill her instantly, she will press the Fire trigger. "Let go of the charger. Let go and we can all go home."

A muzzle flash is followed immediately by a short sharp crack, and a piece of Alison's left breast blows out. Her eyes go wide. Not like she's been shot. More like someone nudged her while walking past her on a busy street.

She takes a step forward, wobbles, unbalanced. The linear beam of laser sighting, which isn't visible outside the building but only on the darker inside, once more finds its target. A flash, a crack, and a portion of her shoulder collapses in a spray of blood and bone.

She's still standing when she looks me in the eye, says, "Mother loved you very much. So. Very. Much." Then, working up a painful smile. "Boom, boom, Ike. Out go the lights."

She collapses into a neat pile of blood, flesh, and bone, but not without pressing the red FIRE trigger as her final parting gift.

CHAPTER 72

The siren screams.

The blasting caps begin their rapid-fire detonation simultaneously on both the lowest and the highest floors, making the building tremble and rattle on its foundations. Alison's body has fallen right beside me, the utility belt that surrounds her narrow waist only inches from my hands. But they might as well be a mile away.

From where I'm seated, I spot the eight-inch knife attached to her belt. If I can reach the belt, I can make a grab for the knife, cut away the tape that binds me along with the tape that binds my family. It's possible we can make it out of the hotel. Make it out via the concrete stairwell while the blasting caps blow, only moments prior to the big blasts that will destroy the bearing beams, undermining the structural support of this old concrete structure.

But I need to get my wrists free. Now.

The blasting caps now detonate on the intermediate floors. Above us and below us. I struggle with my hands. Feel the bones in my wrists bending, breaking, as I struggle to pull free.

Then, a snap in my left wrist.

For a brief second, I feel my head spin. I'm sure I will pass out. A scream works its way up from my gut, while a searing hot pain shoots up and down the nerve bundle in my arm. I must have initially broken the wrist during my battle with Alison on the cliff face…when we fell hard back onto the solid, flat mountain surface. Now the break has gone from bad to severe. But the break, and the lubricating blood from the broken skin, turns out to be a blessing. Because it allows me to pull my hand free of the tape.

Swallowing my pain, I grab the knife from her belt, cut the tape that holds me to the beam. I scream against the electric pain, but I have no choice. I must free my one unbroken wrist or die. When the job is done, and I haven't passed out, it's time to cut my ankles free. But at least this time, I can use my good hand. Standing, I sprint the fifteen feet to Henry, cut him loose.

The blasting caps on the floor below detonate. One after the other. Rapid-fire succession. Shaking the old ten-story building like it's caught in a tornado.

I lose my balance, feet flying out from under me.

I fall. So does Henry. The knife is knocked out of my hand. It slides across the floor. Eyes locked on Ellen, I see the despair painting her face. The desire to live.

Crawling to the knife, left wrist broken, the snapped-in-two sharp edge of white bone exposed, I snatch the knife back up with my good hand. Get back up on my feet, the building swaying from side to side. Reaching down, I grab hold of Henry, pull him up.

"Your mother!" I scream. "Go to your mother!"

Stealing a piece of duct tape that bound Henry, I wrap it tightly around my broken wrist. The pain relief from the tape's splint-like support is almost immediate.

"Run!" I scream.

We run to Ellen, but the caps attached to the roof structure directly above us blow, and we go down again. Hard. Onto our sides. My head hits the concrete, knocks me out for a brief second or two. Or maybe it's a full minute. But then, this hotel won't exist one minute from now. Maybe I'm dead and this is a post-mortem nightmare. A dream about trying desperately to escape a high rise that's in the early stage of implosion, the floors about to collapse onto themselves like vertical dominoes. A dream created in hell. I can't move. I can't do anything other than feel the crush of tons of cement coming down on me.

But this is no dream. I'm awake and this is reality.

Once more, I push myself up, the pain in my wrist so intense, so immediate and pervasive, I might consider allowing myself to die if not for the instinctual need to save my family.

"Ellen!" I shout, but the explosions drown out my voice entirely.

I pull Henry along by his collar. Somehow he manages to get back onto his feet. We come to Ellen, fall to our knees. As I slice through her tape, Henry pulls the layers away, like peeling an onion. He is a different young man from the one I've come to know. He is no longer fragile or sickly. But instead, strong and determined. He strips the piece off his mother's mouth. She screams. But her scream can't be heard above the apocalypse of explosive charges. Sweat pouring off my brow into my eyes, I slice through the tape wrapped around her wrists and ankles.

I point at the stairwell with the knife.

Henry and I lift Ellen up by her shoulders, and together we make for the stairwell opening, as the blasting caps directly behind us begin their detonation cycle, one by one.

CHAPTER 73

The stairwell interior vibrates like a severe earthquake. Lucky for us, it's the strongest part of the structure.

"Hold onto the banisters!" I scream, my voice more audible inside the enclosed space. "Go like hell! Down! Down! Down! Don't look back!"

Ellen goes first, Henry follows. He's having trouble keeping his footing. Having overexerted himself while freeing his mother, he's now too weak to make it on his own. We come to the first landing, and I cut in front of him, lean down, pick him up, torso-over-shoulder in a classic fireman's hold.

A blast occurs on the top floor. A blast big enough to rattle my back teeth. It's the first of the major charges.

The building sways so relentlessly, we're thrust against the stairwell walls.

"Keep going!" I shout, Henry on my shoulder, my bad arm now almost useless, like an appendage that requires amputation.

"We're not going to make it!" Ellen wails.

"We have to make it! Just go!"

We're descending the stairs two at a time. The top of the stairwell disintegrates, the shredded concrete pouring down on us like a lethal rain. Peering down between the rails I see we only have five, maybe six stories to go. But the blasts are coming faster now, taking out the top floor beams, weakening the upper superstructure. I know what's coming next, because I spent most of my adult life trying to imagine it happening.

The true implosion.

In just a matter of seconds, the bearing beams on all floors will blow rapidly, one after the other. Then will come a moment of silence. A moment so profound, it will seem like God has issued the order, and the entire world will be aware of it.

The thought barely passes through my head when the last of the blasts are detonated. We are thrust against the old cinder-block walls. It's all I can do to hold onto Henry while Ellen clings to the metal rail like she's about to drop into a black bottomless pit. The oxygen is sucked out of the air and the world around us flashes with red and white heat, stinging our eyes, piercing our flesh, battering our brains, rattling our bones.

Then, just like that, the blasting stops. In its place comes the silence. The dreaded silence. The stillness. The most peaceful, most quiet, most serene nano-moment in time. The precise moment before the big bang.

"Here's it comes." I swallow. "The final stage."

The thunder begins from the top down, as the rooftop slab drops onto the floor below it, and the floor below that, and the floor below that, and the Wellington Hotel proceeds to undergo a feat of remarkable engineering and pyrotechnics.

Its total inward collapse. Its true implosion.

CHAPTER 74

The house of concrete and steel cards falls. The ten-story Wellington Hotel collapses under its own weight. Each steel-reinforced concrete floor, starting at the top, falling one on top of the other, in perfect succession.

The dust cloud blinds us, the cacophony of colliding materials and blasted main charges stings eardrums. Dust chokes lungs. We don't run down the remaining stairs but instead jump, Henry atop my left shoulder, my hand gripping Ellen's right arm, as we come to the first floor, the exit door already having been removed, the light from the morning sun shining through it not like we are escaping the implosion onto solid ground, but instead sprinting through a thick, acrid, dust-filled fog into heaven on earth.

We make it through the door, but don't dare stop running as the building collapses to mid-level, then a half second later to three-quarter level, and a half second beyond that to the bottom and basement floors.

The shockwave produced by the tons and tons of solid, now demolished building coming into contact with the earth blows us out through the storm fence and into a street filled with fire trucks, cop cruisers, EMT vans, and crowds of people.

I lose my grip on my family. Feel my body flipping head over heels until I find myself lying on my back in the middle of the city road, dazed, confused, nauseous, the world spinning in slow motion all around me. I look over one shoulder until I see Henry, then the other until I see Ellen, both of them lying on their backs. Honestly, I can't say whether they are dead or alive. I only know they are with me. That the building and its implosion hasn't buried them.

It's then, and only then, that I close my eyes and pass out.

FINAL STAGE

CHAPTER 75

Opening my eyes, I'm blinded by the light. It comes from an artificial source installed in a collapsible fixture mounted to the ceiling of an EMT van. Already my left wrist is being tightly bandaged and placed in a stainless steel splint. I'm just glad I wasn't wide awake for the removal of the duct tape.

The blue-uniformed woman applying the temporary cast to my arm isn't alone. Seated beside her is Nick Miller, who, despite the dirt and dust cloud from the Wellington Hotel's implosion, and what no doubt has been a full twenty-four hours without sleep, looks dapper in his pressed shirt and blue and white Repp tie. Ball knot tied perfectly, of course.

"Are you God?" I say, through the thick dust paste that coats the interior of my mouth.

"Depends on who's asking."

"Not the answer I'm looking for." A wave of pain shoots up and down my arm. It serves not only to remind me that I'm still alive, but also that Ellen and Henry are still out there. "What about my family?"

I try and raise myself up.

"Easy," says the woman working on my arm. "This is temporary. You need surgery for that arm. Right now. You understand?"

"Your family is fine, Ike," Miller says. "A little banged up like you. But no worse for wear." He purses his lips. "How in the hell you outran that blast, I'll never know."

"One day I'll tell you about it, if you're buying the beers. But take it from a Master Blaster. It's all in the timing."

In my head I see the "Hot Shot" computerized detonation device gripped in Alison's one good hand. Under normal circumstances, the timed detonations would have fired far too rapidly for us to escape their wrath. My educated guess is that a badly bleeding and confused Alison unknowingly slowed the pace of the detonation sequence just enough to afford us the time we needed to make our escape. It's the only logical explanation. The only possible explanation.

"Beer sounds good," he says. "And bourbon."

"Alison Darling?"

"Dead."

"You sure about that? There isn't going to be one of those Fatal Attraction dead-babe-jumps-out-of-the-bathtub moments?"

He shifts his attention to the EMT.

"He about ready?" he says.

She nods, pulls a pair of medical scissors from the tray, cuts away the excess surgical bandage.

"Done," she says. "Until you get to a hospital." Turning to Miller. "You will personally see to it that Mr. Singer gets himself to a hospital, pronto, Detective?"

"We'll get him there, mucho pronto," Miller says. "But first, we need to make sure we have a secure city." He turns to me. "No more boom boom, isn't that right, Ike?"

"Boom boom," I say. "Out go the lights."

First thing I do after climbing out of the van is find Henry and Ellen. Both of them are seated on the back bumper of another EMT van, silver blankets wrapped around their shoulders. Ellen is drinking something from a white Styrofoam cup, and Henry is drinking a Pepsi from out of the can. Both their faces are still pale from the concrete dust that showered them after the blasts.

I hug them both as tightly as my muscles will allow, my eyes welling with tears, my throat constricting so much I find it impossible to form the simple words, I love you. But I think by now they know exactly how I feel. No matter what comes at you in life, in the end, it's all about family.

"You did good, Dad," Henry says after a time, his face full of wrinkles and more than a few age spots. But it also bears a smile. An almost youthful smile. A smile that says, I just saw death and lived to tell about it.

"And you, my brave son," I say. "You saved our lives."

Ellen isn't smiling, but I can almost feel the relief on her. It's as palpable as her beating heart. I know how much she loves me, but I also know that as soon as things calm down, we will have some talking to do. Talk about the past. About trust. About where we go from here.

But I don't focus on the thought for too long. Because when Ted Pendergast approaches me, his gloved hand slapping my shoulder, I sense he's got some news for me. For Miller.

"Nemo's found something," he says, half out of breath.

"Explosive?" Miller says, his face growing taut, as if to say, Not again. Please, not again.

Rookie Cop shakes his head.

"Human," he says. "Human remains."

Miller turns to me.

"Alison Darling is confirmed dead," he says, exhaling every bit of oxygen from his lungs. "Sometimes I just love it when I'm right."

CHAPTER 76

She lies at the bottom of a pile of rubble, some five hundred tons in total weight. Her eyes remain wide open, despite her skull being crushed, her limbs and torso mutilated to the point of unrecognizable to anything other than God and the devil.

But there is something that has not been harmed. Something that remains untouched by either explosive or the crush of heavy rubble.

Her smile.

It's as if she died happy, regardless of the pain, the struggle, the fear, the violence…the vengeance in her cold heart. Having exacted her revenge on Ike Singer, on God, on Albany itself, she appears to have died happy. And that's something most people will never know.

The black chopper scheduled to retrieve her up on the site of the imploded building under the cover of a dust cloud is not coming for her, both the pilot and her Chinese contact having recognized the situation for what it is.

A complete failure.

No choice but to abort before the Department of Homeland Security and/or the National Guard hone in on their position and either force them to land, or worse, attempt to blow them out of the sky.

Now the chopper races east for the Massachusetts border, and beyond that the Atlantic Ocean, where in a matter of an hour it will find its landing pad atop an ocean-going yacht owned by BigBlast, Inc. Soon, company executives will find another researcher at the Albany University of Nanoscale Science and Engineering who will be willing to share information for the right price. There is never any shortage of individuals willing to take a risk for considerable funds in return. Never any shortage of blasting engineers willing to smuggle both information and product. Never any end to the thirst for good old American ingenuity and blasting high-tech know-how.

CHAPTER 77

Henry and Ellen are settled in a hotel located on nearby lower State Street, courtesy of my employers, the Albany Police Department. Detective Miller and I proceed to examine the sites of the two massive remote-controlled detonated explosions that Alison Darling set inside downtown Albany. The first one occurred at the Albany Family Court Building. According to Miller, luck was on our side since only three people died in a blast that tore away most of the front marble steps, along with the stately building's colonnade and front façade.

Making a cursory examination of the now fenced off structure from inside Miller's cruiser, I am at once shocked by the extent of the damage and humbled by the power of the nano-thermite charge she utilized. As I study what by now Homeland Security considers the detonation device utilized in the blast—a simple retrofitted, medium-sized e-cig device that in my estimation contained mere ounces of liquid thermite explosive—I shake my head and feel my heart sink at the potential destructive forces that have been unleashed by nanoscience.

It's the same story for the second explosion that smashed most of the concourse level at the Empire State Plaza, the modern, white marble-sided state worker office complex built by then Governor Nelson Rockefeller in 1968. A building constructed for the people, by the people. Very few deaths due to the time of the explosion (3 AM), and judging by the detonation device (what's left of it), a relatively small amount of liquid thermite explosive, compared to the hundreds or even thousands of pounds of C-4 and/or dynamite that would have been required to cause the amount of damage I'm witnessing firsthand. For the first time in history, massive explosions are capable of being carried out by a single human being with a pipe bomb the size of your average vaping device.

Back inside the cruiser, Miller slips the key into the dash-mounted starter.

"We've got two choices here, the way I see it," he says. "We can either comb the city for more explosives, in which case we would be busy for days or weeks. Or we can safely assume that Alison blew up everything she wished to blow up already."

"Excepting me and my family," I say.

"What exactly happened out there in the country?"

"How much time do you have?"

He shoots a glance at my bandaged wrist and arm. "You need to get to the hospital, pal. Like five minutes ago."

"I'll be okay for a few more minutes."

"Whaddaya say we grab a couple coffees, talk it over, then get you to the emergency room?"

"No arguments, Miller. You're buying."

We grab the coffees and park down by the river at the old, now abandoned Port of Albany, amongst the old tin-sided warehouses, algae-encrusted piers, and rusting, dockside-mounted cranes. We sip our coffee and stare out at a gray-blue river that runs slow in the late summer, the gulls feeding off the occasional fish that breaks the surface in search of insects. Survival of the fittest.

I am at once reminded of parking here in my pickup sixteen years ago, shoving the barrel of a gun in my mouth. But, at the same time, I remember making the decision to toss the gun into the drink. Making the decision to live.

It takes the better part of a half hour and most of our coffees. But by the time I'm done, I've led Miller through the entire Alison Darling ordeal. From the barn explosion, to the first Alison knock-knock joke text, to the piano explosion, to the kidnapping of Henry, to the assassination by landmine of the APD cop, to our being made to play a sadistic game of cat and mouse with Alison while trying our damndest to avoid being blasted to bits by one of the super nano-thermite rounds she was shooting from her special pistol.

Miller takes a minute to soak it all in.

"Nano-thermite rounds, huh?" he says, swirling the last inch or so of coffee left in his cup. "I thought that stuff was science fiction. At the very least, I've always been told there isn't a gunmetal on earth to facilitate a bullet like that."

"It is sci-fi," I say. "Or was, until now. I've known for a while that nanoscience engineers were working on the development of a thermite-tipped bullet, for obvious military purposes. But I had no idea the concept was in development until Alison herself spelled it out for me. They're trying to develop a gun for it too. Makes sense. She got quite a few rounds off at us with the piece she was using, until it went bad on her and cost her half her hand."

"And Alison Darling was in charge of the project." He exhales. "No wonder she was selling out to the Chinese."

I turn to him quick. "What do you mean the Chinese?"

"That's right. You wouldn't know since you've had such a, let's call it busy night."

I set my coffee cup into one of the free console cup holders. My left arm is resting on my thigh, so that I feel the throb, throb, throb, of the wound.

"Body belonging to a security guard at the University Nanoscience building where Alison works, or worked, was discovered only hours ago. He was murdered. Assassinated. Executed. The e-cigarette he was inhaling from exploded in his face, destroying almost all if it. The e-cig was a booby trap. After everything that went down with those e-cig device bombs earlier, and your pointing the finger at Alison, I sent in a team to examine the place. What we discovered, besides missing nano-thermite explosive and ordinance from the facility's secured basement area, were documents confirming that not only was she working for the Chinese company that was contracted to implode the old Wellington Hotel, she was providing their mother company in Shanghai with precious military information on nano-thermite explosive tech and other assorted corporate secrets."

"So why even bother going after me and my family? After all these years?"

He cocks his head over his shoulder while a seagull dives into the water headfirst, comes flying back out like an ICBM with a small fish caught in its bill.

"I've been studying killings and killers almost all my life, so I feel like I'm pretty good at sizing up their profiles by now."

"Educate me, Miller, before my hand falls off at the wrist."

"Okay, here goes. The beef she had with you was entirely personal. My guess, and this is a fairly educated guess based on everything that's exploded tonight, is that she'd been planning this night for a long, long time. She's not the type to explode with anger. She's more the kind of person who holds everything inside while putting on a happy face, knowing that one day, she would implode.

"She always kept in mind that when the time was right, she would go after you. But she wasn't about to do it with something so banal and garden variety as a gun or a knife, or two or three pressure cooker bombs for that matter. That's the stuff for amateurs and lone wolf terrorists. She was going to use special explosives. High-tech explosives. Explosives that possess more power than anyone can imagine. Her motives were double-edged. I believe she was testing out the thermite rounds, plus her other nano-scale IED goodies, in order to demonstrate their effectiveness and their ultimate worth to her Chinese buyers."

I turn quick. So quick, an electric shock–like pain from my broken wrist shoots up my arm, up my face, into my brain.

"You saying my family and I were guinea pigs in this setup, and that's all?"

He shakes his head. "Not at all. Like I said, this was also very personal. She had a hard-on for you for a very long time. She knew that explosives would be a language and a world you understood, and something you feared and respected more than anything else. The master blaster becomes the master bomb disposal man. What better way to torture you than with nanoscale thermite tech? What better way to illustrate that no matter how much you wronged her, her mother, and her father, in the end, she came out on top. She was a direct extension of that power and she wielded it not only over your life and death, but that of your wife and sick son."

I feel winded at his explanation, but I suppose it makes perfect sense. For a psychotic woman obsessed with revenge. Or, what the hell, maybe she was just a nutcase and that's that.

Miller goes on, "An unmarked and unidentifiable chopper was spotted flying off the grid between the Massachusetts coast and Albany at the exact same time the Wellington went up with you and your family inside it. My guess is they were coming to retrieve her and provide transport to mainland China where she'd be granted asylum, probably under a new identity. We've seen this kind of thing before. But that's really for the FBI to make sense of at this point."

"Nothing much to retrieve inside the Wellington, Miller."

"Somehow the guys in the chopper figured that out, and abandoned their mission before they got blown out of the air by some trigger-happy air/army reservist scouring the area for terrorists. Don't forget, bombs have been going off inside the city all night. The whole world is watching us."

"Where's the chopper now?"

"From what I'm told, it made a U-turn, headed back out to sea, most likely landing on a boat somewhere offshore. Coast Guard is working on intercepting the vessel now."

We sit and stare out at the water for another minute.

"I've strayed only once in my marriage," I say after a time, my eyes focused on my broken wrist. "It was wrong. Dead wrong. I never should have done it to Ellen or to Henry. But how the hell could I have known that it would lead to something as complicated and deadly as this, sixteen years later?"

"I can't answer that for you. But what I can do is offer you some advice now. Look into a better security system for your house. Alison had the run of the joint for the week you were gone." He shoots me a look. "You can't go back there until the place is swept. You realize that, don't you?"

I nod, the throb, throb, throb in my wrist now resonating in my temples.

Miller turns the engine over.

"Who knows what she planted inside and out of the farmhouse," I say. "But those landmines in the driveway…they must have been planted when I was still in Massachusetts getting the Suburban repaired."

He shakes his head. "I didn't blow up when I came out to see you that night. Your pizza man didn't light up either."

It strikes me then. "She must have been there the whole time. Out in the woods at the front of the property. Waiting us out. Waiting to start her deadly game. No wonder the patches of gravel where the charges were buried appeared to be freshly disturbed."

Miller looks at himself in the mirror, adjusts the ball knot on his tie as if it needs adjusting, and then slaps me on the thigh. The slap makes my wrist hurt, but I don't say anything about it.

He says, "She was right there, only a few feet away from us the entire time. Shit, she could probably smell that pizza from Smith's."

"I still feel entirely responsible for what happened. For all those deaths tonight."

"Listen, pal," Miller says. "You've heard it before but I'll say it again. Takes two to tango. We all make mistakes."

"Ellen," I say. "Tell her that."

"You're alive. Your son is alive. She's alive. My guess is she'll forgive you given time."

Time that Henry doesn't have.

He backs out, then throws the tranny in drive, takes off across the wide open empty port parking lot.

"So what now, Ike?" he says, as we approach Broadway in the direction of the Albany Medical Center. "You gonna leave the APD for the building blasting business once more?"

Recent memories flash through my mind. Duct-taped to an I-beam up on the top floor of the Hotel Wellington. My family duct-taped to the I-beams beside it. The blasting caps detonating, the charges about to blow, running for our lives, coming within a single step of being buried by tons and tons of concrete and steel rubble.

"The true implosion," I whisper. "A perfect true implosion."

"Excuse me?" Miller says, hooking a hard right onto Broadway.

"The true implosion. It's what I had always wanted to accomplish with Master Blasters. What my partner and I had always wanted to accomplish. Only a handful of demo experts in the world can make it happen. Alison Darling made it happen."

"With you inside the building."

I nod. "Maybe it's not what I had in mind, but in a way, I feel like I achieved the true implosion and now it's finally time to call it a day on the dream. Because the dream is over. The bad dream anyway. It's the least I can do for Ellen."

He shoots me a look, forms a crooked grin.

"You still have a job with the department," he says. "Far as I know."

"That job is boring," I say, not without a laugh. "Excuse me. Used to be boring." But then, knowing that innocent lives were lost tonight, I suddenly realize there's nothing to laugh about.

"What will it take to make you stay on, Ike? You wanna become a permanent part of the force?"

"A raise would be nice."

"I'll talk to the chief, and he'll talk to the mayor, and Albany will make it happen. You've earned it."

He hooks a left onto State Street, in the direction of the pile of wreckage that used to be the Wellington Hotel, and the Family Court Building, which is now mostly a blasted away ruin. If I didn't know any better, I'd say the place looks like a war zone.

"Safety first and last," I whisper.

"'Scuse me?" Miller says.

"Safety first and last. It was the Master Blasters motto. Something that died along with Alison inside all that blasted concrete."

But something else dawns on me then. Something pleasant in the midst of all the destruction.

"Knock knock," I say after a beat.

Miller looks at me like I've lost my marbles.

"Who's there?"

"Itsmy."

"Itsmy who?"

"Itsmy boy's twentieth birthday today, Detective Miller." Me, smiling. "Kid has beaten the odds, and beat the reaper for another year."

He looks at me quick, a grin plastered on his face.

"Isn't that all any of us want, Ike?" he says. "Because who the hell knows how much time any one of us has got?"

"No truer words, Detective," I say. "No truer words."

We take it slow up the State Street hill, a white smoke and dust-filled plume from the Wellington Hotel true implosion rising up through the clouds, like the hand of God touching heaven itself.

THE END

AUTHOR'S NOTE: Some information specific to the making of IEDs and other homemade explosives has been deliberately left out and/or fabricated for the sake of both safety and the overall protection of innocent individuals.

ABOUT THE AUTHOR

Winner of both the 2015 PWA Shamus Award and the 2015 ITW Thriller Award for Best Original Paperback Novel, Vincent Zandri is the *New York Times* and *USA Today* bestselling author of more than 30 novels including *The Remains*, *Moonlight Weeps, Everything Burns*, *Orchard Grove*, and *When Shadows Come*. He is also the author of numerous Amazon bestselling digital shorts, *Pathological*, *True Stories*, and *Moonlight Mafia* among them. Harlan Coben has described *The Innocent* (formerly *As Catch Can*) as "...gritty, fast-paced, lyrical and haunting," while the *New York Post* called it "Sensational...Masterful...Brilliant!"

Zandri's list of domestic publishers includes Delacorte, Dell, Down & Out Books, Thomas & Mercer, and Polis Books, while his foreign publisher is Meme Publishers of Milan and Paris. An MFA in Writing graduate of Vermont College, Zandri's work is translated in Dutch, Russian, French, Italian, and Japanese. Recently, Zandri was the subject of a major feature by the *New York Times*. He has also made appearances on Bloomberg TV and FOX News. In December 2014, Suspense Magazine named Zandri's *The Shroud Key* as one of the Best Books of 2014.

A freelance photojournalist and the author of the popular "lit blog" The Vincent Zandri Vox, Zandri has written for *Living Ready Magazine, RT, New York Newsday, Hudson Valley Magazine, The Times Union* (Albany), *Game & Fish Magazine*, and many more. He lives in Albany, New York. For more go to www.VincentZandri.com.